The Guilty Mother

DIANE JEFFREY

ONE PLACE. MANY STORIES

HQ
An imprint of HarperCollins*Publishers* Ltd
1 London Bridge Street
London SE1 9GF

This paperback edition 2019

21 22 LSC 10 9 8 7 6 5 4
First published in Great Britain by
HQ, an imprint of HarperCollins*Publishers* Ltd 2019

Printed and bound in the United States of America
by LSC Communications

For my mum and dad,
with much love and many thanks.

PROLOGUE

~

Melissa

October 2018

The screaming inside had stopped. But the thoughts in my head still clamoured for attention. I studied my hands, turning them over to examine my palms. Perhaps my future was written on them, along my lifeline. I started to twist an imaginary gold band around the third finger on my left hand. One, two, three times. The smooth skin here, where previously there had been a wedding ring, proved that I was once married. No, not once. Twice.

The nausea came in waves every time we went over a bump in the road. I wanted to tell the driver I thought I might throw up. The taste of fear was foul in my mouth and I needed some fresh air. But the driver couldn't have heard me even if I'd shouted. You're supposed to look out of the window when you're carsick, but the one in here was small and too high. When I craned my neck, I could just make out flashes of grey sky between bare branches, or occasionally the upper floors of tall buildings we

1

passed. Looking up made me dizzy. Lowering my head, I stared again, in shame, at my hands. Gnarled and dry-skinned, they might have been a sweet old lady's hands rather than those of a cold-blooded killer.

I felt as though I was retracing my steps, travelling back in time. Five years ago, I'd been taken away in a white van just like this one, and now I was being taken back again. It wasn't the same place, it wasn't even the same city – this was London, not Bristol, but people here would scrutinise me and judge me and determine my fate, just as they had done before. At least this time there would be two or three friendly faces among the sea of hostile ones. Two or three people who believed in me.

I hoped it would be three. It was my lucky number.

When I'd been taken away last time, my only thought was that I'd never see Amber and Ellie again, never again hold them in my arms. This memory forced itself on me now. It still seemed so fresh and was so physically painful that I gasped.

Just as I was wondering how far we had left to go, we stopped. I was helped out of the van. We'd reached our destination, but my journey was far from over. I took in my surroundings. It was early and there were only a few people milling around in this side street. Maybe they weren't even there for me.

I inhaled deep breaths of air as if I'd been starved of oxygen and gradually the queasiness abated. It occurred to me that I was more appropriately dressed for a funeral service in a church than an appeal in a court of law. I smoothed down my black skirt as best as I could with my right wrist now handcuffed to the female officer's left one. Then, my legs feeling weaker with each step downwards, I was ushered to the holding area beneath the majestic court buildings.

PART ONE

CHAPTER 1

~

Jonathan

April 2018

I watch helplessly as Noah hits Alfie for the second time.

'Give it back!' Alfie wails.

'Stop it, you two,' I snap, giving them a stern stare in the rear-view mirror. They haven't seen me, and they might as well not have heard me either. I shift my gaze to the dashboard clock. They're going to be late for school. Again. That's the third time this week. And it's only Wednesday.

Switching off the radio with a sigh, I glance at them in the mirror again. Alfie tries to hit Noah back, but Noah dodges his younger brother's fist and then laughs at him, which upsets Alfie even more. He starts to cry.

'Noah, you're three years older than him,' I scold. 'Try and act your age.' I wince. Sometimes my mouth opens and my parents' words tumble out. 'Please give Alfie back his spinner.' Now I'm pleading. That sounds more like me. Life would be easier if I gave in to Noah's demands and allowed him to sit in the front.

As I pull up at the bus stop a few feet away from the entrance to Kingswood Secondary School, Noah hands over the toy. Then he leaps out of the car and strolls away without so much as a goodbye.

I drive around the corner to the junior school. Stopping on the yellow zigzag lines, I flick my hazards on. Alfie and I get out of the car.

'I'll come in and apologise to your teacher,' I say, grabbing Alfie's bag from the passenger seat.

'I can go in by myself,' he says, slamming his door shut and peering up at me through his mother's chocolate eyes. Invisible fingers pinch my heart.

'I know you can, but we're late and—'

'*Dads* never come in.' The way he says it implies it's only mums who do, and now the hand gives my heart a hard squeeze. 'Anyway, she knows you have a problem with punctuality. She's used to it,' he adds. 'Plus if you park there …' he points an accusatory finger at my Ford Focus '… you'll get another fine.'

I can't believe I'm hearing my nine-year-old son correctly. I ruffle his hair and hand over his bag before getting back in behind the wheel. A wave of sadness breaks over me as he turns away. He reminds me so much of his mother. Too much. Putting the key into the ignition, I watch him sprint through the school gates.

Fifteen minutes later and fifteen minutes late, I slide into the chair at my workstation next to Kelly, our junior reporter, who grins at me. I smile back, pretending not to notice as she hastily closes the Facebook window on her laptop.

A drill starts somewhere in the office so I take my earplugs out of their box and push them into my ears. Now I've been officially made chief reporter, I'm to have my own private office. As far as I can see, this is about the only perk to a promotion that amounts to a token increase in salary and a large increase in my workload. At the moment, however, everything is being refurbished to our new editor's requirements. The need to get rid of the open-plan office space for our reporters is about the only thing we've agreed on since she took over six months ago.

The idea now is to put up a combination of Perspex and plywood walls to create cubicles with the aim of reducing not only noise levels in the workplace but also the stress levels of the journalists working there. In addition, it's supposed to boost productivity at *The Redcliffe Gazette* – or *The Redcliffe Rag* as we call it, although I imagine in Kelly's case she'll be able to spend more time on social media without feeling like she's under surveillance.

I've booted up my laptop, replied to a few emails and fetched myself some coffee before Kelly speaks to me.

'What was that?' I pull out one of my earplugs and try not to stare at the diamond stud in Kelly's otherwise perfect button nose.

'Just remembered. Saunders wanted to see you in the Aquarium as soon as you got in.'

'Thanks,' I mutter.

'You're welcome.' Not picking up on my sarcastic tone, or maybe choosing to ignore it, she turns back to her computer screen.

'Did she say what she wanted?'

Kelly shakes her blond bobbed head. Claire doesn't usually call me into her office first thing in the morning. This can't be good.

I raise my hand to knock on the door of our news editor's glass-walled office, but she has already noticed me, and waves her hand for me to come in. She's standing at the open window, blithely flouting the law by lighting up a Marlboro. My favourite brand. I gave up years ago, just before Noah was born, in fact, but every time I come in here, the old habit beckons to me and I feel like a cigarette.

Between puffs, she purses her thin lips and flutters her long eyelashes at me. It's a look I know well. It means this isn't open to discussion. Nope, I'm not going to like this.

Suppressing a sigh and adopting a military at-ease stance, I give a fairly good impression of a patient man while I wait for Claire to finish her cigarette. Eventually she stubs it out in an ashtray on the windowsill, and closes the window.

A petite, slim woman, Claire has a long, straight nose and an angular jawline, high cheekbones and hollow cheeks. Her cropped hair is dyed jet black. A pencil lives almost permanently behind her right ear, but I've never seen her use it. She has striking green eyes, which bore into me now.

She gets straight to the point. 'I'm sure you've heard about the Slade woman's appeal application,' she says.

'Yes, of course.' It doesn't sound very convincing, even to me. I worked late last night, updating an online story, so I didn't watch the news, and this morning I turned off the radio in the car because the boys were fighting. I have no idea what Claire is talking about, but I'm not about to admit that.

'I'd like you to look into it,' she continues, arching an eyebrow at me. She's not fooled. 'All we know is that new evidence has come to light. Find out what's going on. Interview family members. There's a front-page news story here, I'm sure of it. I don't need to tell you that a good article could attract digital display ads for our online paper, too. I want to run this scoop for *The Gazette* before *The Post* even gets wind of it.'

The Rag is only a small-market weekly newspaper. We're under-staffed, underpaid and overworked and we're all multi-tasking. But Claire is very ambitious and has set her sights on having a bigger circulation than *The Bristol Post* one day and a larger online readership than their website, *Bristol Live*. Personally, I doubt that will happen any time soon, if ever.

'I'm thinking a big front-page splash,' Claire continues, spreading her arms in an expansive gesture. 'I'm thinking exclusive interviews with her son and her husband. I'm thinking never-before-seen baby photos …'

Claire continues in this vein and I tune out. I'm thinking pizza and *Paddington 2* with Noah and Archie after this evening's homework. Then I groan inwardly, remembering I've got to go to a Chekhov play tonight to write a review for our monthly print magazine. I can hear the rise and fall of Claire's voice, but it sounds muffled, as if I've put my earplugs back in. Lost in my thoughts, I nod and shake my head in what sounds like the right places and grunt periodically.

I snap out of my reverie when Claire barks, 'Understood?'

'Yep.'

'Good.'

I still haven't a clue what she's on about. Slade. It's a very common surname in the Bristol area, but it does ring a bell. An alarm bell. A distant, dormant memory stirs lazily in a corner of my mind. I can't quite bring it to the surface. Something unsavoury, though, I'm certain of that. A knot forms in my stomach. Although I can't recall who this woman is, a voice in my head is warning me not to rouse this memory. Some strange sixth sense is telling me to stay away.

'We're done.' I'm being dismissed. 'Oh, and Jonathan? Send Kelly in here, will you? How that girl got an English degree with grammar as terrifying as hers is beyond me.' Claire pauses and tucks a non-existent strand of hair behind her ear, knocking the pencil to the floor. I find myself wondering if she used to have long hair as I pick it up for her.

'Yes, of course.' I leave the office. Poor kid. If there's anything sharper than Claire's features, it's her tongue, and I think Kelly is about to be on the receiving end.

'It's your turn,' I say to Kelly, slipping back into my swivel chair. I follow Kelly into the Aquarium with my eyes and then I watch Claire through the glass of her office as she paces the floor, shakes her head in an exaggerated manner, wags her finger, and finally stands still with her hands on her hips. I can't hear what she's saying from here, but everything in her body language indicates she's giving our trainee reporter a severe tongue-lashing. Kelly has her back to me, but I can tell from the way she's hanging her head and hunching her shoulders that she's not taking this well. Claire looks up and catches me staring, so I swivel my chair round to face my laptop.

I allow myself to gaze at the wallpaper image on my screen for several seconds. It's a holiday snap, taken nearly four years ago. Alfie and Noah, all smiles, are sitting on Gaudí's mosaic bench in Park Güell in Barcelona. Mel, sandwiched between the boys, is looking directly at me as I take the photo with my phone.

It's a terrible shot, blurred and overexposed, with Noah doing rabbit ears behind his mother's head. But it's the last picture I ever took of Mel. It was our last summer as a family.

Get a grip, Jon. Get to work!

When I type "Slade Bristol appeal" into the search engine and hit enter, I get several hits. The most recent articles online – from *The Plymouth Herald*, *The Bristol Press* and *The Bristol Post* – were posted yesterday. Words catch my attention as I scroll down. *Will the Court of Appeal grant Melissa Slade leave to appeal? … Melissa Slade to appeal against her murder conviction.*

Melissa Slade.

Seeing her full name brings it all flooding back. My hand starts to shake over the touchpad of my laptop. I'm reluctant to go any further. But then I spot a piece from *The Redcliffe Gazette* at the bottom of the results page. Recognising the headline, I click on it. I feel my brow furrow as I catch sight of the byline: *J. Hunt*. I start to read the article, but I can't take any of it in. It's as if I'm reading a foreign language.

I go back to the top and start again. The words themselves remain meaningless, even though I'm the one who wrote them. But I know the gist of what they say.

I glance at the date. December 2013. Just after Slade's trial.

Eight months before our holiday in Barcelona. That was another lifetime. A different life.

A few seconds ago, I'd been staring at the holiday photo I'd taken of Mel and our boys. Now I find myself looking into Melissa Slade's mesmerising green-blue eyes as she smiles her wide white smile at me, her sheer beauty at odds with the headline below her picture.

MELISSA SLADE SENTENCED TO LIFE FOR MURDER

This woman killed her daughter.

I'm not doing this. I'll tell Claire to find someone else.

I'm suddenly aware of Kelly next to me, her loud sniffing filtering through my earplugs. I didn't notice her come back. I delve into the inside pocket of my jacket, hanging across the back of my chair, and take out a clean handkerchief, which I offer to Kelly. When she has blown her nose, she manages a watery smile.

She says something, so I take out my earplugs and get her to repeat it.

'Why's she so hard on me?'

Claire can be hard on everyone. Because of her own quick competence and keen intelligence, she has little patience with people when she thinks they're not pulling their weight. 'I'm not sure, Kelly,' I say. 'Claire's a perfectionist and expects high standards from everyone.'

I intend that to end the conversation, but I notice Kelly's lower lip wobbling.

'What did she say exactly?' I ask. I don't want her to start sobbing again. I don't know how to deal with that sort of thing.

'She said my latest copy was "unreadable due to numerous grammatical errors and spelling mistakes".'

'Well, that doesn't sound too big a problem to sort out. Do you type up your stuff with the spellcheck on?'

I end up proposing to have a look at one of Kelly's feature articles, more as a welcome distraction than out of the kindness of my heart. It's an interesting story, about Bristol's homeless,

11

but it's not particularly in-depth. While I correct it, I give Kelly a few pointers and tell her to find and interview someone living on the streets to add human interest to her article.

'And get some photos,' I say.

Next I read through a draft of one of Kelly's pieces for the arts and entertainment page of our monthly print magazine. It's a follow-up on an on-going local celebrity scandal, the sort of gossipy article I wouldn't even glance at normally, but Kelly has written it in an appropriately sensationalist tone, and it only contains one spelling slip-up.

'This is good, Kelly,' I comment, which elicits a small smile.

She takes this as invitation to talk to me about her idea of setting up a weekly entertainment vlog.

'I'll have a word with Claire,' I promise. 'She should probably consider a rejuvenating facelift.'

Kelly grins, then pinches her eyebrows into a quick frown.

'For *The Rag*, I mean,' I add hastily. 'Keep it,' I say, as Kelly tries to hand the cotton hanky back to me. She scrunches it up in her hand.

She looks at me, a puzzled expression on her face, as if she's trying to work me out. 'I think my granddad is the only person I ever knew who carried cloth handkerchiefs on him.'

I'm not sure how to answer that, and I'm about to make a joke about her unflattering comparison, but I think the better of it. 'I use them to clean my glasses,' I say, shrugging.

It's mid-afternoon before I can talk to Claire again. I've reread several articles on the Slade case, including my own. I'm still a bit hazy on some of the details, but I am clear about one thing. I'm not doing this.

It smells of cigarettes in Claire's office. I suddenly feel like one – the itch has never completely disappeared, even after all these years as a non-smoker. I decide to scrounge a fag if she lights up, but she doesn't appear to need one herself. She leans forward in her chair, resting her elbows on the desk and her chin on her hands.

I start by pitching Kelly's vlog idea to Claire, aware that I'm putting off talking about Melissa Slade.

'We'll discuss it more fully at the next editorial meeting, but why not? She'll be more presentable on screen than on paper,' Claire comments dryly.

There's a short silence, which Claire breaks. 'Was there anything else?'

'Er, yes. About Melissa Slade's request for an appeal ...'

'Yes?'

'Is there anyone else you could assign that to?'

'Jonathan, it's an interesting story and you're the best I've got.'

'Thank you, but can one of the others do it?'

Claire sighs. She takes a stick of chewing gum out of a packet on her desk, unwraps it and folds it into her mouth. 'Is there some reason you can't?'

Yes. There's a very good reason I can't. But there's no way I'm going to tell Claire what it is. I don't talk about it. Not to her. Not to anyone.

'Well, it's just that I'm really busy at the moment. You know?' I can see from the expression on her face that I'm not convincing her. 'Work-wise, I mean,' I add. I don't know if Claire has children, but I do know that she doesn't tolerate anyone using their kids as an excuse for missing a deadline or as leverage for a lighter workload. 'I'm going to the theatre tonight so I can write a review of *The Cherry Orchard* for *The Mag*, I've got a Sports Day to cover at the local comp tomorrow and—'

'Jonathan, I'm giving you the opportunity to get in there ahead of the pack. This is investigative journalism.'

'Claire. I can't do it.'

'Why the hell not?'

'It's personal.' I have to make an effort not to raise my voice.

'So is this.'

'What do you mean?'

'I mean it has to be you. It can't be anyone else. It wasn't my idea. It came from … Your name …' She breaks off, as if she realises she has said too much.

'Who asked—?'

'Anyway, you know as well as I do, there is no one else.'

I rack my brains, trying to think of another journo who could take the job. I have to get out of this.

'You never know, Jonathan. Maybe they got it wrong and Melissa Slade was innocent all along.'

'Yeah, right,' I scoff.

'That would be a great angle,' Claire continues, as if I hadn't spoken. 'She did time when she didn't do the crime.'

An image bursts into my mind. Melissa Slade, sitting in the dock at Bristol Crown Court. Impassive and cold. I was in that courtroom nearly every day. I didn't see her shed a single tear. Not once during the whole three weeks of her trial.

'She was found guilty,' I argue. 'She did it.'

I storm out of the Aquarium, only just refraining from slamming the door behind me.

CHAPTER 2

~

Melissa

I've been seeing someone since I arrived here. A shrink. There's no stigma attached to it the way there is when you're on the outside. All the inmates I know have regular appointments with the prison psychiatrist. Anyway, he suggested it might be therapeutic if I wrote down my version of events. I don't like that term – it sounds as if my version is just one possible account of what happened instead of the truth.

At first, I was reluctant to go through everything again, to relive something that was – and still is – so traumatic. But I've decided to give it a go and see if it helps. And although one day someone else may read my story – my son, Callum, perhaps – I'm really writing it for myself, so I can always skip the parts that are too painful.

So, this will be a sort of diary, I suppose, but I don't intend to write an entry about what's going on in here every day. Where should I begin? I should focus on the events leading up to my imprisonment. It all started when my daughters, Amber and Ellie, were newborn babies. If I could turn back time – and every single day I wish I could – that's the moment I would go back to.

January – February 2012

It wasn't the same when I brought Callum home. Back then, I was on cloud nine. It really was the happiest time of my life, just as everyone tells you it will be. He was a calm baby and this gave me the impression I was getting everything right. To my delight, the pregnancy weight fell off my body in next to no time with a little exercise and no dieting whatsoever. Simon and I continued to see our friends, many of whom had children themselves. My best friend, Jenny, was expecting her first baby, too. Once she was on maternity leave, she popped round nearly every day to see Callum and me and, as she put it, "learn the ropes".

I would spend several minutes a day just watching Callum sleep, marvelling at how perfect he was, this tiny human being that I'd created. I'd devoured at least half a dozen maternity books during my pregnancy, but nothing had prepared me for the tsunami of feelings that hit me with motherhood. Unconditional love like nothing I'd ever known before, but also such intense fear. I was terrified I wouldn't be able to protect him. He was my responsibility, a huge responsibility. From the instant I brought him into this world, he became my world and I became his. My beautiful baby boy, my life.

With Ellie and Amber, however, it was very different and I didn't know why. Perhaps it was because Michael wasn't as supportive and helpful as Simon had been. Or maybe it was due to my age. I was thirteen years older, about to fall into my forties. It might have been because there were two of them. I don't know.

I remember vividly the first time I realised something was wrong with me. It when I caught sight of my reflection in the mirror above the sofa one afternoon. The woman looking back was unrecognisable. My hair was greasy and lank, my face blotchy and my eyes were bloodshot from lack of sleep. It struck me that I'd been wearing my pyjamas for at least three days and nights. The top had baby sick down the front. I couldn't recall when I'd last taken a shower. I looked awful; I felt awful.

Amber – or maybe it was Ellie – started to scream. It was time for a feed. Instead of going to her, I headed for the bathroom.

'Your mummy is smelly,' I threw over my shoulder in a voice that didn't sound like mine. 'She needs a shower.'

I took my time, spending several minutes under the hot jet. Afterwards, I sprayed on some deodorant, put on a bit of make-up and dried my hair. Then I got dressed – into a maternity outfit – I couldn't fit into my normal clothes yet, but at least I felt cleansed.

That feeling didn't last long. It was quickly replaced by a crushing guilt as I came back into the living room and realised both girls were wailing now. Their racket would have been audible in the bathroom – except for when I was in the shower or when my hairdryer was on – and deafening from the bedroom, directly above, but I must have blocked out their cries.

I went through the motions on automatic pilot, laying them on nursing pillows so I could feed them each with a bottle at the same time, and then changing their nappies one after the other. When they'd calmed down and were strapped into their baby bouncers, I went into the kitchen and made myself breakfast. It was three in the afternoon.

Sitting at the wooden table, I remember glancing up at the clock and noticing it was now half past three. My porridge was still in the bowl, in front of me, untouched. I'd been staring at it. I had no appetite. What had been going through my head for the last half an hour? I had no idea.

It didn't even occur to me to clean up the mess I'd made in the kitchen. I walked back into the living room, my legs heavy and unwilling, as if they'd been chained together. I looked at the twins. My baby girls. They were perfect. Amber had dark hair, like Michael and his daughter, Bella, and Ellie was fair like Callum and me.

I remembered waking up in a pool of sweat the previous night after a particularly vivid nightmare. In my dream, I'd fallen asleep, a baby in each of my arms, and they were about to fall to the floor. It wasn't the first time I'd dreamt that. Far from it. It had become a recurring nightmare.

When I thought about the dream, two things occurred to me. Firstly, it reflected my fear that I was a bad mother. But I thought it also proved I cared about my girls. I didn't want them to come to any harm. I found that reassuring because it meant there couldn't be anything chemically wrong with me. Could there?

Looking at them jiggling on their rocker chairs, I could see how adorable they were. I just didn't feel any bond. There was no emotion in me at all. I couldn't connect. No matter how cute they were, or how much they smiled, the bottom line was I didn't love my baby girls. Apart from a sort of detached numbness, I didn't really feel anything.

I tried to discuss this with my husband. 'Do you think I resent them?'

'Possibly,' he said. 'I do too sometimes if I'm honest. After all, we didn't exactly plan this pregnancy.'

That was true. It came about after I'd had a tummy bug. I must have thrown up my contraceptive pill. Of course, I only realised this about two months later – when it was too late – as I started throwing up again, this time with morning sickness.

'Our sex life is pretty much non-existent at the moment,' Michael added, looking at me in a way that implied he blamed me, more than the twins, for that.

'It will get better.'

'And we don't see much of our friends anymore.'

'I'm sorry, Michael. I can't help it. I'm simply not up to social-ising – I feel exhausted all the time.'

It wasn't just that. I no longer seemed to have anything in common with my friends. Their kids were around the same age as my son, Callum, and my stepdaughter, Bella, and they were into terrible teens and GCSEs or A levels with their offspring, as we were, but unlike us, they were done with nappies and night feeds and baby paraphernalia.

'At least you get to go to work,' I said with a sigh.

Perhaps this was my main regret. I'd had a high-flying career in the police force. I'd made chief inspector at the age of thirty-six and I was heading my second major murder investigation three years later when I found out I was pregnant. In the end, I'd had to hand over the command for that particular case to take my maternity leave. Any aspirations of one day climbing another rung on the ladder had been put on hold. I hoped this was temporary, although in the weeks after the twins were born, I couldn't imagine ever having the energy to go back to work.

'Someone has to earn the bread,' Michael said.

'I know. I just feel a bit … housebound.'

'Why don't you go for a run? The exercise would do you good.'

I'd been completely addicted to sport before I found out I was pregnant. I ran two or three marathons a year, and did ultra trails. When I had the twins, Michael bought me a special buggy so I could go for a jog with them. But the winter was dragging on, Amber seemed to have a constantly runny nose and sniffles, and I was constantly tired. I hadn't used the sports stroller once. I hadn't done any sport whatsoever for ages. Michael's suggestion was a good one, but I didn't feel like it.

I wasn't sure how to pull myself out of the dark abyss I'd fallen into. But then one afternoon, Jenny came for a visit. I thought she'd been avoiding me, but perhaps it was just her busy life that had got in the way and kept us apart, even though she only lived up the road, or maybe I was the one avoiding her.

Jenny hadn't given me much notice and as she stepped into the house, I saw it through her eyes. The place was a pigsty. She

19

made us a mug of tea and rang her cleaner. Ten minutes later, a young woman arrived on my doorstep and introduced herself in a strong Eastern European accent as "Irena the cleaner". In other circumstances, her greeting might have sparked some amusement, but sleep deprivation had robbed me of my sense of humour.

'Let's get the girls ready,' Jenny said. 'We'll go out for some fresh air.'

So while Irena cleaned my house, Jenny and I took Amber and Ellie to the park. It must have been just after school finished for the day because there were lots of children. As we walked along the path, Jenny pushing the buggy, I saw a woman sitting on a bench. She looked how I felt, drained and dazed. She was unwrapping a chocolate bar for her little girl, who was jumping up and down impatiently.

But in the other direction a couple of women walked by, one with a pushchair and one holding a toddler by the hand. They were talking and laughing together, their animated made-up faces glowing with youthful energy. They made it all look so easy; they made me feel like a failure, as if I was inferior to these yummy mummies and would never be up to scratch. I burst into tears.

Using one hand to push the stroller, Jenny took my elbow with her other hand, and led me to a free bench a few feet away. She held me and rubbed my back while violent sobs racked my whole body. I'm not sure how long I cried. I was aware of passers-by staring at us, and I was embarrassed, but Jenny didn't seem to be.

'You need help,' she said, when I'd finished, without asking me what was wrong. 'You can't possibly cope with two teenagers and twin babies by yourself.' She fished a packet of tissues out of her handbag and handed me one.

'Bella helps me out when she's home,' I said. 'And Michael ...'

What did Michael do exactly? An image came to me, then, unbidden – Michael raising his eyebrows disapprovingly. I couldn't pinpoint an actual event to go with the image; he seemed to be giving me that look a lot lately. When he came home at a reasonable time and dinner wasn't ready. Or when he came home late and the house was still untidy.

Jenny didn't push it. 'Wasn't your mum helping you out?' she asked instead.

'She was, but we had a row.' I didn't go into details. It was a petty argument, caused partly by my inability to take advice and partly by my mother giving criticism and instructions rather than suggestions and assistance. I needed to pick up the phone and call her, but I wished just for once that she would make the first move.

'I'll have a word with Irena when we get back to your place,' Jenny said. 'We'll set up something permanent with her. Then we'll make a doctor's appointment for you. And from now on, you must have some time out for yourself. Some "me time", as they say. Every day. To do some exercise, to have a haircut and a facial, or just to relax and breathe.'

I stared at Jenny blankly. I could hardly find the energy to get out of bed, or the time to do basic household chores. On an exceptionally good day, I managed to get dressed and clean my teeth before Michael came home in the evening. How on earth was I going to get out and do some sport or get a makeover?

Jenny answered my unspoken question. 'You need a nanny. We'll find you a nanny,' she said.

I wasn't sure if this was a good idea or how Michael would feel about it. We could easily afford it, although Mike was tight with money – well, he called it "frugal" – but I had my maternity pay.

'Thanks,' I said. 'You're a brick.' I welled up again, thinking I didn't deserve her.

'Of course you do,' she said firmly, and I realised I'd voiced that thought. 'You have to stop thinking like that. You're not yourself at the moment, that's all.'

'How did you know?'

'Well, you might have sailed through motherhood last time with Callum, but I found it a bit of a struggle with Sophia.'

I knew that must be an understatement. Jenny wasn't the sort of person to seek attention for herself and she wouldn't have wanted me to feel sorry for her. I hugged her.

In the end, Jenny didn't find a nanny; she found an *au pair*. With hindsight, of course, it was a mistake letting Clémentine into our home. But we couldn't have foreseen how she would change our lives. Especially mine.

CHAPTER 3

~

Jonathan

April 2018

Just as I'm undocking my laptop to leave the office for the day, my phone beeps with a text. It's from Nina, my childminder. I read it, swearing under my breath.

'What's up?' Kelly says, turning to face me.

'I was supposed to go to see *The Cherry Orchard* this evening,' I say absent-mindedly, my finger typing out a short reply on the keyboard of my phone, 'but Nina has let me down.'

I hit the arrow to send the text and look up to see the blank expression on Kelly's face as she ponders this.

'It's a play,' I add, 'by Chekhov.'

'I know,' Kelly says. She doesn't sound at all indignant, but I feel slightly guilty for underestimating her. 'I haven't seen that one,' she continues, 'but I've seen *The Seagull* and read *Three Sisters*. More of an Ibsen fan myself.'

There's an awkward pause and I don't know how to fill it. I

can't stand Ibsen or Chekhov, personally. I'm not a keen theatre-goer at all, except for the Christmas pantomime, but that doesn't seem like the right thing to say.

In the end, Kelly puts a stop to the pause, but adds to the awkwardness. 'Is it for a review for *The Mag*?' She doesn't pause for me to answer. 'I'll go with you if you don't want to go by yourself.'

'What? Oh, no. Nina was supposed to look after my kids. She's not my date.'

Holly, my girlfriend, is my date. Holly is pretty and intelligent – she's a pathologist – and I've been seeing her for about eighteen months now. My heart sinks at having to cancel my plans with her this evening, although part of me is thrilled at not having to sit through the play. But I still need to fake a review somehow.

'Oh.' Kelly actually sounds disappointed and I realise the play is probably more her bag than mine. 'Well, I can babysit if you like,' she says, 'to thank you for your help earlier.'

'That's very kind of you, Kelly, but it's part of my job description to oversee your work, and I couldn't possibly accept your kind offer. I've got two tickets, though. It's on at Bristol Old Vic. Is there someone you could go with?' Her angelic face brightens up and she nods.

'Yeah. My mum's quite arty. I'm sure she'd love to go with me!'

I open my desk drawer and pull out the envelope containing the tickets. 'I'll need some feedback I can use for my write-up,' I say. Kelly nods again. 'I'll give you a hand with your feature on the homeless if you like.'

On my way home, I call Holly to cancel.

'Oh, never mind. That's OK,' she says, although I can tell from the sound of her voice that it's not. 'If you like, I could …'

She doesn't finish her sentence, but I can guess what she was about to say. Even though we've been dating for a year and a half, I still haven't told anyone about her, least of all my boys. Holly is desperate to come round and meet them. It's a topic she has been bringing up a lot lately and that I've been circumventing. I'm sure Holly thinks I'm commitment-phobic, but it's not that. I think I'm doing a good job of moving on, and it's what Mel would have wanted; it's just that at the moment I'm happy with the way things are.

'I'll make it up to you, I promise.'

As I make pizza and watch *Paddington 2* with my sons that evening, I've all but forgotten about Melissa Slade. I can feel her crouching at the back of my mind, ready to jump out at me, but I'm doing a good job of shutting her out for the moment.

But once I've turned off the TV and put the boys to bed, there's no distraction and no buffer against my thoughts, and I can't seem to get Melissa Slade out of my head.

I can't be bothered to boot up my laptop this evening, but on my phone I skim through some more of the online articles from the trial and her first appeal.

Mel was obsessed with the case. She dreamt of having a baby girl – we were trying for another baby at the time – and she didn't believe that this woman could have killed hers. But that was Mel. She was a good person and she only ever saw the good in other people. 'Innocent until proven guilty, Jon,' I remember her saying when we discussed Melissa Slade's trial in the evenings when I got home from the courtroom.

We didn't discuss the appeal that followed in November 2014. Mel had died two months earlier.

I feel a tear snake its way down my cheek. I wish Mel were here now. I'd like to ask her for advice. I don't know what to do. *What would you do, Mel?* But as soon as the question enters my head, the answer comes to me.

You can do this, Jon. The voice in my head is Mel's. The voice of reason. *It has nothing to do with us. Nothing to do with what happened to our family.*

'Innocent until proven guilty, huh?' I say aloud. 'But she was found guilty as charged.'

Leaning back on the sofa, I doze off for a while, but it's a fitful sleep. I wake up with a start and a crick in my neck. I get up and check on Noah and Alfie before making my way to bed.

The following day, after covering Sports Day at the local school, I write a review from Kelly's enthusiastic comments about the play and the programme, which she has brought with her to show me. She has also taken a few photos with her smartphone and I choose one of the better ones. I add Kelly's name to mine at the top of the article.

At lunchtime, I honour my promise to Kelly. At first she's confused when I buy three sandwiches, but she gives her trademark grin when she gets it. There seem to be roadworks all over the city at the moment, so instead of taking my car, we walk to Temple Way and then get on the bus for Cabot Circus. With my mouth full of BLT sub, I brief Kelly before we get off at the shopping centre.

'You need originality. You wrote that the number of Bristol's homeless is twice the national average, which is shocking, and you mention that a local charity has made shipping containers into homes to get people off the streets, which is fantastic, but this is old news. We need the faces behind the facts and figures. You have to add something new.'

Kelly bobs her head vigorously then bites into her sandwich. When she's not grinning, she's nodding, I think unfairly.

As we wander up and down the pedestrianised streets around the shopping centre, I start to think we should have come after work, in the evening. But then we see a woman sitting in the doorway of a shop, hugging her knees to her chest, her sleeping bag rolled up beside her. The shop has "clearance sale" stickers across its windows and has evidently now closed down.

'There's your angle,' I say to Kelly, pointing.

'What? Oh, I see. The irony. Someone sleeping rough in front of an empty building when the council promised to open up empty buildings to house them.'

'No. That's not what I meant. Although, that could work, too. I was thinking more—'

'Bristol's Homeless *Women*,' Kelly finishes my sentence.

'Exactly,' I say. Handing Kelly a bacon sub and a ten-pound note, I tell her I'll be waiting for her in Costa Coffee a few doors up the road. 'Don't forget to take her photo,' I remind her.

While I'm waiting for Kelly, I open the Notes app on my phone and type in the names of Melissa Slade's family members.

Michael Slade, her husband, father of the twin girls.

Simon Goodman, her ex-husband, father of her son.

What was the kid called again? I look up my article online. I haven't mentioned his name, only his age. At the time of the court case, he was thirteen. I check out other online articles, but the boy's name doesn't appear to have been mentioned in the press. Melissa's mother was mentioned in *The Post*, though. I add her name to my list.

Ivy Moore.

Next, I go onto a People Finder site. This one should help me locate some of Melissa's family members as long as they're on the electoral roll and haven't opted out of this online directory. I don't bother with Michael Slade for now – I already have an address for him from five years ago, but I can't imagine that he would have stayed in that house after what happened in it. There must be thousands of Slades in and around Bristol, but it wouldn't surprise me if he has moved away. Either way, he'll be hard to track down.

Simon Goodman throws up about twenty results. I frown. I'll filter them a bit later when I can use a bigger screen. Ivy Moore is a hit, though. Only one result with that name in the area. On the electoral roll. Full address. Under "other occupants" there is a George Moore, presumably Melissa's father. The age guide seems to fit. They're in their sixties.

I've just finished copying and pasting their address into the notes app of my phone when Kelly materialises in front of me.

Getting up, I drain my coffee, grimacing because it has gone cold, and grab my jacket.

'Any good?'

Nodding, Kelly flashes me a wide smile. Her two body language tics are now in sync, I think.

'Back to the office, then.'

The address I've noted down for Melissa Slade's parents is in Hanham, which isn't far from Kingswood, where I live, so I decide to make a short detour on the way home. Hoping to avoid the traffic, I leave the office earlier than usual, punching the name of their road into my satnav at the first red light.

As I pull up in front of Ivy and George Moore's house, I notice there's a car in the driveway. Looks like I'm in luck. Well, looks like they're home at least. I know from my many years as a journalist that they may not be willing to talk to me. I take in the terrace house, wondering if Melissa grew up in it. Did she have any siblings? Did they go to school nearby? I make a mental note to ask her parents these questions. If they let me in.

George Moore opens the door when I ring the bell. He has an instantly likeable face, bushy grey eyebrows cascading out above kind blue eyes. I know him to be in his sixties from the age guide on the online directory, but his hunched shoulders and sluggish movements make him appear a lot older. His hair – what's left of it – is a slightly lighter shade of grey than his eyebrows.

'Mr Moore? I'm Jonathan Hunt. I'm a journalist from *The Redcliffe Gazette*,' I say, holding out my hand. He hesitates, but then he shakes it, which I take as an encouraging sign. 'I wonder if we could have a chat about your daughter Melissa. I've been asked to write a piece about her appeal application and I'd like to give an accurate account.'

'Usually my wife doesn't …'

'Is your wife here, Mr Moore?' I ask gently, thinking that she is probably the decision-maker for this couple.

'Er, no, but she'll be back soon.'

'Then maybe you and I could talk until she gets home.' When he doesn't react, I add, 'Mr Moore, you have my word, I always endeavour to report objectively. I don't write sensationalist articles. I don't misquote or misrepresent. I'm only ever concerned with the truth.'

To my surprise, he opens the door and leads me into the small living room. The television is on and The Beast seems to be making mincemeat out of the three contestants remaining in the final chase.

The room is clean – it has been recently vacuumed judging from the hoover marks on the worn pink carpet – but it houses a lot of clutter. Every spare inch of dark wooden furniture has a magazine or a book on it; china ornaments jostle for space on the window ledges, and paintings by numbers and children's felt art pictures hang on the walls.

I admire the artwork. 'My sons do a lot of craftwork,' I say. 'They like making model planes and cars. And the younger one, Alfie, loves drawing.'

'My grandson, Callum, liked drawing when he was younger. And Lego and Meccano.' Pointing at the pictures, he says, 'Melissa did those when she was a little girl.' His eyes lose some of their brightness when he mentions his daughter's name, as if he's overcome by the nostalgia of a time when his daughter was still an innocent child.

I clear my throat. I don't want to scare Melissa's father by taking notes, and as I expected Melissa Slade's parents to refuse to talk to me, I haven't prepared any questions, so I start with the ones I asked myself earlier.

Melissa is an only child, her dad informs me. The Moores moved into this house when Melissa was five. She attended local state schools. I try to commit this information to memory. I'll need to make a Voice Memo as soon as I get out to the car before I forget it all. Mind like a sieve. Mr Moore relaxes as we talk, but I have to tread carefully. I sense he's wary of me, so I need to keep building up his trust and avoid catching him off guard with tricky questions.

'Would you like to see some photos?' Mr Moore blurts out as I'm trying to think of a line of questioning to fast-forward from Melissa's childhood to her having children of her own.

'Yes, I would.' I plaster a smile on my face. 'Very much.'

Mr Moore gets up and, to my dismay, reaches down five volumes of photo albums from a shelf on the bookcase. We move to the sofa and he comments on some of the photos as he turns over the pages of the first album. It starts with Melissa's baby photos, some of which have lost at least one of their self-adhesive corners and become crooked. Mr Moore straightens them before he flips each page over. By the end of the album, there are pictures of her as a toddler.

It's a good half an hour before we get to the fifth and final album, this one a photo book that Mr Moore tells me Melissa created online. We seem to have gone full circle as, like the first volume, it starts with photos of Mr and Mrs Moore with a baby. I realise that the photo albums have got me to where I need to go.

'Is that Melissa's son, Mr Moore?'

'Yes. That's Callum, our grandson.'

'And that's your wife holding him, is it?'

'That's right.'

I wonder where Mrs Moore is and when she's due home, but before I can ask, George turns another page and from the next photo Melissa Slade stares out at me through bewitching turquoise eyes. She has a heart-shaped face, long blond hair and a huge smile. I find myself transfixed. She's sitting next to a man, who has his arm round her as she holds their baby son.

'That's Melissa with Simon and Callum,' Mr Moore says, using his index finger to point on the photo at each of them in turn.

Thinking that there may be some photos in this album of Melissa with her baby girls, I remember Claire's words. *I'm thinking never-before-seen baby photos.* But I don't like the idea of asking George for a photo to put in the newspaper. Even if I find one that shows Melissa as a loving mother, I'd feel as if I was invading this family's privacy and abusing the trust George is showing me.

'What was Melissa like?' I ask. I realise I've used the past tense, but if George finds that odd, he doesn't show it.

'She was a bright child. A wayward teenager. She and my wife Ivy were always at loggerheads with one another. She was kind and funny.' He smiles wistfully. 'She was a good mother to Callum.'

He pauses for a moment, and I mull over that last sentence, noting Mr Moore's use of the past tense, too.

'We – Ivy and I – don't see as much of Callum as we'd like to. He's all grown up now. I suppose he prefers to hang out with friends his own age. But when Melissa first ...'

He breaks off, staring vacantly at one of Melissa's felt pictures on the wall. This time he remains silent for so long that I don't think he'll finish his sentence. But then he says, 'Well, we used to see more of our grandson.' His voice wavers slightly. 'We tried to help Simon out. We picked Callum up from school, took him to his activities and clubs, that sort of thing. Ivy gave him a hand with his homework assignments. He had dinner with us and slept here when my son-in-law had to work late.'

I note that he refers to Simon Goodman as his son-in-law despite the fact he and Melissa had divorced and she was remarried. I'm about to ask how old Callum is now, but then it comes back to me that he was thirteen years old at the trial. I do the mental arithmetic in my head. Eighteen. 'What's Callum doing these days?' I ask instead.

But before George can answer, the front door slams and we hear a woman's voice. At first I think she's with someone, but I soon realise she's talking to George from the hallway. She's plump and she waddles into the living room, unwrapping a ludicrously long scarf from around her neck.

'So, I asked to see the manager!' she continues, without looking our way. 'So rude! I'm dying for a cup …' She stops mid-rant when she catches sight of me. Mr Moore leaps to his feet and helps her off with her jacket, and I stand up and approach her, introducing myself and holding out my hand. She doesn't take it. 'A journalist? We don't talk to reporters.'

Up close, I can see she's wearing abundant make-up that doesn't completely conceal the wrinkles criss-crossing in furrows across her face. I know she was once attractive from the photographs I've just seen, but the only trace that remains of her beauty is her eyes. She has the same striking eyes as her daughter.

'But he's from *The Redcliffe Gazette*,' George says. They must buy *The Rag*, I realise.

'I heard about your daughter's application for an appeal, Mrs Moore,' I explain. 'My editor has asked me to cover it and I just want to get my facts straight.'

'Perhaps next time you can phone before showing up on our doorstep,' Mrs Moore says. 'George, I'll make some tea while you show your visitor out.' She kicks off her shoes, bends down to pick them up and about-turns to leave the room.

'I'm sorry,' I say to Mr Moore as we step outside.

'Don't mind Ivy,' he says. 'She hates the press. We had reporters and photographers practically camping outside our house for weeks. A proper media circus, it was. We couldn't open the front door without them bombarding us with questions and shoving cameras in our faces.'

'I'm sorry about that, Mr Moore,' I say, a strange mixture of shame and culpability washing over me at the thought that the Moores were hounded by people in the same profession as me.

'The media branded Melissa as guilty from the start,' he continues. 'How could they prove she was innocent when everyone's minds were already made up?'

I go to leave, but he grabs my arm. I turn to face him. He frowns, pinching his thick eyebrows together.

'She didn't do it, you know. My daughter could never have hurt anyone.' His voice is loud, to override his emotion, I suppose, and for his sake I hope his wife can't hear him.

'Who was in the house when Melissa's baby died?' I ask. The words fly from my mouth before the question has fully formulated in my head, and I realise my mistake as soon as I see George's face cloud over.

'Which baby?' he whispers at the same moment his wife shouts his name from within the house, putting an end to our conversation.

CHAPTER 4

~

Melissa

April 2012

I hadn't wanted to host the dinner party in the first place, but Michael insisted it was high time we invited our friends round. It was only Rob and Jenny, he said. They were coming with their daughter, who was a few months younger than Callum. Michael's daughter, Bella, would be there, too. She seemed to spend as much time as possible at her mum's – she was taking her A levels that year and apparently it was quieter for her to study there – but, to Michael's delight, she'd agreed to come to us for the weekend. With Clémentine, our *au pair*, that made eight of us, not counting the twins.

Clémentine helped out with all the food preparation. She was a godsend, that girl, or so I thought at the time, and I'd been hoping she would extend her stay with us after her year was up. I realised just how much I'd come to rely on her in the short two months she'd been with us and I didn't know what I'd do without her. She shopped and cooked and helped me look after the twins. Her patience was boundless and self-confidence oozed out of every pore of her flawless olive skin. No matter what I asked her to do, she did it graciously. She often took the initiative, too, anticipating what needed to be done before I could make a to-do list in my head.

Clémentine had even impressed Michael, who had initially been reluctant to employ an *au pair*. But once my husband, a self-professed wine buff, found out that Clémentine's parents were winegrowers in the Rhône Valley, it was a done deal. The two of them had taken to discussing and tasting wines in the evenings and Michael had started to take Clémentine with him to his oenology classes once a fortnight.

As for Callum, he was besotted with her. His eyes practically popped out of his spotty face on stalks whenever she sashayed into the room, a cloud of Chanel's Coco Mademoiselle invariably wafting in with her. I'd heard him stutter more than once as he tried out his schoolboy French on her and then witnessed him blushing when she answered in her native tongue and he didn't understand. I think it amused Clémentine.

I couldn't fault her except for one thing. For some reason, she always seemed to tend to Ellie, leaving me to look after Amber. I'd tried to talk to Michael about this, but he argued that at only a few weeks of age, it probably didn't matter one iota to the twins who looked after them as long as someone fed them, changed them and talked to them. I sometimes wondered if I wished Clémentine would take Amber more often because she was prone to colic and colds whereas her sister Ellie was considerably calmer. I kept that thought to myself, though, feeling guilty whenever it wormed its way into my mind.

I tried to convince myself it would be lovely to see Jenny again, but in truth I wasn't looking forward to having guests. Despite that, I'd put a lot of thought into making myself presentable for them coming. I'd had my hair layered and highlighted that afternoon, and as I still didn't fit into my pre-pregnancy clothes, I bought a new outfit in Oasis, opting for dark colours in the hope of concealing my bulges.

If I'd spent a little money getting ready for this evening – too much for Michael's liking – I didn't get to spend much time. Amber cried for what seemed like hours and by the time I finally got her down, I was running late. I did a quick job with my make-up and I was doing up my dress when the doorbell went. I appraised the result in the bedroom mirror. Not perfect, but not too bad. It would do.

When Jenny arrived, though, self-doubt consumed me in one big gulp. 'Sleek' and 'slim' were the words that sprung to mind when I looked at her. In comparison, I could only come up with 'fat' and 'frumpy' to describe myself. The same age as me, Jenny didn't appear to have aged at all since I'd known her whereas I would need to apply a whole bottle of foundation to stand any chance of masking my wrinkles. And although she was normally the same height as me, in her kitten heels Jenny towered two inches over me in my slippers.

'Ooh, your hair looks fantastic,' were the first words she said when I opened the door. Good old Jen. She always said the right thing.

As she, Rob and their daughter, Sophia, stood on the doorstep, I noticed with a prick of envy that Rob had his arm around Jenny's waist. It was months since there had been any genuine affection between Michael and me. I thought the twins would bring us closer again one day, but for the moment the unexpected upheaval in our lives had driven a wedge between us.

Michael shepherded everyone into the living room and served pre-dinner drinks. I was already feeling detached from it all, as though I was on the outside looking in. I made an effort to laugh in the right places, but it didn't sound like my laugh; I attempted to make small talk, but it was stilted, as if I were trying to string together sentences in a foreign language.

At the table, at least three discussions were going on at the same time and I couldn't follow a single one. The chatter grew louder and everyone's words merged into a confused din in my head. Once or twice there was a slight hush and I realised someone had spoken to me and was waiting for my response. It all felt as if I'd walked onto a stage and had to play a part, but I was missing my cues and hadn't learnt my lines.

I'd decided against breastfeeding – it just seemed easier not to and I felt too old to do all the nightly feeds myself – so I could have a drink or two, which I'd been looking forward to. I knocked back the expensive wine without even tasting it, hoping it would loosen my tongue, or at least loosen me up. I was relieved when everyone had finished their starters and I could busy myself with clearing the plates and serving the main course.

Everything was forced – my contribution to the conversation, my smile, which stretched into a rictus across my face. I felt like a fraud. I was faking it, feigning an interest when I had no idea what was going on around me. After a while, I couldn't keep up the pretence. When the baby monitor crackled, I leapt to my feet, seizing the opportunity to get away for a few minutes.

But Clémentine got there first. 'It's Ellie,' she said. 'I'll go and get her.'

'She's terrific, isn't she?' Jenny said.

I was so grateful to Jenny for finding Clémentine to help with the twins and Irena to clean the house that I sat down again, nodded at Jenny and left Clémentine to it. I checked the baby monitor every few minutes, willing Amber to wake up, too. I turned up the volume, although it was unnecessary. Whenever Amber screamed with hunger, you could hear her even without the baby phone.

After the meal, Bella packed the dishwasher while Callum sloped off to his room, Sophia in tow, to play on his console. Blaming the wine, I popped to the toilet before flopping down on the sofa in the living room next to Jenny.

Clémentine was already sitting in an armchair holding Ellie. Her eyes fixed on the baby, she didn't notice me studying her. She was wearing a low-cut white top and a short black skirt. Earlier I'd thought, rather unkindly, that she was a frilly apron short of a French maid's outfit, but now I found myself jealous of the way her clothes showed off her cleavage and shapely legs to perfection.

Bella came into the living room to join us, perching on the arm of Clémentine's chair. I observed my stepdaughter reaching across Clémentine to stroke her half-sister's fair head. Bella was only a year or two younger than Clémentine and they got on well at the time.

Rob and Michael had been talking animatedly about something – I had no idea what – and there was one of those abrupt silences you sometimes get at parties when everyone stops speaking for a moment. It was broken by the noise of Ellie guzzling from her bottle.

'I think we need our own bottle!' Michael said, opening a bottle of Armagnac. He arched his eyebrows at me when I asked for a glass, but he poured me some without comment. It must have been a very small measure because when I picked up my glass a minute or so later, there was no brandy left in it.

Turning to Jenny, I whispered so Michael wouldn't hear, 'Have you got any fags?'

'Of course,' she said and stood up, grabbing her handbag from the floor by her feet and slinging it over her shoulder.

Jenny always carried a packet of cigarettes on her for emergencies and evenings out. I sometimes accompanied her outside and smoked passively while she puffed away, but it had been a while since I'd felt like a smoke myself. Holding the baby monitor in one hand and the cigarette in the other, I relaxed a little for the first time that evening.

When we came back in, stinking like ashtrays, Rob winked at us while Michael scowled at me.

'I think I'll go and check on Amber,' I said. 'It's not like her to sleep through a feed.'

'No, she 'asn't cried for a while,' Clémentine said, her French accent more pronounced than usual. 'She's usually so 'ungry.' She turned to look at Michael with her dark brown eyes, and he chuckled.

Bella offered to go for me and Jenny offered to come with me, but I declined both of them and made my way across the room and up the stairs.

I walked along the landing on slightly wobbly legs, wondering if I was in a fit state to carry my baby and taking deep breaths to try and sober up. The door to the nursery was open and I froze on the threshold, my head suddenly clear, as if someone had just thrown a bucket of icy water over me.

I knew before I walked into the room that something was very wrong. I never told the police that, of course, or anyone else for that matter. But as I stood in the doorway, the room somehow seemed unnaturally still. I strained my ears, but I could hear none of the gentle grunting sounds Amber usually made when she slept.

I can't recall walking towards the cot. I can't remember looking down at my baby, if she was face down, or if her face was purplish or pallid. I obliterated those seconds from my memory and left it to my imagination to fill in the blanks.

I remember collapsing to the floor. I remember someone screaming. I didn't realise it was me until everyone else rushed into the room. Kneeling down next to me, Bella, Jenny and Callum all held me. The colour had drained from Callum's face and I thought he might need support more than I did. Bella made him sit down. She was pale, too.

Clémentine lifted Amber out of the cot and thrust her into Michael's arms. I wanted to call out and tell Clémentine to be gentle with my baby, but I said nothing. I knew it was useless. So I just watched as Clémentine put her mouth over Amber's mouth and nose, and then pushed down on her little sternum with two fingers. Rob rang the ambulance from his mobile, although I heard someone – I think it was Michael – say that there was no point. Amber had been dead for too long.

CHAPTER 5

~

Jonathan

April 2018

'She wouldn't tell me her name,' Kelly says. I'm standing behind her, leaning on the back of her chair as I read the article over her shoulder. 'I found her at Pero's Bridge on Harbourside begging for small change.' I've just read this sentence word for word on Kelly's laptop screen.

I start to quote aloud, mainly to prevent Kelly from commenting while I'm trying to read. '"I was abused at home by my father. When I flunked my exams, I started taking drugs. I even stole money from my mother to pay for them. Long story short, my mother eventually threw me out. Can't blame her, really. I was a mess. I thought I'd get away from it all by leaving home, but I've been sexually assaulted several times since I've been on the streets, too."'

'That's terribly sad,' I say, looking at the photo Kelly has taken of a woman in her early twenties. She's wearing clothes that have

41

seen better days, and her black hair is either tangled or in dread-locks – I can't tell which.

'She's around the same age as me,' Kelly says.

Kelly has also interviewed a busker called Rose. 'She was playing the violin in an underpass in The Bearpit,' Kelly informs me, although, again, I've just read that bit for myself. 'She's very good. I recorded her. Do you want to hear it?'

'Er, maybe later. I'll just finish—'

'She's got a bed in a hostel at the moment rather than sleeping rough.' In the photo, Kelly has captured Rose, bow poised above her instrument, concentration displayed on her face alongside numerous nose and ear piercings. Her drab clothes – khaki trousers, black vest, black fingerless gloves and grey beanie – contrast sharply with the colourful graffiti on the walls behind her.

'So, what do you think?' Kelly asks, when I look up from the screen.

'It's excellent,' I say, sitting down in my chair and rolling it towards Kelly's workstation so that I can still see her computer screen. 'I like the fact you've done a piece on three women – the one we saw at Cabot Circus and these two. Their different stories and circumstances make it an interesting read.' Kelly seems encouraged by these remarks. 'It needs a few nips and tucks, though. But I can help if you like. First up, that headline has to go.'

Kelly looks crestfallen. 'It took me ages to come up with that,' she says.

'Well, it's just my point of view, but you have a fascinating feature here, and "Gimme Shelter" is a clever … um, pun, but well …'

'What do you suggest?'

'How about: WOMEN SLEEPING ON THE STREETS, colon, Bristol's Female Beggars and Buskers?' I move my hand from left to right to indicate the headline, my fingers and thumb showing capitals; then I repeat the gesture, conveying a smaller font for the subheading. Noticing Kelly suppress a smile, I slide my hands under my thighs.

'Alliteration.'

'It sounds more upmarket, more newsworthy. Secondly, it's great that you have these women's accounts, but perhaps you could use your voice as a journalist a little more instead of reporting all of it verbatim.'

As I continue to make suggestions, Kelly makes changes to her article.

'You should ask Claire to run the story online as well as in print,' I say when we've finished. 'That way, you can add the video of Rose playing the violin.' Kelly's face lights up at that idea.

An hour or so after the news meeting that afternoon, Claire summons me into her office.

'How are you getting on with the Melissa Slade case?' she begins.

'Um … I've interviewed the parents,' I say. I feel myself reddening as an image of an irate Ivy Moore flashes before my eyes. Her words echo in my head. *We don't talk to reporters.* 'I need to work my way through the other family members to get a clearer picture.'

'You should get in touch with her first husband, Simon Goodman,' Claire says tucking a non-existent strand of hair behind the ear that doesn't have the pencil. 'I'm sure he'll be able to throw some light on the details of the appeal.'

'Yep. I'll do that.'

'That article Kelly wrote is brilliant, by the way. She won't take the credit. She wants to have your byline on it as well as hers.'

'No, don't do that. It's her own work. I didn't do much. Just helped her tweak it a bit.'

'It was good of you.'

'Is that all?' I know full well it's not. Claire's got that eyelash-fluttering thing going on, which means she's about to ask me to do something I won't want to do.

43

'No. I wanted you to take Kelly under your wing, mentor her for a while.'

'Well, I've been overseeing her copy. I can certainly continue to do that.'

'I was thinking more along the lines of taking her with you—'

'But she has her own patch. And she doesn't need me to hold her hand. She's quite cultured, you know. Very bright.'

'—when you're working on the Slade case,' Claire continues as if I haven't interrupted, 'so she can see how good investigative reporting is done.'

'Do I have a choice?' I don't want to work on the Slade case anyway, but if I must do it, I'd rather do it alone.

'Not really, no.'

There's a pause during which my mouth opens and closes like a goldfish's as I grapple for a valid argument. Before I can come up with anything, Claire says, 'We're done.' I resist the urge to swear until I've left the Aquarium and closed the door behind me.

'Grab your coat, Kelly,' I say curtly, striding past all the work-stations towards the door leading to the stairs. She catches me up before I make it down the two flights of steps to the exit.

'Where are we going?'

'To meet a man called Simon Goodman.' Out of the corner of my eye, I catch the expression on Kelly's face and realising I've snapped at her, I add, more gently, 'I'll bring you up to speed on the way there.'

Simon Goodman hadn't been hard to find. He'd launched a campaign for his ex-wife's release back in 2013 when she was found guilty of murder. He seems to have been inexorably proclaiming her innocence ever since. His email address was on the melissaslade.org.uk website and so I wrote to him, asking if we could talk.

Kelly and I walk the short distance to the Watershed Café and we're sitting at a table when Goodman arrives.

'Jonathan Hunt?'

I've been looking out of the window, enjoying the view of the Floating Harbour and I was expecting Goodman to be wearing a uniform rather than in plain clothes, so he's the one who spots me. He shakes my hand, considering me through narrow blue eyes as I introduce my new mentee.

'I don't have much time,' he says.

Kelly takes this as her cue to get up and fetch the coffees, leaving me to make a start.

'Do you mind if I take notes?' I ask.

'Not at all. In fact, I'd prefer you to.' He takes a seat opposite me. He's at least ten years older than me, pushing fifty at a guess, but he's wearing it well. He has thick dark hair, which shows no sign of receding or greying, designer stubble and a long straight nose.

Goodman is based at Bristol's Central Police Station in Broadmead, which is why he chose to meet at the Watershed Café – it's about halfway between his place of work and mine.

'Superintendent Goodman—'

'Simon.'

'Simon …' I pause. If he's uncomfortable at what must be a role reversal for him – after all, he's the one who generally gets to ask the questions – he doesn't show it. He unbuttons his shirt at the neck and then steeples his hands, waiting. I'll bet he's good at interrogations whereas I've come unprepared, as usual. I decide to begin by checking a few facts. 'You and Melissa were colleagues. Is that how you met?'

'Yes. We met in 1995. We were both at the Bridewell Police Station. A whirlwind romance, really, but in the end, working together and living together, it became too much. I was obsessed with my job and when I was married to Melissa, I made the mistake of never switching off from it. We often worked on the same cases. We carried on working on them at home. I didn't give her enough attention.'

He pauses, but I'm so surprised at the candid account he has just given me of his marriage and its breakdown that I don't know what to say. I try to come up with another question. Fortunately, he saves me the trouble.

'As you can probably imagine, Melissa has suffered terribly in prison at the hands of other inmates because she was a police officer.'

I think the fact she's a convicted baby killer might have helped make her a target for her fellow prisoners, but I don't share this thought. 'Was she good at her job?' I ask.

One side of Simon's mouth turns down, which I interpret as an expression of disapproval. He's obviously not impressed by my interview technique. 'Yes, she was. Very good indeed.'

'And you had one child together?'

'Yes, a son: Callum. He's at university now, but he comes home every weekend and helps out with the campaigning. And before you ask, Melissa was an excellent mother, too.' His irritation is palpable.

'Sorry.'

Simon lets out a long sigh. 'No, I'm sorry. Melissa was vilified in the media when she was arrested. Everyone had made up their minds she was guilty long before she appeared in court. I'm hoping the media might be kinder to us this time round. I've read some of your articles about the case online, and, well, I know you try to report objectively.'

I wince, as the headline of one of my articles springs to mind. SLADE: THE BABY SLAYER. And then another one: FROM COPPER TO KILLER. They hadn't been my original headlines – I can't remember them now. Claire's predecessor had changed them as they weren't sensational enough for his liking. He'd kept my impartial tone in the articles themselves, though.

'I'll do my best to stick to the facts,' I say. 'As I told you in my email, I've been asked to write about Melissa's application for leave to appeal, but I'm not familiar with the ins and outs of it all.' I need to brush up a bit more on the case itself, even though I covered it. I should have done that before meeting Goodman. I ought to get hold of the court transcripts, but I don't really want to wade through them.

'Well, as I'm sure you know, her conviction was upheld at the first appeal four years ago,' he says, stroking his stubble. 'But since then, we've uncovered fresh evidence and an application has been made to the Criminal Cases Review Commission. We have high hopes we'll be granted another appeal.'

Kelly comes back carrying a tray of mugs. I wait until she has sat down and we're sipping our coffees. Then I ask, 'May I ask what this new evidence is?'

'The twins slept on mattresses that contained added fire retardant chemicals. Studies have shown that Sudden Infant Death Syndrome can be—'

'Cot death?' Kelly asks.

'Yes. Cot death. Research shows it can be caused by toxic gases, which are the result of an interaction between these chemicals and common household fungi. A baby who sleeps on its tummy, like Amber did, would breathe in dense fumes. But even a baby who sleeps on its back would be repeatedly exposed to these potentially fatal gases.'

'But this isn't new,' I say. I remember reading something about this before, back when Mel was expecting Noah. Mel was obsessed with doing everything right. We had read up about SIDS, so we bought a mattress along with a special cover for it. And Mel made me give up smoking. 'Surely they banned mattresses containing those chemicals?'

'No, it's not new. And yes, the chemicals were banned. Eventually. But Melissa's ex-husband—'

'*Ex*-husband?'

'Yes. Well, he wasn't then. He is now. She divorced him.'

'Of course.' I nod knowingly, although this is news to me.

'As I was saying, her second husband was a bit of a cheapskate by all accounts.' Dislike flashes across his face, but he quickly hides it. 'He decorated the babies' bedroom to surprise Melissa. The mattresses he got were brand new, but they didn't conform to British Safety Standards. Michael says he doesn't remember where he bought them.'

'So, are you saying that the mattresses weren't tested at the time?'

'No, they were analysed when Melissa was arrested. They found phosphine, arsine and stibine in the air immediately above the mattresses.' I stop him for a moment and ask him to spell all three gases. When I've written them down, he adds, 'It's just that the evidence presented in court against Melissa was more compelling.'

'Then I don't get it,' I say. 'What are the grounds for Melissa's appeal this time? What's this new evidence?'

He takes a deep breath. 'In Ellie's post-mortem, high levels of antimony were found in her liver and body tissue from the flame retardant in the mattress,' he explains. 'We've only recently managed to get hold of the toxicology report. This information wasn't disclosed to Melissa's defence team and, as you can imagine, it could be considered exculpatory evidence.'

'Let me get this straight,' I say. 'New evidence has been uncovered that points towards cot death, and it is in fact old evidence that was somehow buried? Is that what you're saying?'

'That's the gist of it, yes.' Simon drains his coffee, glancing at his watch as he does so. 'I have to go, I'm afraid.' As he stands up, he adds, 'You can always send me an email if there's anything else you'd like to know.'

When Simon Goodman has left, I huddle over my notebook, ostensibly to scribble down a few more notes, but really to collect my thoughts. Talking to Goodman has made me uncomfortable. The whole Melissa Slade case is bringing up memories that I want to leave alone. I don't want to associate her past with mine. I wish I hadn't allowed Claire to push me into covering this case.

Putting down my pen a few seconds later and looking up, I notice Kelly furrowing her brows. I realise this is all rather technical. It's hardly surprising she's lost.

'That was complicated, wasn't it?' It comes out sounding patronising and I instantly regret my question.

'No, I followed everything he said about cot death and the poisonous gases and the new evidence that has come to light. It's not that.'

'Then what?'

'What I don't understand is that he said Amber slept on her stomach ...' She pauses mid-sentence, apparently thinking something through.

'Yes, I don't know why. You're supposed to sleep babies on their backs.'

Kelly shakes her head. 'That's not what I meant,' she says. 'Superintendent Goodman said Amber breathed in the fumes directly, but then he talked about the results of Ellie's post-mortem. And he mentioned twins. Did he get them muddled up?'

'No, he didn't,' I reply, realising it's my fault that Kelly's confused. I've given her a piecemeal account of the events.

'Then, which one died?'

'I'll start again from the beginning,' I say, 'and this time I'll tell you the whole story.'

CHAPTER 6

~

Melissa

April – July 2012

When a baby dies unexpectedly, there's always a thorough investigation. The police interviewed everyone who had been in the house when Amber died. I'd recognised the officer who asked me the questions, although I hadn't known his name until he introduced himself. Constable Patrick Carter. Tall and skinny with short ginger hair, he was sympathetic and kind towards both Michael and me. A young female constable took notes during the interview.

Even though the police came to our home and I was sitting on my own sofa, it was unsettling to be the one answering the questions instead of asking them. There were lots of questions. Had I had an easy pregnancy? Did I have complications giving birth? Were the twins premature? How old was Amber? Had she been a healthy baby? Why did she sleep on her tummy? Had I given her any medicine, to help her sleep for example? Could I describe my relationship with my son when he was a baby? How did I get on with him now? Was I on good terms with my step-daughter? What was my marriage to Michael like?

Despite the sobs that punctuated my sentences, I tried to give comprehensive, coherent replies. The pregnancy had gone smoothly even though I was expecting twins at the age of thirty-nine. I'd experienced no difficulty giving birth three weeks before the due date. Amber was twelve weeks and two days old when she died. She'd had numerous colds during her short life and she'd suffered from colic. I'd taken to laying her on her stomach as this seemed to ease her tummy pain. I'd given her Calpol occasionally, but nothing else. Callum and I had always been close. I got on well with both Bella and Michael.

I asked myself questions, too. Over and over again. Should I have attempted to resuscitate Amber as soon as I realised she was dead? What went wrong? And above all, why me? But I could come up with no answers.

A week later, the coroner's officer called. Dr Holly Lovell, the pathologist who had performed the post-mortem on Amber, had recorded a verdict of sudden infant death from natural causes. There would be no inquest. The woman on the phone was compassionate, reassuring me that there was nothing Michael or I could have done to prevent Amber's death.

In the days that followed, I tried to keep busy, organising Amber's funeral. Michael and I had decided on a small ceremony and a cremation. I also took over with Ellie and spent as much time with her as possible. She became my therapy. I started to drink to ease my pain, but although initially this took my mind off the situation, it quickly became another problem to deal with.

Clémentine cried so much that anyone would have thought Amber was her baby. She was no use to us in that state and as I was tending to Ellie now, we didn't need her anymore, but Michael didn't think it fair on the girl to send her home just yet. He said she'd pull herself together before long and be good company for me. But she hovered around me most of the time, looking sullen, and I wondered if Michael was expecting her to keep an eye on me.

My mother, who had made amends for her part in the argument we'd had back in January, rang every day, which I appreciated. Callum threw himself into his studies without me having to ask him if he was up to date with his schoolwork, and he cooked dinner every evening, although no one had any appetite. Bella wanted to go to her mother's but Michael said she should stick with us at a time like this. I think he needed her around in much the same way as I needed Callum.

To begin with, I checked up on Ellie about every ten minutes when she was sleeping during the day and I got up several times during the night. Or I would stay in her room, sitting in the rocking chair, watching her little chest rise and fall.

'There was nothing genetically wrong with Amber,' Michael said after about a week, 'and Ellie was always a much healthier baby. You don't need to worry.'

Jenny, who was very supportive after I lost Amber, agreed with Michael. 'You're paranoid,' she said, 'which is perfectly understandable. But you know, it's true what they say. Lightning doesn't strike twice. You need to remember that.'

Jenny always said the right thing. But this time she was wrong.

At first, I didn't panic. I thought I was dreaming. One evening, a month or so after Amber's funeral, I walked into the nursery and found my baby lying lifeless in her cot. Certain objects seemed out of place, as though the room was untidy, but I didn't immediately grasp why. In a trance, I straightened the rug on the floor by the cot. I folded up the soft woollen blanket and picked up the cushion, placing them on the rocking chair where they belonged. Then I looked around the room, trying to work out what felt wrong. My heart didn't even skip a beat until I clocked the blond hair. That was when I understood this wasn't a nightmare. This was Ellie, not Amber.

The realisation was like a light bulb exploding painfully in my head and it galvanised me into action. She was still warm; there was still a chance. Lifting Ellie out of the cot, I screamed for Michael, but he didn't come.

Laying Ellie on the floor and kneeling beside her, I attempted resuscitation. Images of Clémentine trying in vain to revive Amber forced their way into my head, but I ignored them, somehow recalling my first aid training in the police force and going through the manoeuvres automatically. I had my mobile on me and while I was doing this, I called the emergency services, putting the speaker on and setting down the phone on the floor next to my daughter while I tried to get her heart to beat again. The ambulance crew took over when they arrived. But they couldn't bring my baby girl back to life either.

With Ellie, it was nothing like the first time. No reassurance or kindness over the phone from the woman at the coroner's office; no sympathy or support from our best friends, who seemed to suspect before we did that something was going on. I rang Simon, my ex-husband, to ask if he'd heard anything at work, but he was evasive in his replies. Whatever he knew, he wouldn't tell me.

An inquest followed. And an inquiry. Michael and I were interrogated separately. At the station this time, by my own colleagues. As I was being led down the corridor to the interview room, I passed Patrick Carter. He'd come out to the house after Amber died, asking his questions gently and using such sympathetic words. This time, he didn't even greet me. His face and neck flushed blood red as he looked the other way. I didn't see Simon.

I knew all the tricks, so I was aware the interrogation room was designed to make me feel ill-at-ease. I recognised the deceptive tactics, the good cop/bad cop act, the playing me off against Michael. I also knew that if they could read my body language and see I was telling the truth that I would be fine, so I was careful not to appear as guilty as I felt. I followed the advice of my solicitor to the letter. Fortunately, my colleagues looked as uncomfortable as I felt and it was over quickly. After that, the police questioned Bella and Callum even though I'd told them they weren't even home the night it happened. No one was home except me.

Then, early one morning, about three weeks after I'd found Ellie dead in her cot, they came for me. I was still in my pyjamas when they arrived and Michael was in the shower. Six of them arrived in two police cars. I knew four of them personally. Perhaps out of courtesy, this time there was an officer with the same rank as me. DCI Nicholas Baker. All this could only mean one thing.

I let them in and offered to make tea, but they refused. Out of nerves, I tried to strike up a mundane conversation – about the weather, probably, but they remained unresponsive, perching awkwardly on the edge of the armchairs and sofa and avoiding eye contact, while we all waited for Michael to get dressed.

When he came into the living room, Michael sat down beside me and took my hand. My head started to spin and I only caught snippets of what DCI Baker said. Inconsistencies ... not natural causes ... suspicious death ... unlawful killing ...

At one point, Michael let go of my hand and turned to me with loathing in his eyes. He hadn't once questioned my innocence. Not once. It was only much later – in court – that I realised he was probably too busy feeling guilty himself. The expression on my husband's face shocked me far more than the chief inspector's words. Michael was sitting right next to me, but he was already distancing himself from me. I was alone in this. I'd been alone for a long time.

Then Baker cautioned me. You do not have to say anything ... anything you do say ... Words I'd uttered countless times, never imagining that one day they would be spoken to me.

I remember, as I was being led away, glancing over my shoulder at my home – the house in which I'd lived with my husband and my son; the house in which my daughters had died. My world had already been turned inside out and it seemed to tip over then. I wasn't sure if it would ever be upright again.

CHAPTER 7

~

Jonathan

May 2018

She's pissed off with me. She doesn't have to say anything – I can tell from the silence over the phone. Hardly surprising. It has taken me over a week to call her after cancelling our night out at the theatre. And I've just given her the impression that I'm only doing it now because I want her to do something for me.

'All right,' she says eventually, to my surprise. 'Where do you want to meet up? At yours?'

That was probably deliberate, and if so, I deserved it. I've never invited her to my house, for obvious reasons.

'I … you … my …'

She remains silent. She's not going to help me out here. Picking up a ballpoint pen from the pot on my workstation, I start spinning it around on my thumb and index finger.

Taking a deep breath, I try again. 'Holly, I haven't told Noah

55

and Alfie about you and me yet. But I will. I just need a little more time.'

'It's OK,' she says, but her tone of voice belies her words. I'm not being fair on Holly. I really do need to sort this out. Soon.

'There's a nice new French restaurant on Chandos Road. They do delicious steaks, apparently.'

'It'll be nice to eat out for a change.' It doesn't sound like a dig this time. I think she's being sincere, but her words remind me that she usually cooks for the two of us at her place and I wince. 'I'm a vegetarian, don't forget,' she adds.

'Right,' I say, doodling absent-mindedly with the biro on the back of the voucher on my desk. 'I'll check the menu and get back to you.'

'Will you ask me over dinner, then?'

That grabs my full attention as for a split second I think Holly is fishing for a marriage proposal. Then I pick up the note of humour that has crept into her voice. 'Ask you what?'

'You said you were calling to ask me out on a date and ask me for a favour.'

'Ah.' The way she puts it makes me sound – and feel – like a total bastard, but that's not quite how I phrased it. 'Well, no, I can tell you now, if you've got a moment.'

'I'm all ears.'

'Are you at work, by any chance?'

'Yes, of course. Why do you ask?'

'I was wondering if you could get your hands on an old report for me.'

'A coroner's report?'

'Yes.'

'That depends. How old? Was the post-mortem done here? Can you give me the name of the deceased?'

'Yes, the post-mortem was carried out in 2012 by your office. The name is Ellie Slade. The Slade baby?' There's another silence, longer this time. 'Holly, can you hear me? Holly?'

'Yes, I'm still here. I'll try and get hold of Ellie's report for you. It shouldn't be a problem. I can definitely show you the one on Amber's death if that's of any use. She died a few weeks before her twin?'

'I'm aware of that,' I say, 'but Amber's death wasn't—'

'I know. I'm the one who did Amber's post-mortem,' Holly finishes. That shuts me up. It hadn't occurred to me that Holly might have been the pathologist who did the report. She and I met long after Melissa Slade's trial and we've never discussed it. I wonder why she carried out Amber's post-mortem, but not Ellie's.

Holly promises to see what she can dig out and when I've said goodbye, I google the restaurant on my laptop. Damn it! It doesn't look veggie friendly. I opt for a Thai restaurant in Clifton instead. Holly lives in the suburb of Cotham, so Clifton will be as handy for her as Redland. Distracted by Holly's involvement in the Slade case, it takes me longer than it should to make the reservations online. Then I text Holly the address of the restaurant. But when I ring Nina to ask her to look after the kids, she's unavailable.

'Bollocks!' I mutter, ending the call.

'How old are they?' Kelly asks, making me jump. I hadn't realised she'd been listening in.

'Who? My boys?' I swivel round in my chair so that I'm facing her. 'Noah's twelve and Alfie's nine.'

'The offer's still open,' Kelly says.

'What offer?'

'I'll babysit if you like.' Kelly is looking at me earnestly.

I'm not sure who else I can ask, but I hesitate even so. Perhaps it's because I've never liked to mix my private life with my professional life. Or maybe it's because she used the word "babysit", which my sons would object to. Or is it because I doubt her capabilities?

'I could use the cash,' Kelly adds.

I'm about to ask if she's had any experience *childminding*, but

57

I check myself. 'Thank you, Kelly,' I say instead. 'That would be great, if you're sure you don't mind.'

'Not at all. So, is Holly your wife, then?'

'Er, no, my wife ...' I trail off as I notice Kelly peering at my wedding ring. She doesn't know, and she doesn't need to know. 'Holly's just a friend,' I say. 'Here, you may as well have this.' I hand her the voucher I've been fiddling with.

'What's this?'

'It's for two free meals at a posh French restaurant that has just opened in Redland. You're not a veggie, are you?' I realise I didn't ask before buying her the bacon sarnie the other day.

'No way. I love meat.'

'Is there someone you'd like to take out to dinner?'

'I'm single at the moment.'

'Oh. Well, do you have any brothers or sisters? Or what about asking a friend?'

Kelly's face clouds over and I wonder if I've said something to upset her. 'My sis ...' She doesn't finish her sentence. Then her smile comes back, although it seems a bit forced. 'My mum likes juicy steaks. I'll treat her. Do I need to write up a review?'

'You got it.'

'OK. Cheers for this.' She waves the voucher at me, winking conspiratorially.

I spend the rest of the afternoon updating stories from my patch, making phone calls, proofreading Kelly's copy for the next print edition and writing up my notes on Melissa Slade.

The whole time I'm working, I have Holly on my mind. Holly is sexy, smart and funny. She's perfect for me. She's perfect, full stop. I met her through an online dating website and when I first started seeing her, I was slightly put off by the thought that the hands touching me had been manipulating dead bodies all day. But Holly made me laugh; she made me feel like myself again. But a year and a half later, I'm still holding back.

She's kind and patient, she loves kids, although she doesn't have any, and I know she'll make a great stepmum. But I'm not sure if my boys are ready. Until recently, Alfie still crept into my bed in the middle of the night and Noah has only just started bringing home good marks and reports again from school. I was so devastated after Mel's death that the boys suffered not only because they'd lost their mum, as if that wasn't bad enough, but also because their father was struggling to look after himself and consequently doing a lousy job of taking care of them. We seem to be finding our feet now. I'm worried that if I bring Holly into the equation, it might upset the balance. And I don't want my boys to think I'm replacing their mother.

An instant message pops up from Claire and so, banishing Holly from my mind, I get up and head for the Aquarium.

'How are you getting on with Melissa Slade?' Claire says without preamble as I close the glass door and breathe in the smell of stale cigarette smoke.

I consider her question. It's strange, the way she has formulated it. I feel an aversion towards Melissa Slade, even though I've never met her. Perhaps, given what happened to me, I should feel a connection. I have something in common with Melissa Slade, but it seems to have sprung from a very different experience. I hope I never do meet the woman. I don't think I'd get on with her at all.

'I'm not much further along than when we discussed it the other day,' I say. 'I've spoken to Simon Goodman, her first husband. He could be a useful contact, I think, as long as we stick to the facts and don't paint his ex-wife in a bad light.' I tell Claire about my brief conversation with the superintendent.

'It's a bit thin for the moment. We'll sit on this for a while until you've talked to a few more family members. What about the husband?'

'You mean Michael Slade? He's an ex-husband now too. He's next on the list.'

'OK. Try and find something *The Post* won't. There's a story in here somewhere, I can feel it, and I don't want them breaking news before us. Timing is everything. Keep me in the loop.'

'Of course.'

'That's all.'

Back at my workstation, I attempt to find out where Michael Slade lives. I try my usual People Finder website, then Facebook, Twitter and Instagram. Nothing. There are several Michael Slades, but none of them is the right one. The man seems to have gone underground after Melissa's trial. His name barely pops up again, even around the time of the appeal.

Out of ideas, I fire off a short email to Simon Goodman, feeling sure he'll know where Slade lives. An hour later he writes back, asking me to ring him and giving me two or three windows to call him over the next couple of days. I sigh, frustrated and confused as to why he won't answer my question by email.

The rest of the afternoon goes by quickly as I have a mountain of work to get through. It's ironic that our print edition has never had a lower readership and yet I've never had so much to do. The Internet and new technologies have revolutionised journalism and I need to constantly add different perspectives to stories I've posted online as the situations evolve. Readers expect to be able to follow what's happening in real time. With members of the general public tweeting about events they've witnessed and uploading their own videos to websites, journalists have to analyse and portray the bigger picture. It's also a job you take home with you. In a connected world, you can't ever really disconnect. I can't wait to go out this evening and get away from it all for a few hours.

Despite getting caught in traffic on the way to and from dropping Kelly off at my house, I arrive at the restaurant a little early, before Holly. When she breezes in, her dark hair is sitting beautifully on her slender shoulders even though there's a gale blowing outside, and the knee-length colourful dress she's wearing shows off her figure to perfection.

She kisses me on the cheek and I pull out her chair for her.

'Here you go,' she says, handing me the brown A4 envelope she was carrying under her arm. 'I've photocopied the reports for both the Slade twins. I'm not supposed to … you know …'

'Don't worry,' I say. 'I'll be careful how I use it.'

I sit down again, putting the envelope on the table. Trying not to eye it longingly, I ask Holly how she has been and how her day was.

'It's OK, 'Holly says, when I get on to the weather. 'You can open it. That way, if you want anything clarified, I'm here.'

So, once we've ordered food and we're sipping wine, I slide out the printed pages and start by speed-reading Amber's report. *Sudden infant death. Natural causes.*

'Upper respiratory tract infection and inflammation of the mucous membranes of the nose,' I read aloud. 'What's that in layman's terms?'

Holly looks up from her phone, which she has been playing with while she waits for me to finish reading. 'Basically, Amber had a cold,' she says. She slept on her stomach to relieve colic and there are signs of asphyxia, which would suggest she suffocated in her sleep. Her blocked nose would have hindered her breathing and I expect she ended up with her face turned down into the mattress.'

I nod. This confirms what I thought. Cot death. It's also the reason I hadn't thought to ask Holly for Amber's post-mortem report.

'I found nothing suspicious. There was nothing at all to suggest violence or abuse,' Holly continues. 'There was no bruising other than slight haematomas around the nose and mouth and a broken rib, both of which were certainly caused by attempts made to resuscitate the baby. I didn't see the need for an inquest.'

Something in Holly's words and tone of voice niggles me. She almost sounds defensive. And that's when it comes back to me – I feel like slapping my forehead with the palm of my hand. I skimmed an online article about this only the other day, but if Holly was named in it, I missed it. In court, the pathologist who had examined Amber's body stuck to her interpretation of her findings. I hadn't been in court that day, but by all accounts, she was resolute in her argument that Amber's death had been an unpreventable tragedy. She would not change her verdict despite pressure to reconsider during cross-examination by the prosecution.

Holly puts her mobile away in her handbag. I say, 'I remember now. In court they tried to make out Melissa Slade had murdered both twins.'

'Yes. She was charged with two counts of murder. They said it was very fortunate for her that Amber had been cremated and that her little body couldn't be exhumed for another examination.' I think I see tears in Holly's eyes, although I'm not sure why. I give her hand a quick squeeze under the table.

Letting Holly recover her composure, I turn to the second report. This one is very different. *Minor retinal haemorrhages. Bruises. Blood in the lungs. Fibres in the lungs. Fractured second right rib. Fractured first left rib.* The cause of death is given as asphyxia consistent with deliberate smothering and/or shaking.

'Why didn't you do Ellie's post-mortem?' I ask Holly.

'Quite simply because I was away on holiday,' she replies.

'Do you agree with its conclusions?'

'The post-mortem was carried out by my colleague Roger Sparks. He's the best pathologist I've ever worked with. He's one of the most meticulous people I know. His conclusions were confirmed in court by other experts, including an eminent ophthalmologist and one of the best paediatric neurosurgeons in the country.'

She hasn't answered my question, so I ask her again.

'I think it's more a case of Roger disagreeing with *my* findings,' she says. 'He thought both deaths had been deliberate. But I was the one who examined Amber and I'm as certain as I can be that she died of natural causes.'

'And Sparks performed the post-mortem on Ellie,' I say, thinking aloud. 'Could Ellie's bruising and broken ribs have been caused by efforts to resuscitate her?'

'That was the big question in court,' Holly says, shrugging. 'Probably not.' She doesn't elaborate.

'So, one unfortunate natural death and one deliberate murder.' The details of the court case come flooding back to me now.

'That's how it seemed.'

'That's also the verdict the jury delivered. She was accused of two murders, but found guilty of one.'

'It doesn't make much sense though, does it?'

'No,' I agree. 'No, it doesn't.'

I look down again, turning to the last page. Two words seem to jump out at me, as if they have been highlighted. *Antimony* and *liver*.

'This is the toxicology report? The part that went missing and has now resurfaced. The evidence that might free Melissa Slade ...'

'Yes, that's right,' Holly says. 'All hell broke loose in our office when that turned up. Roger Sparks is denying any involvement in a cover-up – actually he's denying he wrote the document at all – but it was found among his papers and on his computer when he retired. It all reflects very badly on us.'

'I can imagine. Do you believe him?'

'I don't know what to believe anymore,' she says. 'Anyway, I hope this helps.'

After that, Holly is uncharacteristically quiet. The food is delicious and I top up Holly's wine glass several times, but that doesn't help. She evidently has something on her mind. I assume it's me dragging up the memories of the dead Slade babies, so I stay clear of that subject for the rest of the evening.

When I pull up in front of Holly's place, near Saint Michael's

Hill in Cotham, she turns to me and I think she's going to invite me in, as she always does. I haven't told her yet that I don't have my usual childminder and I didn't ask Kelly to sleep over at mine, which is what Nina does. Nina sleeps on the sofa bed in the sitting room, even though there is a bedroom in my house that no one ever sleeps in. I couldn't bring myself to explain that to Kelly, so I won't be able to stay the night with Holly, but I can come in for a while. I look out of the car window at the beautiful old building, once a large house now converted into modern flats, and tip my head towards it, raising my eyebrows suggestively.

But Holly isn't on the same wavelength. 'Thank you for a lovely dinner, Jonathan,' she says, and it sounds rather definitive. She normally calls me Jon and I'm not sure I want to hear what's coming. 'I think it might be a good idea if we took a break for a while,' she continues. 'I can't keep hanging on forever.' She looks down, at her hands, clutching her handbag on her lap. 'I want to be part of your life instead of watching it from the sidelines, but you won't introduce me to your family or your friends.'

'Holly, I—'

'It's too late, Jon. I came tonight because I wanted to tell you in person, but I'd already made up my mind.'

She gets out of the car and I watch her walk away. I sit in the car for several minutes with the engine idling, looking up at Holly's window, berating myself for messing up so badly with Holly and for messing her around.

When I get home, the boys are asleep and Kelly is dozing in front of the TV on the sofa. I pay her what I normally pay Nina and use the Uber app on my phone to request a ride to take her home. While we're waiting for the driver, I bring her up to speed with the latest in the Slade case.

'So, let's get this straight,' Kelly says. 'It was originally thought the mother lost one baby and murdered the other one?'

'That was the way the evidence pointed at the trial and the jury's verdict, yes.'

'And now fresh evidence – a missing post-mortem report that has resurfaced – suggests both babies died of cot death?' She sounds incredulous.

I consider this before answering. 'Well, that's what Superintendent Goodman and Melissa's defence team are hoping to prove. That report is their main ground for appeal. And it has happened before. There are precedents.'

'What do you mean?'

'You're too young to remember, but there were several women in the nineties and noughties who were imprisoned for killing more than one of their babies. It turned out their babies died of Sudden Infant Death Syndrome and their convictions were gross miscarriages of justice.'

Kelly doesn't appear to have listened to me. 'Is it possible the missing report your *friend* gave you is inconclusive and Melissa Slade killed *both* twins?'

'I suppose we can't rule that out,' I concede, getting the instant sensation I'm betraying Holly. She was sure of herself, so sure that she stood her ground in court. 'She was my girlfriend, actually,' I blurt out, 'but she's not anymore. As of this evening.' I don't know why I say that. It only makes me feel even more disloyal towards Holly.

'Oh.' Kelly doesn't sound very sympathetic, barely breaking flow. 'Or maybe neither Amber nor Ellie died of cot death but Melissa Slade is innocent,' she says, steering the conversation back on track.

'Hmm,' I say dubiously. 'But then, what killed them? A genetic disease?'

'Possibly. You'd think that would have shown up in the post-mortems, though. I wonder if the question is not *what* killed them, but *who*? No one seems to have considered it could have been murder, but that Melissa Slade wasn't the murderer.' She starts to say something else, but she's interrupted by the sound of a car horn.

'Looks like your Uber's here,' I say, unnecessarily.

As Kelly leaves, I try to think over the different theories we've just come up with, but I can't concentrate. My thoughts keep racing back to Holly. I tap out several texts on my mobile, but end up deleting each one. In the end, I write three words. *I'm so sorry.*

CHAPTER 8

~

Melissa

December 2013

Murder. In my experience – and I'd worked on a few murder investigations in my time as a police officer – the fact that someone had deliberately killed someone else was a given. Our task was to collect evidence and use it to identify the murderer.

But in this instance, the big question wasn't who had done it, but had murder been committed at all? If the answer was yes, then I was the murderer. It all seemed back to front.

Much of the evidence against me would be circumstantial, but a lot of it would be based on expert opinions. Since the medical experts, in particular the pathologists, had differing opinions, I was charged with two counts of murder in the end. My case was committed to the Crown Court, where my trial – for the alleged murders of both my babies – began six weeks later. It was expected to last a fortnight.

I could feel the eyes of every single person in the courtroom on me as, flanked by two security guards, I was led in that first morning. My legs threatened to give way and it took all my concentration to put one foot in front of another.

I could still feel everyone staring at me after I'd taken my place in the dock. At first I kept my eyes down, but then I became worried about how that would make me seem. Did I look guilty? So, I glanced around me. It was far bigger than the courtroom at Bristol Magistrates' Court, where my committal proceedings had been held.

And yet, this courtroom, with its wooden pews and wood panelling and very little natural light, was forbidding and claustrophobic. There were far more people here than at my committal hearing; the gallery was packed to the hilt. I tried to find a sympathetic soul to concentrate on, but as I scanned the crowd, I saw only unfriendly faces. I desperately needed my husband and my best friend, but Michael and Jenny, who would be called as witnesses for the defence, weren't allowed in court until it was time for them to give evidence.

As they were sworn in or affirmed, I studied each juror in turn, peering through strands of hair that had fallen in front of my face. There were six men and six women. Five of the men and three of the women looked very young, barely out of their teens, and I doubted they had children of their own. Some of them had chosen the affirmation rather than the oath. I didn't know if there were any conclusions to be drawn from this.

Two female jurors appeared to be around the same age as me. I had no idea if that was a good thing or a bad thing. Would they sympathise with me or judge me? One of them was matronly and I imagined she had a large family. The other was skinny and wearing shabby clothes. She stumbled over the words of her affirmation as she read it. I hoped this was due to nerves. If she struggled with reading, what chance did she stand of grasping legal proceedings? As soon as this thought entered my head, I realised I shouldn't have judged her. She would be judging me.

Finally, there was a woman of African descent, whose age I could not determine, and an elderly man in his sixties, a grandfather, perhaps, who might have been part Asian. They were the only two people in the jury box who weren't white. Both of them took the oath. The man was bearded and sprightly. His kind face was distorted and his forehead was crinkled into a frown. I could tell he didn't want to be here and I could relate to that. The woman stared at me and I tried not to flinch as her large black eyes locked on to mine.

I observed the members of the jury as the judge gave them their preliminary instructions. They looked as intimidated as I was as we listened to Mr Justice Hardcastle, an imposing man, whose deep voice and dress – a black and purple robe with a red sash and a short wig – instantly commanded respect.

I continued to try and gauge their reactions during the Crown's opening speech. I saw the grandfather scribble notes. As witness statements, mainly by my fellow police officers, were read out before the court, the black lady yawned. When the prosecution's first witness, Dr Holly Lovell, stated that Amber had died of natural causes, I observed the thin scruffy woman wipe away her tears. Two of the young men on the jury were clearly perplexed as Dr Roger Sparks, who had examined Ellie, then refuted his colleague's post-mortem findings for Amber and argued that both babies had been deliberately smothered.

Boredom, sympathy, confusion. At first, I found it impossible to predict which way each member of the jury would vote. I didn't even know what verdict I was hoping for. I didn't need other people to judge me; I judged myself. Whatever they thought of me, my conscience was what mattered. And even if I were found not guilty, I'd still have a guilty conscience. It would never be completely clear. How could it be? What sort of a mother can't look after her babies? What sort of a mother lets them die?

By the time the case for the prosecution was closed several days later, I thought I would be found guilty. Guilty of murdering

Amber and Ellie, my baby girls, my own flesh and blood. I told myself that when you're to blame, you get what you deserve. I tried to resign myself to my fate.

But deep down, I felt a cowardly glimmer of hope. I found myself wondering if the jury could find me guilty beyond all reasonable doubt. That's the key phrase, isn't it? Beyond all reasonable doubt? I didn't hear those words uttered in the Crown Court as often as I would have expected, but they were embossed in my head and I'm sure they crossed every juror's mind. Could these twelve people listen to everything that was said and honestly conclude that there wasn't a shred of doubt or a scrap of evidence to suggest I might be innocent? That's all it would take for me to be able to walk free.

This thought then made me morose. I'd ask myself what it would actually mean to walk free. As I was on bail, every evening I was allowed to go back home. Home to a husband who no longer loved me. To a house where my babies' cots were now empty. Was this what I wanted? Would I return to a career catching criminals alongside colleagues who would always wonder if I was one myself? Was that even possible?

As the first witness to be called by the defence, I had to take the stand before Michael or Jenny. I hadn't wanted to give evidence, but my barrister, Martin May QC, had argued that the jury would draw an "adverse inference" from this. In other words, it wouldn't look good.

May had grey-white hair that curled up at the nape of his neck and when I'd first met him it had struck me that even without his wig he would look at home in a courtroom. In his silk robe he looked as if he belonged on the set of a film. Even his demeanour and gestures gave him the aura of a movie star. He exuded confidence, but didn't seem arrogant.

My barrister had never once asked me if I was guilty or innocent. I supposed he must have thought I'd killed my children, which bothered me. I wanted him to believe in me. But I trusted him and his optimism. His game plan, as far as I understood it, was to sow some seeds of doubt in the minds of the jurors so that they would give me the benefit of the doubt. He'd been over the questions he would ask me and I felt ready. That part went as planned.

May had also anticipated many of the questions that Eleanor Wood QC would put to me during the prosecution's cross-examination. She was a dainty woman, but her forceful voice was at odds with her appearance. She made me nervous and I was only too aware of how some of the questions – no matter what answers I gave – would make me seem.

Wood made me out to be a bad mother, resentful of my twins, the result of an unwanted pregnancy, because I'd had to give up a promising career and my sporting activities to bring them up. She highlighted my postnatal depression, which rendered me incapable of looking after my babies properly, and she even managed to hint that my decision not to breastfeed the twins was proof of my lack of love for them.

The fact that I'd found both my babies dead in the evening also pointed towards suspicious deaths rather than SIDS, Wood argued in her potent voice. Mothers were tired and short-fused late in the day whereas cot deaths almost always occurred during the night.

As I listened to the barrister's accusations, a growing feeling of shame engulfed me. I wanted to call out: *No! No! That's not how it was! That's not who I am!* But at the same time, I recognised myself in her description. I'd been an unworthy mother. I hadn't cared for my babies the way I should have.

I was a trembling mess when I left the witness box to walk back to the dock. I hoped that once my husband had given evidence, no one in the courtroom would doubt my innocence. And Jenny, as a character witness, would have a better impact on the jury than I must have had. I convinced myself that the worst was over.

Michael was called to the stand next. He took the oath, which surprised me as he was an atheist. My heartbeat slowed down slightly and I started to breathe more easily. After all, May was on my side and, like me, Michael knew what was going to come up and had prepared his answers.

But Michael didn't stick to the script.

'Where were you on the evening Ellie died?'

Until now, Michael had said he was out. He'd gone for a walk to clear his head. He'd told the police this and he'd told me this. I'd shouted for him when I'd found Ellie, lifeless, in the cot because I'd thought he was home, but he didn't come. So, when he said he was out, I had no reason not to believe him.

'I was in a different part of the house.'

I felt my head jerk up.

Martin May QC, however, recovered quickly. 'So, you didn't hear your wife call you?'

'No, I did not.'

But it was the first thing Eleanor Wood QC asked in cross-examination.

'In your statement to the police, you said you weren't at home at the precise moment the defendant, your wife, found your daughter Ellie dead. But you've just said – under oath – that you were in a different part of the house. Were you or were you not at home, Mr Slade?'

'I was at home, but I was in a different part of the house.'

Why had Michael changed his story? Was it because he was under oath?

'Can you be more specific?'

'I was in a bedroom at the back of the house.'

'Mr Slade, were you alone?'

'No, I wasn't.'

'Could you tell us who you were with?'

'I was with Clémentine Rouquier. Our French *au pair*.'

'And what were you doing in the bedroom at the back of the house with your French nanny?'

In the gallery, someone sniggered loudly.

'I ... er ... She was my mistress.' Michael now started to weep in the witness box. 'While my wife was trying to save our baby, I was with my mistress.' He was crying loudly now. I saw the expressions on the faces of some of the jurors and realised to my astonishment that Michael was eliciting sympathy.

'Did your wife know about your affair?'

Michael didn't answer immediately. The question didn't seem relevant and I expect, like me, he was waiting for May to object. 'I think she might have, yes,' he mumbled. And then I understood why Wood had asked that.

I hadn't known he was having an affair. Of course, any wife would say that because the shame of people knowing you were a weak woman who turned a blind eye to your husband's infidelity is almost greater than the shame of everyone finding out your husband was sleeping around. But I genuinely hadn't suspected a thing. I should have done. After Amber died, I asked Michael to send Clémentine home to France, but he insisted she should stay. She was of no use to us, wandering around the house with her long face, but he kept her on. It wasn't until after Ellie died that he paid her three months' wages, bought her a plane ticket and took her to the airport.

I could see the skeletal woman and the black woman staring at me. They were obviously nearly as taken aback as I was. Although I was reeling from shock, I had enough lucidity to realise how I would come over now. Everyone would think that I'd perjured myself to cover for my husband, so as not to destroy his reputation more than I already had done, or so as to hide my own embarrassment. I'd said he wasn't at home. He'd said he thought I knew about the affair. The jurors would now think I was unreliable, dishonest, a liar. And of course I was all of those things.

Until now, though, I'd assumed that Michael trusted me implicitly, but I found myself wondering if he believed I was guilty of murdering our babies. Did he admit to committing adultery knowing it would make me look worse than him? If the jury believed I knew about Clémentine and him, they might even deduce that Michael's affair had given me a motive: *revenge*.

Perhaps that was taking it too far. But whatever my husband's reasons, his confession had just sealed my fate. There was no way Jenny could make up for this. No way I was ever going home.

CHAPTER 9

~

Jonathan

May 2018

Michael Slade doesn't seem to be at home. I give a shrug in the direction of my car, parked in front of the gate at the bottom of the driveway, where Kelly is waiting out of the rain – by her own admission, she hadn't dressed for the sudden change in the weather. Taking a few steps back, I consider the house. It has an off-white façade with red bricks on the side. Judging from the size of the place, it has at least four bedrooms, maybe more. In my inexpert opinion, the property must have cost a bomb. Granted, it's right on the A369 and you could probably hear the traffic if it wasn't for this downpour, but it's also situated on the edge of the Leigh Woods Nature Reserve.

I thought Michael Slade might have moved away from the Bristol area altogether, but he's barely outside the city boundary. I wonder how he could have afforded a place in this rather coveted corner of suburbia, especially if he paid any of Melissa's legal fees, but this is definitely the address Simon Goodman gave me and I saw Slade's name on the letterbox on the gatepost. There's a flashy red Mercedes Benz SLK in the driveway, which smacks of a midlife crisis. It also suggests that Slade is in, although I hadn't really expected him to be home during the day, even at lunchtime.

I ring the doorbell once more and this time the intercom sputters into life.

'Third time lucky,' I mumble, and then stoop to give my name through the microphone. As I bend down, a raindrop falls onto the back of my neck and rolls down the top of my spine, making me wince. The speaker splutters back at me incoherently. 'I'm sorry, I didn't catch that,' I say loudly, wiping the nape of my neck with my hand.

A few seconds later, the front door swings open and I find myself face to face with Michael Slade. He's several inches shorter than me, although his position on the doorstep gives him a temporary boost to my height, and he's ten to fifteen years older. He's wearing a navy T-shirt tucked into a pair of light green Bermuda shorts, which I find disconcerting, and no socks or shoes.

'Damn thing doesn't work very well,' he says, pointing at the intercom on the wall. 'Neither does the one at the gate.'

'Jonathan Hunt. *The Redcliffe Gazette*,' I say, holding out my hand. He doesn't take it. 'The gate was open.' I nod my head towards the end of the drive. 'I hope you don't mind.'

'This about Melissa?' he asks gruffly.

'That's right. I've been asked to write a piece—'

'I'm not interested.' He starts to close the door, then stops and stares at something over my shoulder. Following his gaze, I turn to see Kelly swinging her long bare legs out of the car. She straightens up, smoothing down her skirt and opening her umbrella. Then she closes the car door and walks up the short drive towards us in her sandals.

I turn back to Slade, whose eyes are still very much glued to Kelly. I seem to remember Michael Slade had a reputation for being a womaniser. I'm not sure how I know that – some blurred memory I can't quite zoom in on. Clearly he still has an eye for the ladies.

Reaching my side, Kelly smiles politely at him, and then shoots me a puzzled look. I'm not sure if the message is *What's going on?* or *What's with the beachwear?*, so I just shrug at her again.

'This is my colleague—'

'I'm working from home today,' Slade says, 'but I can spare a few minutes.' He steps back and holds the door open for us. Kelly has made an impression on him, but he doesn't seem interested in knowing her name, so I don't bother to complete my introduction.

'What is it you do for a living, Mr Slade?' Kelly asks him politely as we traipse behind him along the hallway and into the living room. I'd been about to ask him the same thing. Kelly's taller than him, too, I note, in those chunky sandals anyway.

'I'm a chartered surveyor,' Slade replies over his shoulder. Then in a patronising tone, he adds, 'I work in property and building consultancy.'

I feel offended on Kelly's behalf and then I remind myself that on more than one occasion I, too, have underestimated her intelligence.

Slade offers to make some tea and disappears, leaving Kelly and me alone in the living room. I dry my glasses on my handkerchief and then put them back on. I look around. Slade seems to have decorated the whole room without any colour. The sofas and curtains are oatmeal; the rug with some geometrical pattern on it is a light fawn. Even the coffee table is off-white. The cream walls add little variety.

Over the central fireplace, there's an ornate gilt mirror at such a crooked angle that it can only be deliberately hung that way. A charcoal sketch of a young naked woman kneeling by a fountain hangs on the wall opposite us. It strikes me as vulgar rather than erotic.

'Who knew there were so many tones of white?' I whisper.

'I know, right?' Kelly whispers back. She's staring at the picture and doesn't look at me. 'It's like fifty shades of beige in here.'

I chuckle, taking in the double doors at the far end of the room that lead into a conservatory. I imagine there must be terrific views when it's not belting it down outside.

The weather has been glorious for the last couple of weeks. Ever since Holly left me, in fact. Until today. I've been wallowing in self-pity and feeling very down, and my mood wasn't lifted in the slightest by the sun. But I'm a lot happier today, despite this torrential rain, although I've a sneaky suspicion it may be a high before another low.

'Tastelessly decorated interior, but awesome house,' Kelly comments, breaking into my thoughts. 'Biggish.'

'He's in the right business.'

'I noticed the Merc, too. Is he compensating for something, do you think?'

'I have no idea what you mean.' I arch an eyebrow at her, my mouth twitching. You couldn't fail to notice the car, and I'm impressed Kelly recognised the make. Then I reprimand myself for thinking that way. I'm being judgemental again, not to mention sexist.

'Oh well, he's been hospitable so far,' Kelly says. I have it on the tip of my tongue to retort that if she hadn't alighted from my Ford Focus at exactly the right moment, we wouldn't have been admitted inside this awesome biggish house.

Before we left the offices this morning, I told Kelly what Simon Goodman had said on the phone when I'd called him to ask for Michael Slade's address. He'd warned me that Slade could be very arrogant and prone to exaggeration. He also said Slade was sly. It was plain to me that Melissa's first ex-husband wasn't particularly fond of the second one. I think the subtext was that I should take anything Michael said – if he deigned to speak to me at all – with a pinch of salt. It occurs to me now that Slade might open up more to Kelly than me. He seems quite taken with her, after all.

'Do you want to handle this, Kelly?' I ask.

'What? Interview him, you mean?' When I nod, her face lights up briefly and then falls. 'But I haven't prepared anything,' she says.

I don't tell her that I haven't, either. Just then Slade appears in the doorway holding three mugs at precarious angles. He has put some slippers on. I whisper to Kelly, 'Just wing it. You'll be fine.'

Once we've sipped our teas, Kelly fishes a smartphone out of her handbag. 'Do you mind if I record this?' she asks, fiddling with her mobile.

'I'd rather you didn't,' Slade says.

'Ah. OK. Do you object to me taking notes?'

'No, that's fine, I guess.'

Kelly swaps her phone for a notebook and pen and uses one of her thighs to lean on. 'I'm very sorry if this drags up traumatic memories for you, Mr Slade,' she begins, 'I can't imagine—'

'Michael, please,' says Slade, with what he probably hopes will pass for a winning smile on his face, but looks more like a lecherous leer to me.

'Could we start with the evening Amber died? Were there many people in the house?'

'Not a lot, no. Some of our friends. Our family. That's all.'

'Can you tell me who was there?'

'Well, Melissa, obviously, her son Callum, my daughter Bella, our friends Robert and Jennifer Porter, and their daughter Sophia.'

'So, including you, that would make seven people.'

'That sounds about right. Plus the twins, obviously.'

I wonder what she's going to ask next. If it were me, I'd steer

Slade firmly onto the subject of the babies. He has just given Kelly her cue.

She pauses briefly before saying, 'Mr Slade, were you satisfied with the coroner's verdict of Sudden Infant Death Syndrome for Amber?'

Nicely done!

'Call me Michael.' He sighs. 'Amber was a sickly baby. She always had a cold and tummy ache. I was forever telling her not to, but Melissa positioned Amber on her front in the cot. It all added up logically. So, yes, at the time, I accepted the conclusion of cot death.'

'At the time?'

'Well, with hindsight, it seems less likely, doesn't it?'

Kelly doesn't miss a beat. 'What do you mean, Mr Slade?' she asks gently.

'Well, given that Melissa was found guilty of murdering Ellie, it ... one has to ask oneself ... it stands to reason that ...'

'You think she might have killed both babies,' Kelly offers, when Slade doesn't seem inclined to finish any of his sentences.

'Well, yes, obviously.'

'You believe your wife was guilty, then?'

'My *ex*-wife,' Slade says. After a second or two, it becomes clear he isn't going to answer the question, but his silence does that for him. Simon Goodman had told me Slade blamed Melissa. I got the impression he was reluctant to give me this address for that very reason.

'Was anyone with Melissa on the evening Ellie died?' Kelly asks, undeterred.

'No. Melissa was alone when she claims to have found Ellie dead in her cot. I was at home. She said she shouted for me, but I didn't hear her. I must have been in a different part of the house.'

'Was anyone else at home?'

Slade pauses, just a fraction of a second too long, before

answering. 'No, not as far as I remember.' He stares into his mug. 'It was a long time ago. I've forgotten some of the facts.'

It strikes me that you'd recollect such dramatic events very clearly, even five years later. The police would have questioned Slade about this, perhaps even several times. He must have been over every detail of what happened that evening – who was where, and what everyone did and said. And yet, here he is, pretending his memory is hazy.

And then it comes to me. Michael Slade admitted on the stand – in front of a courtroom full of people – that he'd been cheating on his wife. That's what I was trying to recall earlier when he was ogling Kelly.

I see Kelly narrow her eyes at him. She doesn't believe him. I'll fill her in later.

'Do you know where your daughter and stepson were?' she asks.

Another pregnant pause. 'No, I can't say I do,' Slade replies eventually. 'Bella made the mistake of moving into her mother's house permanently. She stayed with us for a while after we lost Amber – I did everything I could to keep her – but she may have left by then.'

'Mistake? Why was it a mistake for her to move in with her mother, Mr Slade?'

'Bella's mother, Margaret, had no control over her. Bella went a bit wayward before she went AWOL.'

'Your daughter ran away from home?'

He nods. 'Some boyfriend her mother didn't approve of. I think she ran off with him. I think she sends her mother the odd card, but as far as I know, no one has seen her since.'

'How long ago did Bella run away?'

'I'm not sure if you'd call it "running away" at her age. She was eighteen – an adult.'

'I see. And how long ago was it?'

'She left her mother's home about four years ago.'

81

I'd like to hear more about this, but Slade's bitter voice wavers a little, and I wonder if he's going to cry. I decide to keep quiet. It's not my interview.

Kelly scribbles notes furiously in her notebook. I think she's giving him time to pull himself together. I glance down at her lap, but although her handwriting appears very neat, my glasses are smeared now and I can't make out what she has written.

'And Callum?'

'He was around less often for a while, then not at all after Melissa was arrested. Melissa's ex collected Callum's stuff and he lived with his father for a few years until he went to university.'

I'm intrigued that Slade refers to Goodman as "Melissa's ex" when the same term could be applied to him. 'Her ex?' I say before I can stop myself.

Slade snaps his head up. He looks surprised, as though he'd completely forgotten I was there. 'Simon Goodman. Melissa's first husband. Callum's father,' he says, standing up to signal that we've outstayed our welcome.

I drain my tea, and Kelly and I stand up too. This time Slade does shake my hand when I offer it at the door. I hand him a business card and Kelly does the same. Then she picks up her umbrella from where she left it on the doorstep, and holds it over the pair of us. It covers half of me and half of her, and we both get soaked in the few seconds it takes us to walk briskly down the driveway to the car.

'That raised more questions than it answered,' Kelly says wryly as I turn the settings for the heater and the windscreen wipers as high as they will go. 'He didn't seem at all concerned about Bella even though he hasn't seen her for at least four years.'

'No, you're right.'

'I think we need to find her. She might be able to help us.'

'If her parents don't know where she is, there's little chance that we—'

'And he was definitely lying about who was in the house. For

Amber's death as well as for Ellie's. I got the impression someone else was there. Both times.'

'Ah, about that—'

'He looked down a lot,' Kelly says. 'Did you notice that?'

I did, but I assumed he was admiring Kelly's legs.

'He was deliberately avoiding eye contact,' she continues. 'A sure sign he was being dishonest. Do you think he's protecting someone?'

'Kelly, I was reminded of something earlier,' I say. 'Slade was having an affair. With the *au pair*. It came out in court. I think that might be why he was being evasive.'

'Oh. Wow. I see.'

Neither of us speaks for a second or two. I let Kelly take in what I've just told her while I concentrate on overtaking a learner driver.

Then Kelly says, 'It's odd. Simon Goodman is convinced his ex-wife is innocent whereas Slade—'

'I know. I got the feeling he'd have been quite happy for her to go down for murdering both babies.'

'Do you think *he* might have done it?'

'What? Killed the babies? And framed Melissa? The first time it didn't look enough like murder, so the second time he made it clearer?'

'Too far-fetched?'

I consider this. My gut feeling tells me Melissa is guilty as charged; guilty as sin. And Ex-Hubby-Number-Two seems to believe she killed both babies even though she went down for only one count of murder. Unless that's just what he's pretending to think.

'I'm not sure we have anything to suggest that *Michael* Slade is a killer,' I say. 'But I agree. He's a slippery sod.'

'I've got a feeling he knows more about what happened to those babies than he's letting on. He's hiding something.'

CHAPTER 10

~

Melissa

I haven't always been a monster. Until a few months ago, I was just a bad mother, but prison has changed me. From bad mother to beastly monster. Quite a journey. You have to toughen up in prison to survive, as I soon learnt. Especially when you're a police officer and a convicted baby killer.

December 2013

I was taken directly from the holding cells underneath Bristol Crown Court to Her Majesty's Prison Haresfield Park in Gloucestershire. I arrived late in the evening and my personal property was immediately confiscated, labelled and logged. I had the choice between a smokers' or a non-smokers' welcome pack. I'd only ever been an occasional social smoker – the odd fag with Jenny – but I opted for the smokers' one. Then I took a shower before putting on my prison-issue clothing, although I was told

I could wear my own clothing here before long. I was given a prison number and allowed a phone call. The only number I knew by heart, apart from my own mobile, was our landline. So I rang Michael, but we didn't have much to say to each other.

The next day, I went through the reception process. I was interviewed by the health care team. A doctor then examined me and strongly advised me to sign up for the prison's drug and alcohol awareness course. I watched a video about prison life. I had more interviews and assessments. Everyone was friendly and I was fine all the while I was in the induction unit. I felt safe, separated from the other prisoners.

Finally, a prison officer escorted me to the single cell I'd been allocated in one of the main units. Lying on my bed that night, I thought about my babies. I heard their cries all the time, not just when I slept. It was like having bad tinnitus. It drove me mad, but I didn't want it to stop. It was all I had left of my baby girls. Mostly, it was just background noise, white noise, but that night I really listened.

I could distinguish Amber's agonised squalling from Ellie's hungry mewling. I could tell my twin daughters apart. Even now, I could hear them, calling for me, as if I was still their mother. I don't know why, but I'd thought their cries in my head would stop when I was sent to jail, as though my life sentence would turn a page in my life story and begin a different chapter.

I didn't think I would fall asleep. The strong smell of bleach didn't quite mask the lingering reek of vomit, although my cell looked bright and clean. I tossed and turned on the narrow bed, shivering under the starched sheets. It was a far cry from the king-sized bed I used to share with Michael with its soft Egyptian cotton bedclothes, infused with the smell of washing powder mixed with the scent of our bodies. I felt terrified and isolated; lost and unspeakably sad.

But I was mentally and physically exhausted, and my eyelids grew heavy. I could feel sleep taking hold of me. Just as I was nodding off, there was a thud from the other side of the wall. Followed by another one. The third was accompanied by a squeal. It went on for at least a minute before it dawned on me that the inmate in the next cell was banging her head against the wall. I wondered if she'd always been disturbed or if everyone in here ended up with psychiatric problems. Perhaps I'd lose it, too. Maybe I'd get out of prison one day only to go to an asylum.

The headbanging continued. I'd have expected the twins to screech in fright at the racket, but abruptly they stopped crying and became silent. Any sympathy I felt for the woman in the next cell was now booted out by anger. How dare she silence my children! Not so long ago, I'd been wishing myself that Amber wouldn't squall so much. Life is full of little ironies.

'Be quiet!' I yelled at the wall.

But there was another thud and another shriek.

I tried again. 'Stop it!' I tried to bang the wall myself with my hand, but it only served to make my wrist throb in pain. The sound my fist had made was muffled compared to the sound my fellow inmate was making with her head.

Yet another bump and yelp.

'Shut the fuck up!' I shouted at the top of my voice.

And this time, she did, leaving an eerie calm. Third time lucky.

From that evening on, three became my lucky number. It started off with little things. Lying in bed that very night, I crossed and uncrossed my fingers three times. I told myself that if I didn't, I'd never hear from Amber and Ellie again. The next day, I twisted my wedding ring around my finger once, twice, three times. Of course, they'd confiscated the real one when I arrived. For my own security, they'd said. So I had to turn the ghost of my gold band around my wedding finger. Otherwise something bad would happen to Callum. I couldn't take that risk. I knew then that before long, I'd have to do everything three times. Or else.

To begin with, I spent as much time as possible in my room, still do, really, although we're allowed out for several hours a day and encouraged to take part in "purposeful activities" during unlock. But I find that in my cell, I can escape from prison – in my head, at least – by losing myself in the fictitious world of novels. HMP Haresfield Park has a good library.

It took me a while to muster up the courage to go into the recreation room. I've never watched much television, but I thought I should make an effort to fit in. Insults were hurled at me as soon as I entered the room and the air buzzed with hatred. All eyes were on me instead of on the screen.

I sat at the back, leaving two seats free between me and the next girl, who promptly got up, turned her nose up, as if I was giving off a foul stench, and moved further away from me to another chair. Everyone else laughed at this, and I wished I hadn't come. Scanning the room, I wondered if the girl from the cell next to mine was there.

Thankfully, *Downton Abbey* was on, and soon my fellow prisoners lost interest in me and focused their attention on the television. After a few minutes, a waif in her early twenties walked in and sat down next to me. A couple of the others turned round and stared. I could feel my heart thumping against my chest and the pounding in my ears drowned out the voices of Hugh Bonneville and Maggie Smith, as if someone had switched the volume down. What was she going to do to me?

But then she smiled and I sighed with relief. She didn't care who I was. As she flicked her shoulder-length, dark hair, I was reminded of Bella. A wave of sadness broke over me as I realised I'd probably never see my stepdaughter again.

'You're new,' she whispered.

I nodded, hoping to avoid striking up a conversation with her, even though I'd come in here intending to start to blend in. I could see several white scars on her left forearm – shallow, parallel and of uneven length. A lot of the prisoners had similar marks, although, again, I didn't know if they'd self-harmed before or after being sent to this place.

'There's another newcomer,' she continued. 'The copper who slaughtered her twins.' Her voice was louder and a few of the women in front of us made angry shushing noises. 'Have you heard about her?'

I couldn't reply. I realised that it wasn't that she didn't care who I was; she didn't know who I was. But she knew about me.

'I'd like just five minutes alone with her,' she continued, thumping her right fist into her left palm. 'I'd teach her a lesson. That baby killer bitch!'

I got up as she spat out these last words and made my way back to the safety of my room. It was clear to me I was going to have to confine myself to my cell, a prison within a prison.

But the next day they came to me in my room. Five of them. Four to hold me down and one – the dark-haired girl with the scars – to do the dirty work. Or the "handiwork" as she called it. They called her Gemma when they egged her on.

I lifted my head to see what she was doing. She was holding a pen and a needle, a little bigger than an ordinary sewing needle – a tapestry needle, perhaps.

One of her friends pressed a razor blade to my neck. 'Lie down and keep still, pig!' she ordered.

I could hear whimpering. It took me a few seconds to realise it was me.

'Yeah. Shut the fuck up!' Gemma said and then she laughed. The others joined in. I was slow to get the joke. Then it dawned on me. Those were the words I'd shouted through the wall at her the other night. Gemma was my neighbour and it seemed she'd taken it into her head – once she'd stopped using it to bang on the wall – to get me back for yelling at her.

My hand was pushed down into the bed while Gemma worked on it, poking her tongue out in concentration. I clenched my fist, but that didn't stop her. I was utterly helpless. As I lay on my bed, writhing and squealing in pain, thoughts chased each other through my head. Had that needle been sterilised? Somehow I doubted it. What was she drawing on the back of my hand? Would I get an infection?

A prison guard burst in, but not before Gemma had finished her task. I was taken to the prison infirmary. It wasn't the GP who had examined me during reception. This doctor was a small, round young woman with hamster cheeks, pulpous lips and flawless skin. She had very long auburn hair, held back by a bright red Alice band. I read the name on the lapel of her white coat. Dr Nolan. She looked like an older version of the BBC Test Card Girl and she spoke with a soothing Irish lilt.

The prison doctor dabbed at the back of my hand gently. 'The good news is, stick and poke tattoos fade quite a bit over time,' she said. She had a pleasant voice. She didn't ask me what BKB stood for. Maybe she already knew. Baby Killer Bitch. It was my moniker now. I no longer had an identity or a name. Just a nickname, carved onto the back of my hand, and a prison number.

I nodded and bit my bottom lip to stop it wobbling.

'What will happen now?' I asked. I meant, what would happen to me. Would I be tested for AIDS? Would I have to go back to my room or could I stay here a while? That sort of thing.

But Dr Nolan assumed I was asking after my fellow inmates. My attackers. 'Well, Gemma was due up for parole in a fortnight or so,' the doctor said. 'I think the prison guards wanted her to be released more than she wanted it herself.'

I wondered how they got hold of razors and needles inside.

'I probably shouldn't tell you this,' she said, 'but you'll learn soon enough. There's a blind spot when you're outside in the exercise yard. Sometimes family and friends throw small packages over the wall. This prison is understaffed and overcrowded. The guards work hard and they do their best, but you know …'

I wasn't sure why she told me that. I didn't think I'd spoken my question aloud, but her words made me think maybe I had. Or did she tell me that so I could defend myself? Retaliate?

Doctor Nolan kept me in the infirmary for the evening. Under observation, she said, but I think it was probably out of kindness. It was far better than my cell. As I dozed, my mind wandered to my home. I imagined I was in my big comfy bed with the soft sheets, next to Michael, before any of this happened.

When I'd phoned Michael on arriving here, he told me he was going to put our house on the market. He said it was too big now. I suppose it was. With the twins' deaths and my arrest, and Callum, Bella and Clémentine all gone, Michael would be living there on his own.

But I'm sure that was only part of it. Our home housed spectres and shadows now. The bad memories had eclipsed years of good times, leaving in their wake shattered dreams and broken hearts that would never heal. And it occurred to me that even if I was released from prison one day, I no longer had a home to go back to.

CHAPTER 11

~

Jonathan

June 2018

For once, the boys don't bicker in the car on the way to school. I let Noah choose the radio station on the condition that he speaks to Alfie only if he has something nice to say. Noah doesn't say a thing to his younger brother the whole journey. Result! Parenting is all about bribery. According to my elder son, no one listens to the radio anymore, so Noah plugs his smartphone into the USB port and we're subjected to ten minutes of hip-hop from a streaming app. Compromise. Another essential ingredient to bringing up kids.

I am such a crap dad.

After dropping my sons off – on time for a change, I smile to myself. I decide that the day has got off to a good start.

But then my mobile goes. The ringtone is so loud I jump.

'Jonathan, there's been a bit of drama,' Claire's voice trills through the car speaker. She's too loud as well. I turn the volume down. 'A car hurtled off the M5 and plunged fifty metres down an embankment about – ooh – an hour ago now.' I imagine Claire looking at her watch as she paces around the Aquarium in her heels. 'A driver and one passenger.' She sounds oddly excited. I hate the fact that other people's misfortunes make great fodder for our news stories. 'The driver is still trapped in the wreck and fire crews are on site.'

'OK, on my way,' I say, trying to keep the reluctance out of my voice. Great. I can only imagine what the traffic will be like. A road accident at rush hour.

'M5 northbound, just after Junction 15.'

'Got it,' I say chirpily.

Or, as Alfie would say: Bring. It. Off.

~

I don't get into *The Redcliffe Gazette* offices until way past two in the afternoon. As soon as I burst through the door, Kelly waves to me from across the room, which is still, after about three months of construction, more open-plan than booths. Thankfully, the workmen seem to be taking yet another day off, so at least it's peaceful. Kelly appears to have been looking out for me. The last thing I feel like doing right now is proofreading another of her articles.

As I make my way over to my workstation, I notice Claire has a visitor – or a victim – in the Aquarium. Sinking into my swivel chair with a sigh, I pull the hanky out of my pocket and wipe the sweat from my brow. I can feel my shirt sticking to my back.

'Hot out?' Kelly asks as I sit down.

'Just a bit.' I've been regretting booking up our family holiday in the South of France this year. If I'd known we were in for this heatwave, I'd have chosen a different destination. Like Iceland or Greenland. Or Kazakhstan.

I'm not just hot; I'm hungry, despite the sandwich I bought

from the motorway services on the way back. Not to mention grumpy.

'Not now, Kelly,' I say, as she pushes a green cardboard folder apparently containing a wad of papers across my desk. At first glance, I'd assumed she was handing me her latest work, but there are a lot of pages in that folder, so it can't be that. I don't have time to surmise about what she wants to show me. I need to get to work. 'I'd better get this online first.'

'Oh.' Her face falls.

'I'll take a look later. Handing the folder back to her, I connect my laptop to the docking station. 'Who's that with Claire?'

'It's Superintendent Simon Goodman.'

'What?' I whirl round. So it is. 'What's he doing with her?'

'No idea.'

As I watch, Simon gets up and shakes Claire's hand. I turn back to my computer, pretending to be hard at work. Out of the corner of my eye, I watch him cross the room.

'Jonathan, have you got a moment?' Claire calls from behind me.

'Ah,' I say in a low voice to Kelly. 'All is about to be revealed.'

'What have you got for me on that car accident?' Claire asks before I've even closed the door behind me. Straight to the point as usual. I want to know what Simon Goodman was doing here, but that will have to wait.

'Well, luckily, neither the driver nor the passenger – husband and wife – died in the crash,' I begin. Claire doesn't comment, but her face clearly says, *lucky for some.* 'The man – he was the one behind the wheel – managed to get out of the car by himself. He'd already been taken to Southmead by the time I arrived. Minor injuries. Scrapes and scratches, according to the paramedic I spoke to.'

'Oh dear.' I'm not sure exactly what has caused Claire's disappointment. Was she hoping for a fatality? Or at the very least severe injuries? Or is it because I arrived too late at the scene to get a photo of one of the casualties?

'I've got some good photos of the fire crew freeing the woman from the wreck with hydraulic cutters.'

Claire brightens at this. 'Right. Get those uploaded and posted. Perhaps you can go to the hospital tomorrow for a follow-up. See if you can blag your way in to see the husband or the wife and get a quote? That's all.'

This is my cue to leave, but I haven't finished. 'Was that Simon Goodman in your office just now?'

'Yes.' She doesn't offer an explanation.

'Anything to do with the Melissa Slade appeal?'

She spreads her arms, as if to say, *what else?* but it's obvious she isn't going to enlighten me.

I'm halfway out the door when Claire calls me back. 'Oh, Jonathan? I nearly forgot. Someone rang *The Gazette* and asked to speak to you. She said it was important, so the call was passed to me. A Jennifer Porter? She wouldn't say what it was about.'

The name rings a bell. Jennifer Porter. Then it comes to me. Melissa's friend Jenny. Michael Slade mentioned her. She was one of the guests at the dinner party in their house the evening Amber died. 'Did she leave a number?'

'No. She said she'd try again later. I gave her your extension.'

'OK. And she didn't say what she wanted?'

Claire glares at me through bottle-green eyes that make it clear she has better things to do than repeat herself.

'Right. Thanks.' Now I have two unanswered questions. What was Simon Goodman doing here? And why did Jennifer Porter call me? 'If I miss her again, give her my mobile number.'

Sitting at my desk, I start work on this morning's story about the car accident. I'm suddenly aware that beads of sweat are forming on my face again, but it has nothing to do with the heat.

I've never been to the scene of a traffic accident – not to report on it, although I had to report on a motorway pile-up not long ago and I've covered a couple of drunk-driving collisions. This morning, at the scene of the accident, I felt strangely detached, and as I sift through my photos now, it's as if I'm seeing the car wreck for the first time. In one of my shots, the woman's face is very sharp despite the zoom on my camera. As I stare at her, her features blur and then I see Mel's face, as if the woman has morphed into my wife.

For a few seconds, I gaze at her lovingly, longingly. Mel was deemed newsworthy once. Briefly. Then something else came along, something more dramatic and more recent, and she became old news. That's the way it works. Everyone gets their fifteen minutes of fame. Isn't that what Andy Warhol said? Mel lasted a bit longer than a quarter of an hour. When she made the headlines, it was more of a one-day wonder.

The smell of coffee, as Kelly places a steaming plastic cup on my desk, pulls me firmly back to the present.

'You looked like you could use this,' she says.

'Thank you, Kelly.'

'So, what was Superintendent Goodman doing with Saunders in the Aquarium?'

'I'm none the wiser, Kelly. Our editor wasn't very forthcoming about that.'

'Maybe this will provide a clue.' She thrusts the green folder into my hands. 'He slipped me this when Claire wasn't looking.'

'Who did? Goodman?'

Kelly nods. I see a yellow Post-it stuck to the folder with my name written on it in neat capital letters. I snap off the elastic and open the folder. It contains several printed pages, some of them dated.

'It's a journal,' I say, skimming the first entry. *Callum … beautiful baby boy … very different … something was wrong with me … bad mother … I couldn't connect …*

I look up at Kelly. 'These are Melissa Slade's diaries.'

Her eyes widen. 'Ooh. Can I … when you've finished …?'

'Photocopy it. That way we can both read it.' I close the folder hand it back to her.

Kelly gets up and I get back to work. I've just posted the story on the accident when a call comes through on my extension. It's Jennifer Porter. She has the voice of a child, although, if she's Melissa's friend, she must be a fair bit older than she sounds.

'Simon Goodman asked me to get in touch with you,' she says. 'He gave me your email address, but I thought it would be better to speak to you.'

'I'm so glad you rang. Would you like to meet up somewhere? We could chat over a cup of tea?'

'No. I … I didn't want to get in touch at all,' she admits. 'Can I have your word that you won't quote me on anything?'

'Of course. All off the record. I promise. Where would you like to start? What did you want to tell me?'

I hear a sigh. 'I'm not sure, to be honest. I'd like to help – Melissa was my friend and Callum, her son, is still good friends with my daughter, Sophia.'

'But?'

'My husband, Rob, has been dead against me getting involved with the campaign for Melissa's release. He thinks … well, you never really know anyone, do you? I don't know if I'm doing the right thing.'

I think I understand what Jennifer Porter is trying to say. 'I know what you mean,' I say. 'I've been asked to write about Melissa and the appeal, but I don't know her. I've never met her.' I don't tell her that I never want to meet Melissa. 'I like to report the facts and it's not easy getting to the truth with so much conflicting information.'

'Exactly.'

'Shall I ask you some questions and you can answer what you feel comfortable with?'

'OK.'

I slide a notebook towards me on the desk and pick up a pen. 'Let's start with the dinner party. Can you talk me through that evening?'

Kelly has rolled her chair nearer to me and I put Jennifer Porter on the speaker so that she can follow the conversation.

'It was just a normal dinner party to begin with. Rob and I arrived with our daughter, Sophia, at about seven. The food was lovely. There was good wine. Everything was going fine until we realised that Amber ... was ... It was awful.'

'What about during the evening? Did everyone's behaviour seem normal to you?'

She doesn't answer for a second or two. 'I think so, yes. Melissa had told me that things weren't great between her and Michael, and he didn't say anything, but you could tell. He gave her black looks, that sort of thing. She slipped outside for a cigarette with me and he didn't approve.'

As I scribble this down, Jennifer Porter stops talking, as if she's afraid she has said too much.

'Go on,' I say gently.

'I was just thinking, that could be normal behaviour for some married couples who have just had twins. Maybe Michael was just tired and irritable. Two babies at the same time would put a strain on anyone's marriage.'

'Uh-huh. What about Melissa? How did she seem to you that evening?'

'She'd made an effort.'

'With the meal, you mean?'

'No, I don't think she did much of the food preparation or cooking. I meant with her hair and her clothes. She looked lovely.'

'And this was unusual?'

'Sort of. At the time, yes. She'd been very down since the twins were born. I went round to her place one day and she was unwashed, unkempt, you know. She'd been struggling.'

'Depressed?'

'Yes. She was eventually diagnosed with postnatal depression. Anyway, on the evening of the dinner party, she was wearing new clothes, she'd had her hair cut and she was wearing make-up. I

97

remember feeling very relieved to see her that way. I'd been worried about her.'

'So she showed no signs of being depressed that evening?'

'Um …' Another slight pause. Then she says, 'I don't think it would be true to say that. She drank a lot. Michael was concerned she was drinking too much. That's what he told Rob. Melissa seemed on edge. She wouldn't let go of the baby monitor and kept checking the volume was turned up high so she would hear Amber when she needed a feed. Ellie had already woken up, you see, and … well, we only realised later why Amber hadn't.'

Kelly grabs my Biro and notepad and scribbles something down, then angles the pad towards me. Glancing down, I read *FOOD?*

I don't twig immediately as Jennifer Porter has just mentioned feeding the baby and so I'm visualising bottles of milk, boobs and mashed-up baby meals in jars. Then I nod at Kelly as I get her drift.

'Mrs Porter, you said Melissa didn't do much of the food preparation. Did Michael do the cooking?'

'No. Clémentine took care of most of that.'

'Clémentine? Was that—?'

'Clémentine … Rouquier, I think her surname was. She was their French *au pair*. I'd found her to help out Melissa.' She sounds rueful.

'And she was there that night?'

'Yes.'

I write the name on the pad.

'Are you aware that Michael Slade was having an affair with the nanny? I don't like to gossip, but it might be important.'

'Yes, I know. I was in court the day Michael gave evidence,' I say.

'He was old enough to be her father. They shared a love of French wine, apparently.' I exchange a look with Kelly. 'He was actually fucking her – in the house – the night Ellie died,' Jennifer

Porter continues, her innocent voice at odds with the crude words coming through the speaker.

I struggle to find anything to say to that. As my mouth opens and closes again, Kelly writes something else down on my pad. I arch my eyebrows at her. It wouldn't have entered my head to ask that, but I think I know where Kelly is going with it.

I put Kelly's question to Jenny. 'Would you say that Michael Slade loved his baby girls?'

'I don't know,' she says. Judging from her tone, she's surprised at this question, too. 'I think so. I doubt he could have killed them, if that's what you're driving at.' I look at Kelly, who gives a satisfied nod.

'What about Melissa?'

'What about her? Did she love Amber and Ellie or do I think she killed them?'

'Either,' I say. 'Both.'

She sighs. 'That's what I meant earlier, I guess,' she says, 'when I said you never really know people. She was – *is* – my friend. She wasn't herself in the months after the twins were born, but she was doing her best. On the other hand … no, it's nothing … I shouldn't …'

'This is off the record,' I remind her.

'She'd packed up the nursery, boxed up all the baby stuff as soon as the police had finished with the room. The clothes and everything. It was all disposed of before her trial. How can anyone be so heartless?'

I imagine Jenny's question is a rhetorical one, but I reply anyway. 'It might not have been heartlessness,' I say. 'It may just have been her way of trying to cope with her grief.'

Jenny clams up a bit after that. I make sure she notes down my mobile number in case she thinks of anything else. She also agrees to give me hers.

'It seems heartless to me, clearing out all the baby things as if they never existed,' Kelly says once I've hung up. 'It sounds more

99

like Melissa was getting rid of the evidence than coping with grief.'

'People deal with bereavement in very different ways,' I tell Kelly. 'There's no right way or wrong way.' But as I say that, I begin to doubt myself. Have I been doing the right thing? Have I got it all wrong? I realise that for the first time I'm feeling a sliver of sympathy, and a grudging admiration, for Melissa Slade. I also realise it's time I let go.

CHAPTER 12

~

Melissa

May 2014

During the night, every night, my girls grow up surprisingly quickly. One night they got their first teeth. Another night they started to walk and talk. They often fight with each other over primary-coloured building blocks. They sometimes play together with dolls and teddy bears.

I always go to sleep, dying to see them, but at the same time dreading the moment when I'll wake up, the instant when I'll experience afresh the horror and anguish of losing my babies. This wasn't reality, but yet another dream. Another dream that can never come true. I'll never hear my girls' first words; never see them take their first steps. The realisation leaves my lungs crushed and withered every time.

I've been at HMP Haresfield Park for five months now and I still feel surprised in the mornings that I've woken up at all. I truly believe I might be killed one night by one of my fellow prisoners. They all hate me. I'm a pariah, an untouchable. As both a former police officer and a convicted child murderer, I'm considered subhuman. And treated as such.

When I arrived, I swore never to proclaim my innocence, or rant and rail against the injustice of the judicial system. There are plenty of prisoners who do that, and it doesn't gain them kudos in here. I keep my head down and myself to myself.

I've been given cleaning duties to do. This is supposedly safe employment. I think the others see this as dirty work and it seems appropriate to them that I should be assigned these duties. I work hard to show I don't deem myself above such tasks. But no matter how much I scrub and polish, I don't seem to earn any respect.

The prison officers are concerned for my safety and they have offered several times to escort me whenever I leave my cell. But this would draw more unwelcome attention to me and I'm trying to keep a low profile, so I've always refused. That has scored me a few brownie points.

But I think there may have been a turning point recently. I think I've made a friend. Her name is Cathy, but everyone calls her Bob. That makes me think of Kate in *Blackadder*, although she doesn't look remotely like her. Cathy is small and slim; pretty and pretty tough. She has a skull and crossbones tattoo on the side of her long neck. She could be described as streetwise if there were any streets inside. Like me, she's a lifer. Unlike me, she's popular on the wing.

I found myself sitting next to Cathy in the dining hall about a fortnight ago. Ours was apparently one of the only prisons in the country to have a canteen. In most penal institutions, inmates eat in their cells, or so I'm told. I think I'd prefer to eat in my cell, really, but at Haresfield Park, it's supposed to be a privilege to eat communally in the refectory, and you can easily lose that right.

I think that day, the woman sitting opposite me probably did. She was from a different wing and I'd never seen her before, but she must have known who I was because she suddenly stood up and hurled her tray at me. Half of her meal ended up on my face and in my hair. Fortunately, the food was barely lukewarm, as usual, and I wasn't burnt. But I wanted to cry. I wanted to run away and hide.

'Sit tight,' my neighbour at the table hissed. 'Don't move.' I looked at her out of the corner of my eye. She had the other half of the meal over her. As I watched, she wiped her face on her T-shirt and carried on eating her food, her expression impassive, as if nothing had happened. I did the same. I stayed put, but the prisoner who had thrown the food got up and left the dining room. Some of the women laughed; others threw admiring glances our way.

After dinner, Cathy came into my room uninvited and sat cross-legged on my bed. She scrutinised me through large dark eyes that were partly hidden by her fringe. I stared back. Did she want something? Did she think she'd done me a favour and expect me to pay her back?

'I'm Cathy,' she said. It wasn't worth me introducing myself. Everyone on the wing knew me. Or thought they did. I looked her up and down. Her plaits still had flecks of minced beef in them. 'I know who you are,' she continued, undeterred by my silence. 'So, what's your story?'

'Sorry?'

'I mean, I know what you're in here for, but you're innocent, right?'

'Isn't everyone in here innocent?'

She laughed at that. 'I'm not.'

'Oh. What are you in here for?' I wasn't sure if I should have asked that question. I didn't really want to know the answer and I certainly didn't want to annoy Cathy. But she didn't seem to mind.

'I murdered my husband. He used to beat me up, force me to have sex with him, that sort of thing. It went on for years.' I noticed a scar running down her right cheek and wondered if her husband had caused it. 'One night I'd had enough, so I used a knife to kill the son of a bitch.'

'But isn't that self-defence?'

'Nah. It was premeditated. I was going to make it look like a burglary gone wrong. My bastard husband was loaded. As in filthy rich. Wealthy family. Huge house. The alarm didn't always work. He refused to get a guard dog – he loathed dogs.' She wagged a finger in my face in mock warning. 'Never trust people who don't like animals.'

Cathy seemed to lose track of what she was saying and a vacant expression passed over her face, but in a blink it was gone. 'Anyway, I figured he'd be an easy target for burglars,' she continues. 'I thought I'd get away with it. I thought I'd – literally – get away with murder.'

'So what went—'

'But then I got carried away. Didn't quite go through with my plans. Once I'd knifed him in the stomach and he was squirming on the floor like the coward he was, an idea came to me and I couldn't resist it.'

Cathy had become more and more animated as she spoke and she actually licked her lips at this point. She clearly had no remorse and enjoyed telling her story. She paused again, this time, I think, for effect.

'Go on.'

'Well, then I unbuckled his belt, pulled down his jeans and skanky pants – he'd pissed himself, of course, and I sliced off his dick.'

'You didn't?' I was shocked, but the corners of my mouth were twitching. Cathy was a great narrator and I could feel myself leaning forwards, hanging on to her every word.

'Yeah, I did. It was only small.' She wiggled her little finger. 'Thank God. At least it didn't hurt too much all the times he raped me.' She paused yet again, her face contorted with memories. I was fairly sure she was joking, understating what she'd gone through. He must have hurt her very badly for her to do what she did to him.

Then she resumed her story. 'I laughed the whole time. You'll only feel a little prick, I told him over and over.' She laughed now, maniacally. 'That's why they call me Bob, you know.'

'What? Why?'

'Lorena Bobbitt. You know, the American woman who cut off her abusive husband's penis?'

'Oh, I see.' And then I laughed too.

An image of my father reading the newspaper in his armchair flashed into my mind then. I recalled his reaction to an article about a teenage girl's rapist who had been arrested in Bristol.

'He deserves to have it chopped off!' he'd said to my mother. 'It's a crying shame for scum like him that they got rid of the death penalty in this country.'

It seemed to me that a life sentence was too severe a punishment for Cathy. She was younger than me, early thirties at most. She would have had much of her life ahead of her. So what if she'd had her moment of revenge? Her husband had been abusing her for a long time. He'd got no less than he deserved. Hadn't he?

'His family paid for a top barrister,' she said, as if she'd been reading my mind. 'Screwed me over good and proper in court.'

'I'm sorry.'

'Shit happens,' she said, making a dismissive gesture with her hand. 'But, I got sidetracked. I asked about you. Tell me your story.'

So I did. I didn't have anything to lose. I'd been wary of Cathy, but I found I already liked her immensely, and even though I'd just met her, I trusted her implicitly. I told her everything. Just as I'd told it to Simon. The exact same words, more or less.

CHAPTER 13

~

Jonathan

June 2018

On the way home from football practice the following Saturday morning, my sons are at it again. They're playing a game that seems to have two very simple rules. One: the first one to spot a yellow car and pinch his opponent scores a point. There seems to be an extraordinarily high number of yellow cars on the roads around Kingswood. Two: the loser is the one who bursts into tears first. Or, put differently, Noah wins and gloats; Alfie loses and howls.

I check the rear-view mirror before slamming on the brakes at a bus stop and stunning the boys into silence. Then I get out of the car and yank open the back door, using way more force than necessary. Hauling Noah out of the car, I yell at him, 'You win!'

'It was just a game, Dad,' he whines.

'I'm not talking about the bloody game,' I shout, aware that a few passers-by are smugly observing the dubious parenting skills I'm displaying. 'Get in the front! Now!'

I take a deep breath and get back in behind the wheel. Turning to my elder son and forcing myself to drop a few decibels, I say, 'This has got to stop, Noah!'

'Sorry, Dad,' Noah says meekly as I pull back into the road.

'It's not me you should be apologising to.'

'Sorry, Alfie.'

'I hope you're not going to fight like this when we go on holiday to France this summer.'

'No, Dad,' they chorus.

I've calmed down a bit by the time I park in the driveway in front of our house, but I need some time alone so I send the boys to their rooms to play separately for a while before lunch. They'll be on electronic games or tablets, but never mind.

I open the door to Rosie's room. It hasn't changed; I haven't changed a thing. I take in the pink walls, the rocking chair that Mel fell in love with, the white cot, the teddies sitting on top of the toy box, the rose-coloured bookcase with touch and feel books on it. These books have never been opened; their pages never turned. Everything in this room is unused and amassing dust. *This isn't a nursery, Jon. It's a shrine.*

Since our phone conversation the other day, I've been thinking about something Jennifer Porter, Melissa's friend, mentioned. She commented on how soon Melissa packed up her babies' things after their deaths. Jennifer thought it was heartless, but I'd suggested that maybe it was Melissa's way of dealing with her grief, her way of trying to accept that her babies were dead.

As I sink onto the rocking chair and look into the empty cot through the bars, I realise I have left this for far too long. I have kept this bedroom the way Mel and I decorated it four years ago, afraid that if I tidied away Rosie's things, it would be denying her existence. But Rosie will always exist in my heart and mind.

I've been sending my boys mixed messages, encouraging them

to move on while this room has chained us to the past, attesting to what we might have been. The three of us will never get over what happened, but we can get on with our lives.

I get up and go out to the garage, coming back with some cardboard boxes and a roll of brown parcel tape. Then I get to work.

I'm pulling out tiny clothes from the chest of drawers and putting them into plastic bags when Alfie peeps round the door. I swipe at my tears with the back of my hand. 'All right, mate? Are you hungry?' I ask, my voice trembling. He exits without a word.

Minutes later, he's back with Noah, who is carrying a mug of tea. In silence, Noah hands me the steaming mug and kneels down next to me. He pulls out another drawer and starts bagging up the clothes, while Alfie drags a cardboard box over to the toy box and puts the teddy bears inside.

I'm so touched that I well up again and I tell myself sternly, not for the first time, that I need to focus on what I do have and not what I've lost. My boys lost their mummy and their sister and they need me. As I look at my sons through wet eyes, a huge wave of pride unfurls inside me.

An hour later, I bundle them into the car again. Noah sits in the back seat and chats with his brother. I hear Alfie laugh at his brother's jokes and it chases away the dark clouds in my head. I ask them if they'd like to help me paint Rosie's room next weekend. They jump at my idea of turning her bedroom into a games room for the pair of them. I'll sell the rocking chair, cot and toy box on eBay. I should have done all that a long time ago.

After a late lunch at McDonald's, we drop off the baby clothes and books at Oxfam and then go come home to watch a film.

Noah lets Alfie choose the DVD and all three of us sit on the sofa in the living room. While they're engrossed in *Coco*, I open Melissa Slade's diary. I get as far as the second page, and the boys are up to the bit where Miguel discovers a family photo with the face of his great-great-grandfather torn out, when I decide to fetch a notebook and pen. I need to go through this thoroughly, for once. I'm a single father and I cut corners. My epitaph will probably have an inscription to that effect. But I want to take in every word that Melissa has written.

Sitting back down, I try to block out the film and concentrate on what I'm reading. Melissa starts with an account of her post-partum depression. She relates how she felt in a detached way – her tone is almost matter-of-fact. She doesn't dwell on her feelings, and although this makes her come over as slightly cold, I think I'm beginning to understand her. She has tried to tell her story, but she has had to tell it as if it happened to someone else so she could get the words down.

She writes about how supportive her friend Jenny was and how unsupportive her husband was, and I find my dislike for Michael Slade intensifying. She mentions how she gave up her career and her sporting activities to bring up her twins. This jogs my memory. I remember in one of the online articles – not one of mine – the journo had depicted an uncaring, bitter mother, who had hired a nanny to raise her children so that she could go out and get fit.

Something else occurs to me, but I don't know if it's relevant. Melissa's relationship with her second husband seems to have been far from hunky-dory. On the other hand, she has received no end of support from her first husband. Simon Goodman has been campaigning for her appeal and her release since she went to prison. He's still on her side now. I jot this observation down on my pad and then chew the end of my pen pensively. Perhaps he's still in love with her.

Then I read the entry about the dinner party. I've never met Melissa – and still have no desire to meet her – and yet it's as if I can hear her voice in my head, recounting the events of that evening. She describes the lengths she went to in order to look her best. I can almost picture her desperately trying to stop Amber crying so that she could put on her make-up and new dress before the guests arrived.

When I get to the part where Melissa finds Amber dead in her cot, my own heart stops for a couple of beats. I copy down everyone's reactions, although, again, I'm not sure if they're important. Melissa started screaming; Callum went deathly white when he realised his little sister was dead; Bella rushed to her stepmother's aid; Jenny comforted her friend. Michael and Clémentine, who attempted to resuscitate the baby, and Rob, who rang for an ambulance, managed to stay level-headed.

I read on. The next section is about Melissa's paranoia. She was terrified that the same fate might be awaiting Ellie, too. I imagine Melissa in the bedroom, rocking in the chair, watching her baby's tummy rise and fall. I can see the room in so much detail. Then it dawns on me that I'm visualising Melissa in Rosie's nursery, the bedroom the boys and I packed up this morning.

I know what's going to happen next and I don't want to read it, but somehow I'm compelled to keep going. Another paragraph; another page. Until I get to the end of that diary entry. The bit where Melissa finds Ellie, lifeless in her cot. Then I put the journal down on the coffee table. I can't take any more for now.

I know how it feels to lose a child. It's not something I can put into words, but I do know how it feels. Melissa lost two children. She must have thought nothing could get worse than that. But she was wrong. Heaped on top of the searing pain of losing her twin babies, was the ordeal of being charged with their murders.

My mind wanders to Callum and Bella. I imagine how they were affected by losing their siblings, well, technically half-siblings, although I doubt that made much difference. According to Michael Slade, Bella went back to her mother's for a while, but Callum's mother was taken from him. Locked up for life. I expect Bella and Callum lost each other, as well as Amber and Ellie.

I look at my sons, whose eyes are glued to the screen. Our

tragedy has left an indelible, caustic mark on them for life. Alfie's memories of his mummy fade a bit more every year, and neither he nor Noah ever knew their sister, but sorrow is etched on their father's face as a constant visual reminder that our family is fractured.

My thoughts turn back to Melissa. Could she be innocent? It's the first time I've considered this seriously. Of course if she didn't admit to killing her babies at the time, she was hardly going to fess up in a diary that could have ended up in anyone's hands – and has ended up in mine. After reading part of her journal, I feel a sliver of sympathy for her. But I still don't believe her.

I can't quite shake the impression that I'm somehow being manipulated. By whom, I don't know. Goodman? Melissa? Is her account what actually happened? Or is it fabulation? I have no way of telling. But if Melissa didn't murder Ellie, then this is one hell of a tragedy. Not to mention a gross miscarriage of justice. I'm just not sure I buy that version of events.

As Miguel sings "Remember Me" and I notice Alfie surreptitiously wiping away a tear, I realise my eyes are also threatening to brim over. I can't remember the last time I cried before this morning, and yet here I am, on the verge of blubbering, for the third time in one day. I resolve to get to the bottom of Melissa's story, to get to the truth. For her children's sakes. For her daughters and her son.

CHAPTER 14

~

Melissa

I'd stopped writing my diary. It wasn't really helping and there was nothing more to say anyway. I'd given my account of the events leading up to my imprisonment: the death of my baby girls, my arrest, my trial, my sentence. But now it seems that isn't the end. It has all started up again.

April 2018

When I was arrested, I'd wanted it over. I decided to enter a guilty plea. I knew if I did this at my first court appearance, I could avoid a trial. *Go to jail. Go directly to jail.* My days were shaped by the endless cycle of sunrise and nightfall, the light becoming dark and then light again. But my world was in darkness even during the daytime, and at night I could hardly sleep. My life had become one endless nightmare. I just wanted it to end. The nightmare, that is, although if my life had been coming to an end at that moment in time, I wouldn't have put up much of a fight.

Martin May QC had tried to convince me to plead not guilty, but I wouldn't listen. Then Simon had begged me. And against my better judgement, I'd let him talk me round. I did what Simon said. He told me there was no way I'd be found guilty. I went through a trial and was sentenced to life imprisonment. Simon persuaded me to lodge an appeal. He said my conviction would be quashed and I'd be acquitted. My conviction was upheld and I stayed in prison.

Nearly four years down the line and today Simon was sitting opposite me in the visits room at Her Majesty's Prison Haresfield Park, using much the same arguments as he had back then.

'Your son lost his sisters, and his mother, too,' he said. 'He needs you. You're no use to him in here.'

'*Our* son is an adult now, Simon. And the first appeal was dismissed. Why should this one be successful?'

'He still needs you. Right now he needs you more than ever.' I winced. According to Simon, Callum is in a bad way. 'We've got good grounds for this one, Melissa,' Simon continued. 'The prosecution sat on vital inform—'

'I can't take any more, Si. What if the court orders a retrial?'

'Lissa, you're the strongest woman I know. You're still young—'

'I'm middle-aged.'

'—enough to start again. You can do this. This time we'll win.'

'You said that last time,' I said, sounding like a petulant child.

'Come on, Lissa! Come home.'

'Home? Where is that?'

HMP Haresfield Park has been my home for the last four years. I share a room now with Cathy and we've made it comfortable. As lifers, we're allowed curtains, a phone, which is monitored of course, and a television in our room. We even have photographs of our respective sons in glassless frames on the desks.

Where would I go if I ever got out? I've divorced Michael, and he has sold our house. It has been a very long time since home has been with Simon and Callum.

'Clear your name.' His voice was laced with charm. 'Think of Callum.'

'I have been thinking of Callum. You know I have.'

I thought about Callum all the time. I was terrified of how all this was affecting him. He'd had to go through his teenage years without any maternal support. But what sort of mother was I when I'd let my daughters die? Sometimes I thought I deserved to rot in jail and that Callum was better off without me. I hadn't seen him for several months. He didn't want to come and see me anymore, which was understandable, I suppose.

'Lissa, you can only help him now if you come home. Let's get this guilty verdict overturned. Please.'

Simon put his fingertips together, holding his hands almost as if in prayer with his lips and nose pushed against his forefingers, while he waited for my answer. He was looking at me over the top of his hands with the same puppy expression he'd used on me when he'd proposed.

Unwilling to think about what I'd have to go through – again – if I was granted permission for another appeal, I allowed my mind to wander back to that day. I'd just told Simon I was pregnant. We'd only been together for three months, although we'd known each other for a lot longer. I'm pretty sure we conceived our son on the first night, the night Simon and I wound up at his place, roaring drunk, after celebrating a successful investigation with colleagues.

I'd prepared my speech. I was about to say I'd decided to keep the baby and he could have as much or as little to do with him or her as he wanted. Blah, blah.

But I didn't get to spout my spiel. Simon hadn't missed a beat. 'Marry me,' he'd said, gazing at me with his intense, blue eyes.

To say I was surprised would be putting it mildly. I stood there, gaping at him. The brilliant, handsome Simon Goodman who everyone said was married to his job. And here he was asking me to marry him. You couldn't say no to him. Like in the playground game, Simon says. He was like a pit bull. Once he'd found something to sink his teeth into, he wouldn't let go. And I'd become his goal.

'I want to do the right thing by you. Let's do this together.'

I could see he was still trying to do the right thing by me now. And, as always, he was right. I had to consider Callum. I had to focus on what I had, and not what I had lost.

I looked around the room at the other prisoners talking to members of their family or friends. I could see a few women from my wing here. The first time I had visitors – Simon and Callum – I had to wait for them in the visits room. I'd expected it to have uncomfortable wooden chairs, and tables bolted to the floor. But Haresfield is a "rehabilitative" prison, and I was surprised to discover a warm, welcoming room with low tables and colourful wide foam chairs, part of a programme introduced by the prison staff here to make prisoners feel as human as possible. The idea is that if we feel normal, we'll act normal.

Similarly, we're encouraged to refer to our cells as "rooms", and for those of us who have earned the privilege through good behaviour, we have laptops in our "rooms". Obviously, we don't have any Internet access, but we can use them for our studies or to arrange visits or to leave feedback on the meals, that sort of thing. I've typed my diary on mine.

'What if you made a mistake? Have you ever considered you might be wrong?'

At those words, I snapped my eyes back to him. I felt my eyebrows pinch into a V. I knew what he meant, but I wasn't about to discuss it. I knew I wasn't wrong. I'd done what I had to do.

I felt panic fluttering inside me. I scratched my left arm with my right arm. Three times at the top; three times at the bottom. Then I swapped arms. I'd picked off the scabs from my left forearm and I could see spots of blood appearing on my sleeve. Simon placed his hand gently on mine to make me stop, so I had to start all over again. Top left. One. Two. Three. Bottom left. One. Two. Three. Top right …

I dreaded to think of all the routines I would have to do once I was back in my room. Wash my hands. Check there was no dust under the bed. Unfold my clothes and fold them again. Rituals, the prison psychiatrist called them. If I didn't perform all these rituals, I'd be putting Callum in danger. Deep down, I knew this wasn't rational behaviour, but I'd given up trying to resist the urges. If I didn't go through the motions and something happened to Callum, I would never forgive myself. In any case, it wasn't like I had anything better to do with my time, and once everything was done – three times – the anxiety abated. A bit.

As these thoughts went through my head, Simon's voice faded to static. But I knew he was pulling out all the stops. And I was sure he knew I'd give in.

'All right,' I said, more to shut him up than anything else.

Simon smiled then, his eyes boring into me. I sensed danger. Its colour wasn't a fiery red, but a piercing, ice blue.

I'm not sure if caving in to Simon was the right thing to do. Is this my chance? Will I be given a get out of jail free card this time? I think it has only just hit me as I've been typing all this up. I'm going to ask for leave to appeal. I'm going to get my hopes up, and probably dashed, all over again. A familiar heaviness has lodged itself between my stomach and my heart. I know from experience I'll have to get used to it. It will take up residence there for a while. But I have to do this. For Callum.

CHAPTER 15

~

Jonathan

July 2018

Claire isn't so much hopping mad as stomping. As much as her high-heeled shoes will allow, anyway. I can see her pacing up and down in the Aquarium several minutes before the editorial meeting is due to begin that Monday morning.

Once we've all filed into Claire's office, two other senior members of *The Rag* and I sit in our chairs around Claire's desk while everyone else perches their buttocks on windowsills or props their backs against the walls. Claire begins the meeting with her usual summary of sales, insights, figures, feedback and so on. *The Redcliffe Gazette*'s readership is up, Claire informs us without a smile. There's a timid ripple of applause, but it doesn't catch on. In a funereal voice, Claire congratulates Kelly on her good work. Her entertainment vlog now has more followers than *The Rag* has readers for its print edition. I try not to smirk.

I scan the Aquarium and tune out as Claire directs the

discussions about leaders and stories for this week's online news and print edition. There aren't many of us – twenty at most, including the advertising department, but this room is bursting at the seams. The builders are knocking two offices into one on the next floor up. One day, if the work is ever completed, this will provide us with a larger room for meetings such as this. But for now we're squashed like sardines in the Aquarium, shouting at each other in order to make ourselves heard over the drilling and hammering directly above our heads.

As far as I can tell, listening with only half an ear, everything is running smoothly. So what's the matter with Claire? She's definitely wound up about something. Her shoulders are tensed up, her lips are pursed and she has taken the pencil out from behind her ear to tap on her desk with it.

She places a hand on my shoulder as everyone else troops out after the meeting. I stay seated.

'Is something wrong?' I ask as she closes the glass door behind the last one out. I wonder if I'm about to get a bollocking for something.

She walks slowly back to her desk, her energy seemingly depleted, and sinks into the swivel chair. She looks at the pencil in her hand as if just realising it's there and puts it in the pen holder on her desk.

'No, I'm fine. Thank you. I was wondering if you had anything for me on the Melissa Slade appeal.'

This reminds me I still haven't found out what she and Goodman were discussing. She may already know what I've got. 'I have her journal. Well, what looks like extracts from it. Simon Goodman, when he came to see you, handed some papers to Kelly.'

'Yes. Melissa kept a diary in prison. When she was told about you, she thought it might be useful for you to read it. She edited it so that you didn't have to wade through too much irrelevant material, apparently.'

Edited? Hmm. That doesn't sound like the right word. Redacted, maybe? What did Melissa cut? So Claire already knew about the journal. In fact, she knew more about it than I did. But there's something bugging me more than that.

'What do you mean, when—?'

'Have you read it?'

'Erm … yes. This weekend.' So much for not taking any more shortcuts. I haven't read past the part where Melissa found Ellie. 'What do you mean, when she was told about me?'

'I haven't been entirely open with you, Jonathan.'

'Oh?' It comes out coated with sarcasm. I've been wondering what she has been scheming ever since the day I saw Simon Goodman with her in the Aquarium.

She lets out a big sigh. 'Can I buy you lunch? I can't talk on an empty stomach.'

Without waiting for an answer, she slips off her heels and pulls a pair of flat-soled shoes out of a desk drawer. When she straightens up, she has shrunk by about three inches. I follow her through the silent offices towards the exit. Everyone has gone on their lunch break, including the workmen upstairs. Only Kelly is still here. Damn! I was supposed to grab a bite with her so we could discuss where to go next with Melissa Slade.

I almost ask Claire if Kelly can come with us, but I sense Claire has something she wants to confide in me, so I throw an apologetic look in Kelly's direction as I go past. She nods to show she has understood and turns back to her computer.

The smouldering glare of the sunlight hits me as we step outside and I realise I've left my sunglasses in the car. It takes Claire a minute or two to locate hers in her outsized handbag. Then she starts to power walk in her sensible shoes and I have to do an undignified skip every now and then to keep up with her. Luckily it's only a short distance to the little café that Claire takes me to in a side street behind St Mary Redcliffe Church. I've never been here before, didn't even know this place existed, but Claire is greeted by name as soon as we enter.

'A regular, are you?'

'The usual, please,' she tells the waiter, who materialises, pen poised over his notepad, once we've sat down. 'They do an excellent full English breakfast,' she says to me.

'That what you're having?'

'Yep.' She folds up her sunglasses and puts them on the table, then wiggles out of her light jacket and lays it on the bench beside her.

'Same for me, then.'

The waiter puts his pad and pen into his top pocket without noting our orders in it.

When he has gone, I turn to Claire. 'So, what's your connection with Goodman?'

'Well, my son isn't very well,' she begins, her face falling. 'He has kidney disease.'

'I'm sorry to hear that.' I didn't even know Claire had a son.

'He got into a bit of trouble a few months ago and—'

'With the police?'

She nods. 'He was due in hospital for dialysis and instead he was at the police station. Simon brought him to the hospital.'

Simon. So, she's on first-name terms with him.

'Jack – my son – got little more than a slap on the wrist,' she continues. 'A warning. Minor offence, Simon said, and Jack was a minor himself. No one got hurt. No biggie.'

It occurs to me that it probably was quite a big deal if CID was involved with her son's misdemeanour. Another thought strikes me. Claire would have asked for Simon's number right away. She would have seen in him a useful contact. I'm not nearly as good as her at cultivating sources.

'But he has checked up on Jack several times,' Claire continues, 'making sure he stays on the straight and narrow. It's not easy being a single parent, especially with a teenage son.'

'Tell me about it. Noah's a preteen and that's no walk in the park.'

'Simon understood that,' she adds, as if I hadn't spoken.

He would, I suppose. Callum was a teenager when Melissa was sent down.

'How's Jack now?' I ask.

The waiter arrives with our breakfasts and mugs of tea. As he puts down my mug, some of the tea spills over onto the table. I grab a paper napkin and mop it up, waving the apologetic waiter away.

Claire waits until he has disappeared before replying. 'There haven't been any more incidents, if that's what you mean,' she says, tucking in to her lunch ravenously.

'It wasn't. I was talking about his health.'

'Oh. He's still undergoing treatment. He has dialysis today, actually,' she says. 'Usually I go with him. Or my ex does. He was supposed to go with him this afternoon …' She trails off, stabbing her fork into a sausage with unnecessary force.

I realise that's probably what's bothering her today. The fact that her son has to go to his hospital appointment alone. 'Claire, you should go. I'll cover. I can call you if there's anything urgent.'

I'm not sure if she trusts me to hold the fort, but she nods and says, 'You're right. I'll go straight to the hospital after lunch. Thank you.'

I've hardly touched my meal, my parents having drilled into me from an early age not to speak with my mouth full, but Claire has almost finished. She has a large appetite for such a small woman.

'I still don't get what Goodman was doing here the other day,' I say.

'Ah. As you know, he's been campaigning relentlessly for his ex-wife's release. The Criminal Cases Review Commission has just referred the case back to the court of appeal, and he thinks

121

it would be helpful if Melissa were interviewed by a journalist. Preferably a local journalist.'

I'm aware I'm gaping at her, even though my mouth is full of bacon and beans. 'A local journalist? Who?' Stupid question. Claire doesn't reply, but I already know the answer. I narrow my eyes at her. 'Oh, no. You have to be kidding. I'm not doing it. And anyway, this isn't an American TV series. I can't just waltz up to the prison gate and demand to see an inmate.'

'No. There's a special procedure.' She puts down her knife and fork and pushes an imaginary strand of hair behind her ear. 'You have to go through the right channels. But it's possible for a journalist and a prisoner to meet face to face. In certain exceptional circumstances, of course.'

I arch my eyebrows. 'Such as?'

'For example, when the journalist intends to investigate and bring to public attention the prisoner's case. In this instance, the miscarriage of justice of which Melissa Slade was victim.'

'Allegedly,' I say. Claire shoots green daggers at me. 'What makes you think this application will go through? Isn't it a bit of a long shot?' Now her look has become furtive. There's something else she's not telling me.

'Let's just say I'm fairly confident this will be approved,' she says. I stay silent. It's often the best way to get people to talk, as my job has taught me. 'I went to school with the prison governor, OK?' There it is. I should have known. Claire knows people everywhere who will pull strings for her. 'We're friends on Facebook.' I almost scoff. 'She'll—'

'Bend the rules?'

'This is all above board. Jonathan, why are you being so unreasonable?'

This time I don't answer because it's a rhetorical question. Isn't it? Am I being unreasonable? Simon Goodman did a favour for Claire and now I'm to be instrumental in returning that favour. That's the way I see it. I'm not sure I'm the one being unreasonable here. I'm being used as a pawn in their game. This isn't about trying to dig up a scoop. It isn't about investigative journalism. It's about writing an article, setting the tone so that the media and the general public will demand justice for Melissa Slade. This goes against my beliefs. For one thing, I pride myself with writing unbiasedly, and secondly I don't know for sure that this woman is innocent. I don't *believe* she's innocent.

I slam my fist down on the table, making Claire jump. 'I'm not doing it! I won't be used! What if she's guilty? You can't expect me to—'

'What if she's innocent? Could you just think it over? Can't you at least meet her before you make up your mind?'

I'm seething. My heart is thumping and I'm shaking. I'm about to protest, but I close my mouth. Claire's words echo in my ears. *What is she's innocent?*

What if she didn't kill her baby? Why am I so convinced she's guilty? The doubt started to creep in when I read her diary, but I shut it out. Am I being judgemental? Narrow-minded?

Claire glances at her watch. 'I need to get going.' She opens her handbag and I assume she's hunting for her purse, but instead she pulls out a wad of papers and slides them across the table towards me. 'Have a look at this. It explains everything. Can you sign the forms and leave them on my desk? I'll pick them up later on my way back from the hospital.'

After smoothing down her skirt as she sidles across the bench, Claire gets up, folds her jacket over her arm and heads for the door. So much for buying me lunch. At the door, she turns round and I think she has remembered after all. She strides back to the table.

'One more thing,' she says. 'I need an article in this week's print edition. On the cover.'

'But you said in the editorial meeting—'

'I know what I said. I didn't want everyone in on this. Anyway, the paper hasn't been put to bed yet, has it?' She throws this last retort over her shoulder, already halfway out the door.

My breakfast has gone cold. As I pay the bill and leave, I hear my mother's voice in my head, scolding me for not finishing my meal.

For a while, I wander around aimlessly, somehow ending up in the grounds of St Mary Redcliffe Church. I remember coming here when I was little on a school outing. I sit down on a wooden bench to the side of the building. From here, I can see the piece of tram rail the guide told us about, which flew into the garden when a bomb landed on a nearby street during the Blitz. It has been left, standing almost upright, as a reminder of how close the church came to destruction.

A lucky escape. Was that what Melissa had hoped for? Did she try and get away with murder? Or was she wrongfully convicted? Did she kill one of her babies? Both of them? I have so many unanswered questions whirring around my brain. Too many.

I have to write an article about a miscarriage of justice when I don't know if that's what this is. Claire clearly wants it slanted that way, though. I should have refused, insisted it was against my principles. Instead, I feel bad now about being objectionable. Her son is not well and I wasn't very nice to her. Leaning forwards on the bench, I cradle my head in my hands and groan aloud. *Write the article, Jon. Just stick to the facts.* That's all I have to do, report objectively. Yeah, right.

My thoughts turn to Goodman. How long have he and Claire been in cahoots? I remember Claire told me to get in touch with him that day in her office. I bet he was waiting for my call. Not for the first time, I get the impression I'm being manipulated.

I look at the piece of tramline again. *Almost upright.* Goodman seems like an upright citizen, though. And not just because of his name. He's a superintendent in the CID, for a start. He believes in Melissa's innocence more than anyone and he's campaigning for her release. If anyone knows about justice, it's him.

But then again, he let Claire's son Jack off the hook. That can't have been legal. *Almost upright.* Perhaps it seemed like the right thing to do, with Jack being sick, and Simon has been checking up on him, making sure he stays out of trouble. Unless he did all that so that Claire would fight in his corner, rally to his cause. I groan again, scaring an elderly man, who was walking past the bench. He glowers at me, clutching his heart.

Feeling more confused than ever, I make my way back to the newspaper offices, stopping at a bakery on the way to buy a cinnamon bun for Kelly.

'To make up for not shouting you lunch,' I say, placing my offering in front of Kelly, who is sitting at her desk.

'There was no need, but that's really nice of you. I love Danish pastries.'

I tell Kelly about the piece Claire wants me to write for the next print edition, although I don't mention that I suspect Claire and Simon orchestrated all this a while ago.

'It looks like it's going to be the first article of many,' I grumble. 'I'm uncomfortable with supporting a cause I'm not sure I believe in.'

'But if she is innocent, she deserves to be heard,' Kelly says. 'Too often in this country, victims of miscarriages of justice are simply ignored.'

I ponder this. 'That's true,' I say. 'That's helpful, actually. So, you think she's innocent, then?' If I truly believed, as Goodman does, in Melissa Slade's innocence, it would make it a lot easier to write this.

'Nah. Her diary's incomplete for a start. That alone smacks of dishonesty.'

'Right.' Damn.

'In her last diary entry – the one about her grief – it seems deliberately emotional, almost as if she was no longer writing it for herself but aiming to garner sympathy votes from her readers.'

I ask Kelly to summarise the rest of the diary for me, resolving to read it myself as soon as I get a moment. *Good intentions, Jon.*

When she has finished, I tell her about the forms I'm supposed to fill in for Claire.

'Ooh. At least if you get to see her, you can make up your own mind about her.'

'That's pretty much what Claire said. But I don't want to see her. And I have to write at least one article before I meet her.'

'Why don't you write this one as neutrally as you can? Then if you do interview Melissa Slade at a later date, you might have a better idea of whether she's innocent or guilty.'

Kelly's reasoning is much the same as mine, but it sounds less jumbled when she says it than it did in my head a little earlier. But I don't know if Claire will let me get away with neutral and objective, keywords that have always driven my reporting.

'And we still have time to investigate before the appeal, don't we?' Kelly continues. 'When is it?'

'The date hasn't been set yet, but in three or four months' time, I would think.'

'So, basically, either Melissa killed her babies, or they died of cot death, or someone else killed them. Or possibly Amber died of cot death and Ellie was killed. I'll make a list of everyone involved – people who lived in that house or who were there when the twins died – and we'll work our way through it until we get to the truth.'

I find myself smiling and nodding and realise the role reversal is complete. Kelly is now guiding me and I'm grinning like a loon and nodding like a donkey. She fetches me a coffee and splits her cinnamon bun with me. Then she draws up her list while I read the information that Claire has printed out about prisoners' access to the media. When I've gone through it, I start to fill out the forms.

Before going home, I leave the papers on Claire's desk. It looks like I'll be meeting Melissa Slade. I'm already dreading it. This is one interview I will have to prepare for. And prepare myself for, too.

CHAPTER 16

~

Melissa

June 2018

It creeps up on me when I least expect it. It pounces on me in the dinner hall or lies in wait for me in the shower. It attacks as I lie awake in bed at night or pervades my dreams while I sleep. Grief. Time eases rather than erases the pain of loss, or so it is said. I often wonder how much time it will take. It has been five years since Amber and Ellie died, and my wound is still as open and raw as if it only happened five days ago.

I still break down frequently. At the moment, there's no one to see me cry and act as a bulwark against my sorrow. I was told I would have a new cellmate, but for the moment I'm on my own. I've been alone in my room for several weeks – since Cathy was released on bail, pending her retrial. New evidence has been found showing the extent of the domestic violence her husband subjected her to. A witness has come forward, too, apparently. I'm so happy for her, but, selfishly, sad for me.

I spoke to Cathy on the phone earlier in the week and I've been following her story on the local news. It seems highly likely she'll be found not guilty of murder, but guilty of manslaughter. Provocation, not premeditation, her QC will argue, according to Cathy. She has served over six years in custody and so she should get to walk free. Her retrial is expected to end any day now. Then she'll just have to wait for the verdict to be returned. A foregone conclusion. A slam dunk. A formality. As I told her on the phone, if she ever comes back to Haresfield, it will be to visit me.

I'm glad now that Simon persuaded me to ask for leave to appeal. I don't want to be here without Cathy.

'Your turn next,' he said when he came to visit last week. He brought with him the news that our application to the Criminal Cases Review Commission has been successful. The wait has begun for the appeal date to be set. It's going to be a long wait, I can tell, like it was when I was waiting for the verdict in my trial. No, more like waiting for my trial to begin the first time round. Interminable. Torture.

Martin May QC also came to see me in prison last week. I found it encouraging that he came in person instead of inter-viewing me by video link or sending a junior barrister. I always assumed he thought I was guilty. Perhaps he does believe I'm innocent after all. Simon said he has waived most of his fees. Pro bono. That's just as well. I know the campaign has raised some money, but my legal fees have been sky-high, and Simon and my parents have footed a lot of the bill.

May was very reassuring. 'We'll focus on Ellie's toxicology report in this appeal,' he told me. 'The fact that it was omitted from your daughter's medical records fundamentally discredits the findings of Dr Roger Sparks, the pathologist who carried out her post-mortem.'

He paused here and ran his hands through his curls. I wondered if he was trying not to get my hopes up.

'That's good, right?' I needed it in black and white. Good or bad?

'Yes, indeed it is. We have other points to raise, but the failure to disclose the full medical report is on its own a weighty argument. As you know, the toxicology findings indicate that there was evidence of a natural cause of death.' In a softer voice, he added, 'If we'd had this information from the beginning, you would never have been tried for Ellie's murder, much less Amber's.'

I was on the verge of tears at the mere mention of my babies by name, but I held it together.

'One more thing,' my barrister said. 'You can apply for bail if you wish to do so.'

'What do you think I should do?'

'Only you can make that decision.'

I could sense a 'but' coming, so I waited.

'Sometimes an appellant arriving from prison is in a better frame of mind than an appellant who has been at home waiting for the hearing,' May continued. 'It goes without saying that the impression you make on the judges at the hearing is vital.'

Home. Not for the first time, I asked myself what that meant.

Martin May QC must have taken my hesitation to mean I wanted to ask for bail despite his advice because he said, 'If we ask for bail, your request may be refused. And if you don't ask for bail, I won't have to reveal too much of our strategy to the prosecution.'

Until recently I felt I deserved to be here. I believed I needed to be punished. I was a terrible mother to my baby girls. I didn't show them love. I didn't protect them. I still feel accountable for their deaths. Perhaps I do deserve to stay here forever. But my son needs me and I can't do anything for him if I'm inside. I have to be strong. I have to do whatever it takes to get out of here and help Callum. I can still be a good mother to him. It's not too late.

I looked my barrister in the eye and said, 'I'll stay put. For now.'

CHAPTER 17

~

The Redcliffe Gazette

Melissa Slade: Gross Miscarriage of Justice?
New facts suggest wrongful murder conviction

J.Hunt
Thurs 5 July 2018

Life Sentence
Melissa Slade, a former police officer currently serving a life
sentence for the murder of her baby Ellie, may soon be released.
Mrs Slade's first appeal, in November 2014, was unsuccessful, but
her case has recently been referred back to the appeal court after
it emerged that strong evidence pointing to Mrs Slade's innocence
was not disclosed to her defence team at the time of her trial.

The Twins
Baby Amber died tragically and unexpectedly in April 2012 aged
3 months. Throughout her brief life, she had suffered from

numerous colds, which made her breathing laboured, and a verdict of sudden infant death (cot death) was recorded following a post-mortem.

When Amber's twin sister Ellie died just over four weeks later, however, their mother was arrested by her own colleagues and charged with two counts of murder.

The Trial

The jury, after initially failing to reach a unanimous verdict, finally delivered a majority verdict of 10–2. In a terrifying *coup de théâtre*, Mrs Slade was found not guilty of the murder of Amber, but a guilty verdict was returned for Ellie's murder. Perhaps this baffling finale was caused by the contradictory and confusing expert testimonies given in court concerning the deaths of the two infants.

"At the very least the two cases should have been tried separately," Martin May QC, Melissa's defence barrister, told *The Redcliffe Gazette*, "but it is my belief that Melissa Slade should never have been tried at all."

According to Mr George Moore, Melissa Slade's father, the burden of proof was reversed in his daughter's case. He told *The Gazette*: "Everyone had made up their minds before the trial. Melissa was presumed guilty from the start."

New Evidence

It has since come to light that crucial details from Ellie's medical records were kept hidden from the police as well as from Mrs Slade's lawyers. Indeed, high levels of antimony, a chemical commonly associated with cot death, were detected in Ellie's lungs and liver during the post-mortem. This evidence should have been shared with the defence team and may well have led to unanimous not guilty verdicts on both charges.

Justice
The Criminal Cases Review Commission, which examines possible miscarriages of justice, has now referred the case back to the appeal court.

Superintendent Simon Goodman, the father of Mrs Slade's son Callum, is confident that the conviction will be quashed this time.

"Melissa is innocent and I know that justice will be served this time," said Goodman, who has been campaigning alongside his son for the release of Mrs Slade, now 45, since she was sentenced to life imprisonment in December 2013.

As shown in cases such as those of Angela Cannings and Sally Clark, who also incurred miscarriages of justice, for a mother who has experienced one cot death, there is a higher probability rather than a lower probability that she will suffer another one.

Appeal
Mrs Slade is now waiting for a date to be set for her appeal. If her conviction is found unsafe, she will walk free. She has now spent almost five years in prison, but her family is hopeful she will be home by the end of this year.

CHAPTER 18

~

Melissa

July 2018

I think this will be the last time I write in my diary. For a while, at least. I've already passed the rest of it on to Simon, so there seems little point in carrying on with it. Anyway, the past has caught up with the present, as it were. I've written an account of everything that has led to me being here – in HMP Haresfield, and now all I can do is wait and hope to get out of here soon.

This morning I had some news. I was in my cell, reading, when a guard raced in. He was agitated and told me to come with him. My heart stopped and skipped several beats. I thought that something must have happened to Callum.

But it wasn't that.

'No. Don't worry. It's good news,' the guard said. But he wouldn't say any more.

It was the prison governor who told me. A date has been set for my appeal. The 13th of November. Thirteen. Unlucky for some.

We heard back from the Criminal Cases Review Commission in record time and although it's four months away, it seems imminent.

Now we have a date, all sorts of questions have been chasing each other around my head. Where will I go if I'm freed? What will I do? Will I be able to make up for lost time with Callum? Will he understand? Does he know why I did what I did?

I also find myself wondering a lot about that missing toxicology report. My whole appeal hinges on this. Will it be enough to get my sentence quashed? Why has it turned up now? Could it have been an oversight? If not, who concealed it and why? Did Dr Sparks have an agenda? Was he bribed? Who would want to bribe him? I have no answers to any of these questions.

When I think back to my policing days, I remember sometimes having a theory about a case. A strong gut feeling about something. I knew the truth. I just knew it. And I used the evidence we collected to prove it. Simon, who was probably the best officer I ever worked with, didn't go about it that way. He was – still is – much more open-minded than me. He used the evidence to get to the facts and reassessed the situation with every piece of information and every clue that was uncovered.

Maybe someone had it in their head that I was guilty and Dr Sparks looked for evidence to support this, ignoring data – crucial data – that went against this belief. Even if Sparks was convinced I was guilty, he can't be completely innocent. He must have known his report was incomplete. He would have realised in court that something was very wrong.

I'll probably never find out exactly what happened, but I'm sure someone will pay. And I'd rather be in my shoes than theirs. That said, being in my shoes right now means getting prepared mentally for another appeal. I'm dreading it. I have to appear before three judges. They will decide whether to quash my conviction or order a retrial or dismiss the appeal. I don't know what I'll do if there's a retrial. Sometimes I think I'd rather die than go through all that again.

And yet, I am going through it all again. Every day. I had a go at writing about my trial in my journal some time ago, but it was too painful and not at all therapeutic, so I glossed over the whole experience. But even though I've been repressing these memories, crystal-clear images keep coming back to me now. I can see the faces of the jurors in high definition when I close my eyes. Key moments from the trial thrust themselves upon me, forcing me to relive the pathologists' evidence, Michael's confession on the stand, the deliberations, the verdict.

The deliberations went on forever and in the end, a majority verdict was delivered. On count one, I was found not guilty; on count two I was found guilty. Ten to two for each count. It was bewildering. Ten out of twelve jurors thought I hadn't killed Amber. Were they the same ten who had found me guilty of killing Ellie?

I'll never know what went on behind the closed doors of the jury room. I wonder if the jurors themselves were as confused as I was. The foreman turned out to be the elderly man with the friendly face. When he announced the not guilty verdict for Amber, I thought I was going home. No one, least of all me, could have foreseen the bombshell he was about to drop.

Two jurors had disagreed with that guilty verdict. Who were they? The old man and the black lady? The two women who were around my age? The scrawny one had cried during my trial and I remembered imagining the other one, the plump one, had children of her own. Did they feel, as I did, that it was inconceivable that a mother could commit such a reprehensible crime?

It's not just images that I recall. I can still hear, practically word for word, the brutal allegations Eleanor Wood QC made during the trial. She summarised them all during the closing speech for the prosecution, branding me an alcoholic and a serial baby killer. She claimed I resented my daughters for getting in the way of my career and my life. The fact that both Amber and Ellie had died in the evening couldn't possibly be a tragic coincidence, Wood insisted, not least because babies who died from cot deaths were discovered dead in the morning, almost without exception. She even derided me for failing to get my story straight with my husband the adulterer.

Did Eleanor Wood QC's words sting because I didn't recognise the monster they were describing or, on the contrary, because I recognised the truth? Home truths hit hard right where it hurts.

I've been trying to block these thoughts and block out the memories of my trial. I've been working on my mind-set, trying to think positively. I keep telling myself I need to have faith. Not in God or anything like that – I slid from agnostic to atheist some time ago. No, I need to believe in the justice system. I did believe in it once. I used to fight for justice – that's part of what a police officer does – but the justice system let me down. I have to trust it again. It won't disappoint me this time. But sometimes I get the uneasy feeling that for the system to work for me, I have to work the system.

~

Today got off to a good start with the news that a date has been set for my appeal. I intended that to be my last diary entry, but I'm going to type up what happened just a few hours ago. It was awful.

Three people entered my cell and shook my new-found faith in the justice system to the core. Two guards were bringing Cathy back. Her conviction was upheld. She looked broken. I crossed the room and took her in my arms as she started to sob.

Where can she go from here? That appeal had been her last chance. This will be her home for good now. Cathy come home. Poor, poor Cathy.

I'm gutted for her. And the selfish part of me wonders what this means for me. It means that I'm no longer alone. My friend is back. But if her appeal has been rejected, what hope is there for mine? I can't shake the feeling that Cathy's return is a very bad omen for me.

CHAPTER 19

~

Jonathan

August 2018

I've never been in a prison before, although I've sat outside one plenty of times. A men's prison. HMP Bristol. I used to drive there regularly when Adrian Pike – the man who killed Mel and Rosie – was jailed for a poxy ten years. I'd sit in my car, on the other side of the wall, picturing Pike lying on a hard bed, staring at the ceiling of a tiny airless cell. I could almost smell the filthy toilet without a lid in the corner. Pike would lose sleep, fearing for his life at the hands of his cellmate, a complete psycho with bulging muscles covered in tattoos. The two of them also shared their cell – and sometimes their respective bunk beds – with an intrusion of cockroaches.

Even if all this had been true, it wouldn't have made me feel any better. Nothing could bring back Mel or Rosie. And you can't move on when you don't feel justice has been served. Pike will probably be out by the time he's thirty-five. My wife was thirty-five when she died. She was pregnant. My daughter never got to live in the outside world. Pike may live another forty or fifty years on the outside. Unless I play out my fantasies and kill him. I used to contemplate that in some detail. But a wall keeps people out as well as in, and when I might have been reckless enough to go through with it, he was banged up, safely shut away from me.

Now I'm sitting outside a women's prison, in the car park at HMP Haresfield Park, psyching myself up to meet Melissa Slade.

As I'm early, I go through my interview notes, making sure that I've learnt them by heart, and then I flick through the printed pages of Melissa Slade's memoirs, which I finished a few days ago, rereading the paragraphs I've highlighted. I haven't crammed this much since my A levels.

I shake my head, trying to dispel the image that my mind has projected of a plexiglass screen separating her from me, both of us clutching old-fashioned telephone receivers to communicate. It's not going to be anything like this. For a start, my interview has been scheduled outside official visiting times and it is to be held in the visits room.

It's time, but I can't quite bring myself to get out of the car. Dread churns in my stomach. What am I scared of? Maybe I'm reluctant more than scared. I'm just not convinced I'm doing the right thing. I've been sent here to help fight for justice, but I may end up helping a murderer *escape* justice.

And there's one thought I can't get out of my head. It sends a current of rage through my whole body: This woman may have killed her baby girls; mine was killed. By Melissa Slade's own admission, she was a terrible mother to her daughters. Even if she didn't actually kill them. I never got to be a father to my daughter.

But if Melissa Slade is innocent, and I can't help thinking that's a whopping if, then maybe her baby girls were killed, too. *You can do this.* Mel would have said something like that, and indeed the voice in my head sounds a lot like hers. But still I don't move.

When I do move, it's not to get out of the car. Turning the key in the ignition, I let off the handbrake. Then I drive towards the exit of the car park. I haven't even unfastened my seatbelt and I don't know if I ever had any intention of visiting Melissa Slade.

But when I push my ticket in the slot, the barrier doesn't lift up, the machine spews the ticket back out and an automated voice tells me to pay at the machine. I slam the lever into reverse. *Grow a pair, Jon.* This time it's my own voice. Sighing, I park the car in the same space as before and head for the entrance to the visits centre.

At the gate, I hand over my press card as well as my ID. When the gate buzzes open, I'm taken to a small room, a bit like a cloakroom. Here I have to leave my mobile phone in a locker, but I've had the governor's permission to take in a voice recorder as long as it's used only as an aide-mémoire and not to broadcast the interview. I'm not allowed to keep my wallet on me either, but there are signs informing me that I may take loose change with me for refreshments from the vending machine. After a rub-down search, I go through a metal detector and finally I'm instructed to stand still while the sniffer dog carries out its duty.

I'm a full ten minutes late by the time I walk into the visits room. Melissa Slade is already there, sitting at a brightly coloured low table, her hands clasped in her lap and her head bowed. Next to her is a mousy-haired man who appears to be around my age. For a second I'm puzzled, then I remember I was told a media liaison officer would be within sight and sound of the interview at all times.

'I thought you weren't coming,' Melissa Slade says as I approach, standing up to greet me. I don't tell her I almost didn't. 'I'm so glad you did.' Her voice is soft, almost musical.

We sit down opposite each other. The media liaison officer has remained seated and I nod at him. Melissa Slade flashes a smile at me, but it doesn't quite reach her turquoise eyes, which are dimmer somehow than I remember from the photo her father showed me. Her blond hair is shorter and darker. She's wearing jeans and a baggy long-sleeved T-shirt that doesn't disguise how thin she is, almost skeletal. But she's still hypnotically beautiful. Her face is perfectly symmetrical, right down to her laughter lines, her skin is flawless, her teeth even and white. I realise I'm staring at her, appraising her, and force myself to look away.

'Pleased to meet you,' I say.

She laughs at that, a nervous giggle. 'And here I was, hoping we could be honest with one another,' she says, the ghost of a twinkle illuminating her eyes. Then it's gone, her expression serious as she adds, 'I don't blame you for not wanting to come.'

I feel wrong-footed somehow, but it's undermined by a twinge of guilt.

'Your editor told Simon.'

'Sorry,' I say.

'No, I'm sorry. That wasn't a great opening gambit.'

I chuckle, although it sounds a little forced. There's an awkward pause as I rack my brains, trying – and failing – to remember the first question I wanted to ask her.

I scan the room. It's exactly how Melissa described it in her diary. With its low furniture and cheerful colours, it looks more like a café with a misguided attempt at a trendy interior than the visits room of a prison. Its atmosphere is relaxed and everything in it is designed to make prisoners and visitors feel at ease. This meeting with Melissa is having the opposite effect on me, though. I can feel tension in my shoulders and beads of sweat breaking out on my forehead.

My interview notes come back to me.

'It would help me with my articles if I was in possession of all the facts,' I begin. 'I've read your journal, but is there anything that's not in it that I should be aware of?'

'No.'

'Are you still keeping a diary now?'

'No. I wrote one more entry after giving the diary to Simon. It was the day I got my appeal date. It was the same day my friend Cathy's appeal fell through. I was a bit emotional and so I felt like typing up the day's events. But that's all. I've decided to stop now. There's nothing else to say. For the moment, at least.'

'All right. I believe some of what you originally wrote was edited out. Can you tell me what you deleted?'

'I started keeping a diary here in prison. For myself,' she says. 'It was therapeutic and a way of passing the time.'

'Go on.'

'I didn't know anyone else would ever read it. When Simon suggested I should give it to him so he could pass it on to you, I … there were things, personal things … they're not related to my case. There were also boring things, like what we ate for dinner each day.'

'How much of the journal did you take out?'

'There was so much material. I took out anything I didn't consider relevant to your investigation.'

I ponder this. That's pretty much what Claire said. But Melissa Slade seems to be prevaricating. She hasn't actually answered my question. And her tales of prison life – when she was held down and tattooed or when another inmate threw a plate of food over her – that's not relevant and yet she left that in.

'I see.' I probably don't sound very convinced. I'm not. 'Mrs Slade—'

'Do you mind if we use first names? It's less formal. Do you prefer Jon or Jonathan?'

I do mind and I don't want to be less formal. 'My friends call me Jon,' I say, meaning that she should use Jonathan, or better still, Mr Hunt.

'Jon it is, then.'

I can feel myself scowl. As long as she doesn't expect me to call her Mel. I can't do that. There's just no way. Somehow, to me, she's not worthy of that name. No one could be now.

'And you can call me Melissa. Or Lissa, if you like. My friends do.'

I'm a little thrown by what she has just said, but at least she doesn't go by "Mel". I try to get back on track. 'Melissa, with your appeal coming up, you must be—'

'I didn't want to ask for leave to appeal to begin with,' she says.

That wasn't the route I wanted to go down. I wanted to know if she felt more optimistic this time, what her plans were if she were released, that sort of thing. But Melissa Slade is leading this interview. Perhaps she has prepared for it as much as I have. I decide to play ball. For now. 'Why not?'

She sighs. 'I got my hopes up the first time, but our grounds for appeal weren't very solid—'

'What were the grounds for appeal?'

'Things like the two cases should have been tried separately and that the judge was wrong a few times in the way he directed the jury. I can't even remember. As I said, not very solid. I didn't want to ask for leave to appeal this time in case I ended up disappointed again.'

'What made you change your mind?'

'Simon and Callum. You see, Callum is having a rough time right now. Everyone found out at uni that he was the son of a … that he was my son. He was ostracised by his peers, his girlfriend dumped him and he's taking it all very badly. Well, he's depressed.' She looks dejected but I can't tell if it's an act. 'He has dropped out and come home. Simon says – quite rightly – that Callum needs me to come home too.'

I nod. I remember reading that in one of her diary entries. 'Right. So, you were worried about having your hopes raised and dashed with another appeal, but you decided to go for it for Callum's sake.' I wonder if there's more to it than that.

As if reading my mind, she says, 'Also, somewhere deep inside I felt … I was to blame and this was the price I had to pay.'

'To blame for what?'

'For my babies' deaths. I was their mother. I didn't protect them. They died. On my watch, as it were. Both of them. I felt I deserved to be punished for that.' For a second, she looks like she's about to cry, but then she bites her lip and regains her composure.

'Melissa, I wonder if you would talk me through it all. The moments when you found your two little girls. Just in case there's anything significant that you didn't write in your journal.' I bite down the urge to add *or that you edited out*.

Melissa relates the events, and from time to time I interrupt her to ask a question or to check something that has crossed my mind, but it all tallies with what she wrote in her diary. She doesn't tell me much I don't already know.

As she talks, I study her, as discreetly as possible. I notice that at the difficult parts, for example when she discovers her babies are dead, her voice becomes quieter and almost monotonous, and her eyes become more vacant as if she's distancing herself from her memories or pretending it didn't happen to her. Some of what she says is word for word what she has written. She must have been over it, and through it, so many times, and it's almost as if she has learnt her lines by heart.

I also notice she fidgets a lot, rubbing her arms, or rubbing one leg against the other. It's not until I realise that she has repeated the movements using the other hand and the other foot that I remember the obsessive rituals she described in her diary.

When she has finished, she looks pale and exhausted. Part of me still wants to hate her, but she seems so vulnerable that I find myself thinking I should be protecting her instead. I've put her through an ordeal that hasn't turned out to be helpful to me anyway. For the moment I haven't found out anything new and I can't have much time left. I need to get on with this.

'What do—'

'Would you like a coffee?'

I don't want one, and I think she might be stalling. 'I'll get them,' I say, reaching into my jeans pocket to fish out my change.

I buy three coffees as the media liaison officer, who has said nothing since hello, seems to be nodding off and looks like he could do with a caffeine fix.

'Did any of that help?' Melissa asks as I hand her the plastic cup.

'Yes,' I lie.

'I could do with a cigarette.' I follow her gaze to a no smoking sign on the wall.

'I was just thinking the same thing. Always tastes good with coffee, doesn't it?'

'Or alcohol. None of that in here, though.'

We're making small talk, wasting time. 'Melissa, can I ask you a question?'

'That's what you're here for,' she says with an attempt at a smile. I don't return it.

'What do you think happened? Do you think both your daughters died of Sudden Infant Death Syndrome?'

She doesn't answer immediately, which makes me suspicious. Then she says, 'It's what I think now, yes.'

I'm about to ask what she thought before the new evidence came to light, but she gets there before me.

'When Amber died, I genuinely thought it was cot death, even before the coroner's report. She slept on her stomach and she had difficulty breathing. But when Ellie died, too, well … it seemed like too much of a coincidence. And Ellie was so healthy, so full of life.'

Her voice is quiet and I have to strain to hear her. I lean forwards, my arms folded across my knees, although it seems too intimate a gesture, as if I'm invading her space.

'The only other explanation I could come up with at the time was that maybe they both died of some genetic disease that wasn't found in the post-mortems,' she continues.

144

As she speaks, her eyes flit from left to right and she rubs her arms. I get the distinct impression she's not telling the truth. It sounds rehearsed to me and her body language is all wrong, eyes all over the place and scratching herself like mad with what's left of her bitten nails. I have no choice but to let it go. I've come up with all these possible scenarios myself, anyway. Somehow I feel further from the truth than ever.

'Either way, though, whether your babies died of a genetic disease or cot death, that would be from natural causes,' I say. 'You've never considered the possibility that their deaths were deliberate?'

'No, never.' Her answer comes back at me quickly. Too quickly. As if she's on the defensive. 'I can't think why anyone would have wanted either of them dead. They were only babies, innocent babies.'

I think I'm pushing it, but I pursue this line of questioning. 'Did anyone resent them? Was anyone in your family jealous of them? After all, they arrived somewhat unexpectedly, according to what you've written in your memoirs.'

She gives a hint of a wistful smile. 'Very unexpectedly. It was a complete surprise.'

'I can imagine,' I say. If I were to find out now, at the age of forty, that I was about to be a dad again, it would be a shock rather than a surprise, but I keep this thought to myself.

'No, in court they made out I resented them, but that's not true. Having twin babies made things tense between Michael and me, but he doted on them. And Callum and Bella were very good with them. They helped out. Bella kept a watchful eye on them whenever she was staying with us. And when she was at her mother's, she rang frequently to ask how they were.'

'Do you know where your stepdaughter is, Melissa?' I ask. 'My colleague, Kelly, has drawn up a list of people we need to talk to, but she has been unable to locate Bella.'

'I have no idea. She had problems at home – with her mother, I mean – and left.'

'Why didn't she come back to live with her father?'

'It was such a difficult time. I'd been arrested. Michael was moving house. You'll have to ask him if he knows any more than I do.'

'I already have,' I mutter.

'Oh, that's right.' She sounds vaguely amused. 'Simon told me you went to see Mike. What did you think of him?'

I remember what Melissa said right at the beginning of this interview about being honest with each other. It was intended as a joke, but I think she meant it even though I'm not sure she has held up her end of the bargain. If I'm honest, I think Michael Slade's a prick, but I can't admit that. 'You first,' I hazard.

She leans back and folds her hands over her stomach. 'I met Mike in a bar one evening – I was out for a friend's hen night. He lavished attention on me, and made me feel like the centre of his world. He swept me off my feet. I fell for him completely. Simon was a wonderful man, but he was so wrapped up in his job that he had very little time for me. After a while, we had nothing to talk about but work. I left him for Michael.' She casts her eyes down and I wonder if she regrets that decision now. She looks up again. 'Your turn.'

'Your ex-husband and I don't have much in common and we didn't exactly hit it off,' I reply, watching Melissa's face break into a grin. 'But as my wife used to say, I can be too quick to judge people and I'm a poor judge of character.'

'She doesn't say that anymore?' Melissa puts her fingertips over her mouth, but the words have come out. They hang in the space between us. I, too, have said too much.

I don't answer. The question is too personal. I don't want her to know anything about me. This isn't about me. I'm the one who's supposed to ask the questions, but she has turned it around. Force of habit, maybe. *Once a police officer ...* She glances at my hand, sees the wedding ring and then looks up.

'I'm so sorry,' she says, and I realise she has understood. She doesn't ask how it happened. Instead she asks, 'Have you got children?'

'Yes, two boys,' I tell her. It sounds curt, and I feel compelled to add to this in a softer tone. 'Twelve and nine.'

'Such great ages. I'm sure you're a terrific father,' she continues. 'We'd do anything for our sons, wouldn't we? Run into a burning building to save them; drown to keep them afloat. I know I would for mine. I'd give my life in a heartbeat if I had to. Such unconditional love.'

I nod, anxious to steer the conversation away from this topic. 'You and Michael divorced after you were sent to jail, I believe?'

'That's right. I'd been inside for just over two years when I filed for divorce.'

'I had no idea you could do that from prison.'

'Yes, in certain circumstances. In my case, I'd been living apart from my spouse for the requisite two years and he agreed to the divorce.'

'But you kept his name?'

'I didn't, actually. I'm using my maiden name. But I'm probably the only one using it. Outside I'll always be known as Melissa Slade, the baby slayer, and inside I'm just a number.'

I have a few more questions, but the mousy-haired guy sits up, looks pointedly at the digital clock on the wall and then coughs.

Taking his cue, I stand up. 'Well, Melissa Moore, I think our time is up.' She brightens at my use of her maiden name.

'I won't see you again, will I?' she says.

'I only get one visit, if that's what you mean. But I'll see you in court, as they say. In the meantime, if there's anything you think of, anything at all, you can write to me. And if I need to know anything else, I'll write to you.'

'Absolutely.'

I try to find something encouraging to say. Not: "I hope your appeal will be successful" or "all the best" because I only wish

147

that for her if she's innocent and I still don't know what to think on that score.

'I sincerely hope justice will be done, Melissa.' My last words to her before leaving. Her face falls. She has grasped the subtext.

As I walk back to the car park, reminding myself to pay at the machine before trying to leave this time, some of Melissa's words replay in my head. *We'd do anything for our sons, wouldn't we? Run into a burning building to save them, drown to keep them afloat.* It's only now that her words strike me as odd. Melissa had a son and two daughters. Why didn't she say we'd do anything for our *children*? Why did she say for our *sons*?

She said she would lay down her life in a heartbeat for her son. Wouldn't she have done the same thing for her daughters? I know I would have given my life to save my daughter the day Adrian Pike killed her.

Then I remember reading in Melissa's journal that she didn't immediately feel the boundless love for her twin baby girls that she had instantly felt when Callum was a newborn. Did she really not care about Amber and Ellie?

I dismiss my train of thought. It was just a turn of phrase or a slip of the tongue and I'm reading too much into it. Melissa's daughters are dead after all – she couldn't give her life for them now even if she wanted to.

PART TWO

CHAPTER 20

~

Kelly

August 2018

At midday there's still no word from Jon, so I ring him on his mobile to find out how it went with Melissa Slade. I've been unable to concentrate all morning – I'm that keen to know what she said to him.

'Kelly, I don't like using the phone in the car, even on hands-free,' he says, 'but I'm on my way in. I need to do a couple of things before taking off on my hols tomorrow.'

As soon as he arrives, though, Claire starts waving at him with both arms from behind her glass wall, like she's drowning in the Aquarium. He makes his way straight to her office, pulling a discreet face at me on the way past.

There's something different about him and it takes me a moment to realise I've never seen him without his glasses on before. Plus he's kind of smart in an old-fashioned way. He must be sweating in that tweed suit, though. It's like twenty-eight degrees outside and it's not as if we have air con in here. His hair is sitting right, too, instead of standing on end as it usually does.

For want of something better to do, I fetch a coffee from the machine in the corner. It's gross, but it's caffeine. It's abnormally quiet today and I'm super bored. Resisting the urge to go on Facebook, I examine the list I made the other day of people who may have information about the Slade babies' deaths.

– Melissa Slade
– ~~Michael Slade~~
– Bella Slade
– ~~Jennifer Porter (friend)~~
– Rob Porter
– Sophia Porter (daughter)
– ~~Simon Goodman~~
– Callum Goodman
– ~~George~~ & Ivy Moore (Melissa's parents)
– Clémentine Rouquier (*au pair*)
– ~~Holly Lovell (pathologist: Amber)~~
– Roger Sparks (pathologist: Ellie)
– ~~Martin May QC (Melissa's barrister)~~

John and I both interviewed Michael Slade and Simon Goodman, Melissa's ex-husbands; Jennifer Porter called Jon on the phone, and Jon rang Melissa's lawyer to get a quote for his article. So I've crossed out those names. Jon went to visit Melissa Slade in prison this morning, so I score a line through her name too. He has also talked to Melissa's father. Melissa's mother is still on the list. But she wouldn't talk to Jon, so she's unlikely to talk to me. She hates reporters, apparently.

No one seems to know where Bella Slade is, so we can't interview her. She was there the night Amber died. She may know something that could point us in the right direction, but as Jon pointed out, if her parents don't know where she is, we're unlikely to be able to find her.

And Bella's not the only one who is conspicuous in her absence. As far as I'm aware, the *au pair* didn't stick around for the trial, either.

I go on Facebook after all, glancing around to check no one is looking over my shoulder, even though I'm doing this for research purposes. Clémentine Rouquier sounded like it might be a common French name to me, but to my surprise, only one comes up when I type it in the search bar. There aren't many public posts. I scroll through the stuff that's not hidden by her privacy settings. Photos of bottles of wine and grapes. It's her.

In one of the latest posts, there's a photo of a book cover. *Le Guide Hachette des Vins 2018.* And a second photo next to it of a page inside that book. I read the entry that has been highlighted. I get the gist. *Côtes du Rhône. Appellation d'origine contrôlée. Château des Amoureux.* A rating of two stars, out of three, presumably. I google *Château des Amoureux.* There's an English version, so I click on the Union Jack. The vineyard has belonged to the Rouquier family for more than a century and it is situated in Saint-Martin-d'Ardèche, in the Rhône Valley, near Montélimar, less than two hours south of Lyon.

A plan begins to form in my mind and I jot down the address but then I whirl round, sensing someone looking over my shoulder.

'Tut tut,' Jon says, nodding towards my laptop screen, but I can tell from his tone he's joking.

'It's for work, honest,' I return. 'You're looking cool, by the way.'

'Cool, huh?'

'Yeah. Nice suit.' It amuses me that he got scrubbed up to go and see Melissa Slade in prison. Like he's the one who had to make a good impression.

'*Hot* suit,' he says, chuckling, as he shrugs out of his jacket and hangs it on the back of his chair.

'So, come on. What was she like? Did she do it? Or is she innocent?'

'Hmm. The jury's still out on that one, so to speak.' He plugs his laptop into the docking station. I know he was worried about this visit, but I was excited. I want to know all about it, but he seems distracted.

He swivels round in his chair to face me. I know I've got his full attention when he starts staring at my nose stud.

'She was OK. Pleasant. Polite. Pretty. I thought she'd be self-pitying and attention-seeking, but she was, well … normal, I suppose. But I'm still not convinced she's innocent.'

'Why?'

'I got the impression there was something she wasn't telling me. When she told me about finding her babies dead, she used the same words she'd written in her diary. Some of it was verbatim. It's all a bit … contrived. Rehearsed.'

'So did you get anything useful out of her?'

'No, nothing at all,' he says, still addressing my piercing. 'But she said something I found strange. She said she'd do anything for her son.'

'What's weird about that?'

'I just wondered why she didn't say *children* instead of *son*.'

'She's only got one child now,' I point out. 'Her son.'

'Yeah, that's what I told myself.'

'So, what do we do next?'

'I'm not planning to do anything else,' he says. 'Claire wants me to update the story online and upload some photos I took of the outside of the prison. For the print edition, I'll write an article about meeting a convicted killer, that sort of thing. Simon gave Claire a photo of Melissa holding a twin in each arm and looking radiant for that one. Here, look.'

He slides a photo across his desk towards me.

'Where did Simon get this?' I ask, thinking that the photographer must have been Michael Slade.

'From Melissa's parents, I suppose. The photo alone should do the trick. In any case, after that, I'll have served my purpose. This will no longer be a scoop. It will be national news. It'll be on TV. It's going to become much bigger than *The Rag*. By the time Melissa's appeal comes round in November, there will be journos everywhere.'

'I thought Claire wanted an exclusive. Interviews with family members et cetera.'

'Yeah. I think what Claire actually wanted was for us to set the tone.' He sounds pissed off now and I'm not sure if it's with Claire or me. 'If the first person to report in any detail on a possible miscarriage of justice is on the side of the defendant, or the appellant, or whatever she is, then everyone will follow suit.'

'I don't get it. Are you saying Saunders was hoping to influence public opinion? Why would she want to do that?'

'Let's just say I think she owed Superintendent Goodman a favour.'

'So you're just going to swan off to France and forget about all of this?' The words are out before I can stop them. Jon is my boss. Sort of. I can't speak to him like that.

'Pretty much, yeah. I was determined to get to the truth, too. But we may never get to the bottom of this, you know.'

'But someone knows the truth.' I'm aware I'm raising my voice, and there are people in the room gawking at us now, but I can't stop myself.

'Sure, but if that person is Melissa, no one else will ever find out what really happened to those poor babies.' He combs his hair with his fingers and it stands on end. 'She won't ever confess if she did it.'

'What if Melissa doesn't know what happened? Have you considered that?'

'So now you think she's innocent?' He turns back to his

computer and I think I've lost him and the argument. I can't believe he's going to give up on this story.

'I don't know about that,' I say more softly. 'I'm just saying, someone knows the truth, but maybe Melissa doesn't. We can't give up, Jon.'

He grunts and logs in. 'Look, the month of August tends to be quiet in journalism, as you know. Apart from the fact nothing newsworthy really happens, everyone is away on holiday. You can spend some time working on this while I'm on holiday. If you manage to find anything, you can tell me all about it when I get back. I'll only be gone a week.'

'While you're away, I thought I'd carry on working my way through the list. I'd like to pay Callum a visit. Which uni does he go to?'

'He dropped out, according to his mother. So he's back home, at his father's, I should think. He's the main reason she wants to get out of jail.'

'I see. Is it OK with you if I ask him a few questions?'

'Maybe check with Simon Goodman first.' He grabs a Post-it and brings his emails up on his laptop screen. He scribbles something down and then hands me the Post-it. It has Simon Goodman's email address and mobile number on it.

'I've got a contact for you, too.'

'Oh?' He sounds completely uninterested. Undeterred, I hand him the piece of paper with the address I wrote down a few minutes ago. 'What's this?'

'Clémentine Rouquier, the Slade twins' nanny. This is the address of her father's vineyard. I thought as you were going to the south of France on holi …' I break off when I see the stern look he's giving me. 'It's two hours south of Lyon,' I add, but I think my voice is drowned out by the hammering from upstairs.

'I'm taking a well-earned break, Kelly. It's not a working holiday. It's a family holiday. Just me and my boys. And anyway, we're going to the Camargue. It's nowhere near Lyon.'

I want to point out that this place isn't near Lyon either, and it's probably only a few hours' drive from the Camargue, but Jon opens a small box and takes out his earplugs, a clear signal that our conversation is over. But I notice he puts the piece of paper down on his desk, which I take as a good sign. He won't drop our investigation. Will he?

A drill starts up somewhere in the building.

Jon turns to me. 'Hopefully the workmen will have finished by the time I get back. It's been months.' I'm not sure if he's shouting to make himself heard over the noise or because he has earplugs in, but either way, he's not angry with me, which is a relief.

I write an email to Simon Goodman, explaining that I'll be continuing to report on Melissa's miscarriage of justice during Jon's absence and asking if I can meet up with his son. I don't know what I expect Callum to tell me if I do get to see him. I'd like to find out what he thinks of his mother and what she was like before his baby sisters died. And before they were born, come to think of it, when he was little. That would be a good start.

I check my emails every now and again, but there's no reply from Superintendent Goodman by the end of the afternoon when it's time to go home. Crap! I close down my computer.

Jon starts to undock his laptop.

'Have a nice time,' I say when he has taken out his earplugs. 'The Camargue, you say? White horses and flamingos?' I remember going camping there with my parents when I was little. We were eaten alive by mosquitoes despite spraying ourselves liberally with insect repellent and burning citronella candles.

'And sea and sun,' Jon says, standing up and hooking his jacket over his shoulder. 'This time tomorrow, we'll be on the plane.'

His words from earlier come back to me. *Just me and my boys.* He's married, though. He wears a wedding ring. And I remember seeing photos of the four of them all over the living room when I babysat for Noah and Alfie.

I wonder why his wife isn't going. I don't dare ask him. Besides, it's none of my business. But my mind tries to fill in the blanks. Perhaps she's working and couldn't get time off. Or maybe his marriage has broken down. I'm sure he was seeing that pathologist, Holly. His wife may have found out. Jon's a good guy on the whole, but I can't stand infidelity. If he got caught with his trousers down, it serves him right.

When Jon has left the office, I pack up my own things. Just as I'm about to leave, my phone pings with an incoming mail. I plonk everything down on my desk and fish my mobile out of my handbag. It's from Simon Goodman. He suggests I come round to his place at the weekend. Fab! I fire off a quick reply.

I happen to glance down on my way past Jon's desk and spot a piece of paper, scrunched up in his waste paper bin. Bending down, I pick it up. I know what it is even before I smooth out the creases. It's the piece of scrap paper I wrote the address of the vineyard on. My heart sinks. It looks like I'm on my own with the Melissa Slade case from now on.

CHAPTER 21

~

Jonathan

August 2018

'There's no way I'm going across that, Daddy,' Alfie says.

We're standing on the banks of the River Gardon, admiring the *Pont du Gard*. Well, I'm admiring it. Alfie is staring fearfully at the tourists walking on the lower level of the aqueduct.

'That wasn't part of the plan,' I say.

'Ba-by. How old did you say it was, Dad?' Noah addresses both Alfie and me in the same breath without taking his eyes off the screen of my mobile as he takes photos.

'About two thousand years old.'

'And it's still standing,' Noah muses.

This, of course, is what's troubling Alfie, who was glued to the TV, watching the images on repeat a fortnight ago when the viaduct in Genova collapsed.

'The Romans were incredible builders. We could do with some of them in the offices of *The Rag*, actually.'

'Shame the Italians didn't inherit their skills,' Noah comments wryly.

I'm about to point out that when the Ponte Morandi was built, no one could have foreseen how much traffic would be using it sixty years later, but Noah already knows this. He's very clued-up on current affairs for his age. I bite my tongue and let it go.

It has been a lovely day so far and I want it to continue that way. We visited Nîmes – the amphitheatre this morning and the temple of Diana this afternoon. Despite the heat and the lack of shade, the boys were on their best behaviour, largely thanks to my promise of ice cream after the visits. But I'm sensing they've had enough of Roman ruins for one day.

'What do you want to do?' I ask. 'Go back to the *gîte* and play a game? Go for a swim? Visit something else?'

'I want to watch a DVD,' Alfie says.

'We've watched the ones we brought with us,' Noah argues.

We go back to the hire car with its steering wheel on the wrong side. Noah, who is allowed in the front seat as long as he reminds me to drive on the right every time we set off, activates Siri on my phone. Between them, they find an *Auchan* a few miles – correction, *kilometres* – away. In the supermarket, we stock up on food – baguettes, cheese, crisps, pâté, popcorn and sweets mainly – and buy two DVDs. Noah chooses *Thor: Ragnarok*, and Alfie goes for *The Incredibles 2*, or *Les Indestructibles 2*, as it's apparently called in French. I check the DVDs have the English language version.

I spot a DVD on the shelf with the title *Amoureux de ma Femme*. I only got a 'B' in my French GCSE, but I know what that means. My heart skips a beat as I picture Mel on our wedding day. I was madly in love with my wife.

Then my mind leaps to the piece of paper I balled up and threw into the paper basket under my workstation a few days ago. *Château des Amoureux*. The name of the vineyard Kelly wanted me to go to.

'Let's go and pay, lads,' I say, snapping out of my reverie.

As I open the boot to put the shopping in, Alfie points at the car DVD player. It was a present from my parents for their grandsons and we brought it with us in one of the suitcases. I've kept it in the boot in case we do a lot of motorway or get stuck in traffic so the boys don't get too bored.

'Can we watch my one now?' Alfie pleads.

'We'll be back at the *gîte* in a little while. Wouldn't you rather wait till then?'

'No.'

I'm about to refuse and hand him the packet of *Carambar* chews instead, but then I change my mind. Not just about the DVD. 'All right. Why not?'

Noah hops into the back and gets the DVD player sorted out while I mess around with google and then fiddle with the satnav.

After driving for ten minutes in the opposite direction to the *gîte*, I glance in the rear-view mirror. Both Noah and Alfie are fast asleep with their earphones in. I unplug the power cable of the DVD player from the cigarette lighter socket. According to the satnav, I should be there in another forty-six minutes. Saint-Martin-d'Ardèche, the place is called. As I slow down at a roundabout, I switch on the radio to a station called RTL2, which is playing a U2 track, and I sigh.

'You win, Kelly,' I mutter, then start singing along with Bono.

Half an hour or so later, after several minutes of incomprehensible adverts, a French song – something halfway between rap and hip-hop – comes over the airwaves and through my car speakers. Switching the radio off, I begin to wonder if it was a mistake to come here. At the very least I should have rung ahead. This is a family estate. Clémentine's father probably still runs the place. For all I know, Clémentine doesn't even work in the wine industry herself.

I don't have a clue what to ask her anyway. What do I want

to know, exactly? I've been too impulsive, coming here on a whim – Kelly's whim. My boys are still fast asleep. I could turn round and head back. They'd never know. No one would.

Just then I see the first signpost for Saint-Martin-d'Ardèche pointing across a bridge over the Ardèche River. There's a group of kayakers paddling down the river, and the gorges, dark green and chalky white, are reflected in it. I'm almost here now. I may as well go and see if Clémentine's around.

Once in the village itself, I get a bit lost. The satnav sends me up a tiny road, which is little more than a footpath. At the end of it, I'm instructed to turn left. I look dubiously at the field I'm supposed to drive through and reverse all the way back down the track.

Turning around at the bottom, I spot a couple of joggers. They stop obligingly when I sound my horn and open my window. '*Pour aller au Château des Amoureux, s'il vous plaît?*' I say, my GCSE French coming back to me in my hour of need.

They both turn and point in the direction I'm facing. One of them pulls out his earphones and garbles directions. I don't catch a single word. But I can see the vines stretching across the hillside and a domineering white stone castle perched on top of the hill, nothing but blue sky above it.

Noah stirs and asks where we are. I tell him I have to make a stop on the way back to the *gîte* for work. To my surprise, he doesn't moan. When I get to the Rouquier family's vineyard, both Noah and Alfie are wide awake. I park in front of the main building and see a little wooden sign for "*dégustation*", which fortunately has the translation – wine tasting – underneath.

A Border collie bounds towards us, its tail wagging, as we get out of the car and I leave the boys fussing over it as I follow the sign around the back of the property. There's another sign with the same word on a door and a bell tinkles as I open it. I enter a dark, cool room, my eyes taking a second or two to adjust to the dimness. There's a musty smell in here, overlaid with the odour of tannin and wood. A barrel is pushed to one side of the room with empty wine glasses sitting on top of it, and a couple of high stools are lined up along a bar. I notice some certificates or awards framed and hanging on the stone walls.

A man in his early sixties materialises behind the bar. Damn. I was expecting Clémentine. I'm not entirely sure what she looks like, but this certainly isn't her.

'*Je veux Clémentine,*' I say. The man says nothing, but his eyebrows, shooting up towards his balding head, tell me my three-word sentence isn't quite right. '*Je voudrais voir Clémentine,*' I try again, adding, '*s'il vous plaît,*' as an afterthought.

He gets out his mobile and talks down it in French. Then he ends the call, giving me a tight smile. After a few minutes, just as I'm beginning to think that maybe the phone call had nothing to do with my request, the bell goes again. I whirl round and find myself face to face with a tall, slim woman in her mid-twenties. She's wearing a singlet over denim shorts and her skin is bronzed from the sun. She has the same dark brown eyes as the man. Clémentine.

'*On se connaît?*' she asks me.

I get it when she repeats her question. I reply in English. 'No, we don't know each other, but we have an acquaintance in common.'

She makes her way behind the bar and opens a fridge. Twisting the cap off a plastic bottle of Evian, she takes several gulps. Her hands are stained, from the grapes I imagine. '*C'est bon, Papa,*' she says, dismissing the man. '*C'est l'ami d'un de mes copains.*'

Her father grunts and leaves the way he came in – through a door behind the bar. I climb up onto a bar stool. For a few seconds, neither of us speaks, each appraising the other.

Then I say, 'My name is Jonathan Hunt. I'm a reporter for *The Redcliffe Gazette*. I was on holiday not far from here—'

'Redcliffe? You come from Bristol?' Her inquisitive look is replaced by a wary one. 'Is this about Michael Slade?'

'No, it's more about his ex-wife, Melissa,' I say, wondering why Clémentine would think I've come about Michael. Because of her affair with him?

'Ex?'

'Yes, they divorced while she was in prison.'

'Was?'

'She's still in prison. But she has an appeal pending. I'm investigating a possible miscarriage of justice. Would you mind talking to me? I won't take up much of your time.'

'I have nothing to say. I considered myself lucky that I didn't have to go to court before. I only had to provide a statement. I'd rather not get involved.'

'You don't have to answer anything you don't feel comfortable with and I don't need to name you as a source.' When she doesn't respond, I try a different tactic. 'Please? I've come all this way.'

'I had understood you were on holiday near here?'

'Well, yes …' I'm not sure how to implore with my eyes, but I aim for that expression now.

'OK. As long as this is … off the record … Is that how you say it?'

'Yes. Off the record. You have my word. Your English is perfect, by the way. My French is terrible.'

'Thank you. It's a bit rusty, but I am expanding the export side of my father's business, so I need to practise my English.'

I wonder if this is why she agreed to talk to me. A good opportunity for her to work on her speaking skills. Suits me.

Or perhaps she's just curious. She leans towards me. 'You said a miscarriage of justice? You mean she didn't kill her babies?'

'She was convicted of murdering only one of them, officially, but yes, there's new evidence to suggest that she's innocent.'

'*Only* one,' Clémentine repeats. 'What's this new evidence?'

'A medical report that was kept from the defence.' I can't let Clémentine turn the tables and ask me questions. So, I add quickly, 'You worked there as an *au pair*, is that right?'

164

'Yes. It was supposed to be during one year, but I came home after three months. Then I got another job in the States during six months.'

'As an *au pair*?'

'No, as a waitress, cleaner, general dogsbody at a hotel in California.'

'Hard work, huh?'

'I was given accommodation and it was good for my English. That was the important thing.'

'What was it like working for the Slades?' Clémentine crosses her arms and narrows her eyes, and I realise I'm close to demolishing the trust I've been building up. I need to skirt round her relationship with Michael Slade. I amend my question. 'What was it like working for Melissa Slade?'

'She was moody. One instant she was in a bad mood, the next she was fine. She had no patience with her babies. She didn't 'ave any confidence either. Amber cried a lot. Melissa could never stop her to cry … I mean, stop her crying. Sometimes Melissa, she cried, too.'

'Were you able to calm Amber?'

Clémentine pauses. Then she says, 'I looked after Ellie more.'

'Because she was less fractious?'

'Fractious?'

'Calmer. Did you prefer to look after Ellie because she was easier?'

She hesitates again before answering. It's as though she's struggling to find her words. Not because she needs to work out what she wants to say in English, but because she's trying to give the right answer. 'No. I left Amber to Melissa because I hoped if Melissa pacified her, then she would become a mother more confident … a more confident mother.'

I'm not sure I believe this. I think if Melissa had looked after Ellie more she would have felt like she was doing a better job, but I'm no expert on childcare – my sons attest to that.

'What were the other members of the family like?' I ask, keeping my question as vague as possible.

'They were all nice. Callum was like a younger brother; I got on well with his half-sister Bella.'

'His stepsister.'

'Yes, his stepsister.' Clémentine shifts from one foot to the other, her eyes darting all over the place. Then she looks at her wrist. She's not wearing a watch, but she says, 'I don't have any more time, I'm afraid.'

'I know about you and Michael, Clémentine, if that's what you're worried about. That's not why I'm here. Unless it has any bearing on Melissa's situation, we don't have to talk about it.'

She nods. 'I don't know if Melissa guessed about us while I was there. I didn't know her before she had her babies. Maybe she was different. But she was not a good mother and she was not a good wife when I knew her. She didn't love her children and she didn't love her 'usband. She didn't even like herself. I often ask myself if she found out about us and that's what pushed her.'

'Pushed her?'

'I mean, if she found out that Michael and me, we were in love, maybe that had something to do with why she killed her babies. I blame myself a lot.'

In love. Clémentine can only have been nineteen or twenty and Michael must have been around thirty-nine or forty, around the age I am now. It seems clear to me he took advantage of her, but six years later, she still views their relationship through rose-tinted spectacles.

'So you think she's guilty?' I say.

'Who else would have killed two innocent babies?'

'The fresh evidence that has been uncovered indicates they may not have been killed at all. Either of them.'

She shrugs. 'I hope that's true.'

'But you don't believe it is?'

166

'I don't believe in coincidences.'

It occurs to me that the jury at Melissa's trial probably didn't, either. 'Did you keep in touch with Michael?' I ask.

'No.' She lowers her head. 'He thought it was better like this. I didn't need to be tied down … tied up … involved in this, he said.'

It sounds to me more like he was using that as a convenient excuse to end his relationship with Clémentine, but I refrain from comment. 'What about Bella? You said the two of you got on well. Did you keep in touch with her?'

'No. She wrote to me – twice I think. She wasn't at the trial, but she found out about her father and me. She was furious.' Clémentine has tears in her eyes, but she keeps them locked on mine. 'That was the last I 'eard from her. The last email she sent. After, I wanted to apologise, but I didn't know how to contact her.'

It seems to me that in this day and age if you want to get in touch with someone, you can find a way, but I don't push it.

As if reading my thoughts, Clémentine says, 'I don't think Bella uses the Internet now.'

Something feels off in all this, but whatever it is, it's a dead end. Damn! I think Bella might have an important piece of this messy jigsaw puzzle. 'Do you have any idea where I might find her?'

'I don't 'ave an address for her, if that's what you mean.' She laughs sardonically and I'm not sure why. I get the feeling she's joking but I've missed the punchline. 'The last time I called Michael on the phone, he said she was always in Bristol. In the centre.'

I frown. Then I get a flash from Madame Smith's French lessons at school. "Encore" can be translated into "always" or "still". Clémentine clearly thinks Bella still lives in the city centre. Perhaps Bella's mother's house is in the centre. Clémentine might not be aware that Bella left home. It's not my place to tell her.

'When was that?' I ask, recalling her saying just now that Michael had severed all ties with Clémentine. 'When did you last speak to Michael?'

'Maybe three or four months after the trial had ended?'

I sigh. No one seems to know what has become of Bella. She moved out of her father's house when Melissa was arrested. Then she walked out the door of her mother's house and no one has heard from her since. She vanished four years ago, leaving no trace whatsoever.

'Thank you. You've been very helpful,' I say, trying to sound sincere.

'Will you ... will you see Michael soon?'

'Possibly.'

'Would you say hello from me? Give him my love?'

'Yes, of course,' I lie. Poor kid.

Then Clémentine straightens herself to her full height, as though discarding her relapse into the lovesick teenager she'd once been and becoming the capable career woman she was when she entered this room. 'Were you having the intention to buy wine?' she demands.

I end up buying two cases of *Côtes du Rhône* even though I have no idea how I'm going to squeeze twelve bottles of wine into our suitcases for the flight home and I hardly ever drink red wine anyway. Clémentine and I carry a box each to the hire car, where the boys are still playing with the dog.

'Time to go, kids,' I say. 'Get the DVD player sorted out for the journey back.' Putting the wine in the boot, I spot the packet of popcorn poking out of one of the shopping bags. I toss it to Alfie.

'Lovely boys,' Clémentine says. 'I can tell you're a terrific father.'

I don't correct her. 'Thank you. It was a pleasure to meet you. You needn't worry, I won't mention your name in print at all. May I call you if I think of something you might be able to help me with?'

'If you want,' she replies with a shrug.

On the journey back, I replay in my mind everything Clémentine said. I get the strange impression that she has given me a vital piece of information. She said something I should have picked up on, provided some crucial clue pointing the way to the truth. But I can't put my finger on it.

CHAPTER 22

~

Kelly

August 2018

Bushy Park is in Totterdown, not far from where my mum lives in Knowle, so after lunch at hers, I hoof it, following the directions on the Google Maps app on my phone. I'd imagined Simon Goodman living in a house, for some reason, and I'm surprised. It's a nice enough location, near the city centre. I just thought a fancy property in a safe neighbourhood like Horfield or Henleaze would be more up a high-ranking police officer's street. No pun intended. Perhaps, though, he's single and hates gardening and this ground-floor flat in Totterdown suits him perfectly.

I'm bang on time, so I open the gate, walk up the narrow drive and the stone steps at the end of it and ring the doorbell. It takes him a while to answer the door and when he does, he looks puzzled, as though he can't quite place me.

'Kelly Fox, *The Redcliffe Gazette*?' It sounds like a question, so

I try to be more assertive. 'I made an appointment through you – by email – to talk to your son, Callum.'

'Ah, yes.' Goodman strokes his stubble. 'I'm sorry. It slipped my mind you were coming today. I'm afraid Callum's … not well.'

I know from Melissa Slade's diary that Callum has had a bit of a breakdown and I wonder if that's why Simon Goodman hesitated. Does he mean he's not well mentally? Depressed? Or is he searching for an excuse to fob me off?

'Right, well, I'll send you another email, shall I?' I can hear the irritation in my voice. I should probably keep him sweet, in case Jon and I need to talk to him again, so I fake a smile and add, 'Have a lovely weekend.'

Perching on the wall of the church next to Goodman's flat, I fish my phone out of my handbag. I notice that there's only nine per cent battery power left. I charged up the phone last night but using Google Maps has drained the battery. Still, nine per cent should be enough for a quick call to my mum. I cross my fingers, hoping she'll answer. She does.

'Hi, Mum. Any chance you could pick me up in the car?'

'Sure,' she says. 'Where are you?'

'In Totterdown. Have you got something to note down the address or shall I text it to you?'

There's no answer. I pull my phone away from my ear. The screen is black. It's gone dead. Resisting the urge to throw my mobile on the ground and swear, I put it back in my handbag. I stand up to leave, but sit back down again as I hear the creak of Goodman's front gate. Simon Goodman steps onto the pavement, leaving the gate open behind him. Then he turns right, away from me, and right again, and walks up the street that's perpendicular to this one.

I'm still sitting on the wall when I see him a few seconds later coming back down the road at the wheel of his car. He hasn't noticed me. Either he's absorbed in his thoughts or he's not very observant for a policeman. Once his car has disappeared from sight, I walk back up the drive and the steps to the front door of his flat and ring the doorbell again.

Doorstepping, this is called. When a journalist turns up at someone's home and tries to get an interview out of them when they don't want to talk. Although in this case, it's the father who doesn't want me to talk to his son. I feel like a tabloid paparazzo.

I give up after ringing three times, but as I turn away, the door opens a fraction and a guy five or six years younger than me sticks his head round the doorframe, no doubt trying to hide the fact he's still wearing pyjamas at two in the afternoon. He has dark blond hair that could do with a cut and dark rings under blue-green eyes that would be striking if they weren't so blood-shot. His skin has the pallor of someone who doesn't get outdoors much, or perhaps he genuinely is ill. Despite all that, he's kind of attractive if you're into the bespoke blond bedhead look. It doesn't do much for me.

'Oh. I thought my dad had forgotten his keys,' he says. His breath wafts towards me. Tobacco. And something else. He gives an involuntary giggle and it clicks: he's stoned.

'Callum? I'm Kelly Fox.' I flash my press card like a police badge. 'Your father arranged for me to talk to you this afternoon.'

'I don't think he mentioned it to me. Um … now's not a good time.' I get another whiff of his stale breath and try hard not to wrinkle my nose. Or gag.

'It won't take long,' I say.

'I'm … er … not dressed.'

His eyes travel down to my feet, then back up to fix on my cleavage. I'm wearing a low-cut T-shirt under a fake leather jacket, and suddenly I don't feel sufficiently dressed myself.

'I don't mind,' I say. 'But I could make you a coffee while you freshen up if you like?'

His gaze shifts from my breasts to my handbag. 'You got any aspirin in there by any chance?'

I suppress a smile. He's slurring his words and it's obviously

172

an effort for him to speak. Add to that, he has a broad Bristol accent. He sounds like he's doing an impression of a pissed pirate in pain. 'I've got some paracetamol, if that's any good?'

The fact I've got painkillers on me seems to sway him. He nods, then winces, like the movement has sent a bolt of pain through his head. Stepping back, he opens the door wider for me to come inside.

'I'd prefer tea,' he says.

'Sorry?'

'Rather than coffee. Kitchen's through there.' He points to a door to the left of the hallway. 'Back in a bit.'

As I'm hunting through the cupboards for teabags, I hear water running. Callum has obviously hopped in the shower. I hope he gets a move on. I don't know where his dad has gone and how long I've got, but I don't think I should be here when he gets back.

I fill a glass with water and drop in two effervescent painkillers. Callum appears in the doorway, dressed in jeans and a T-shirt and rubbing his wet hair with a towel. I hand him the glass and he slings the towel over the back of a kitchen chair.

'Cheers. Found everything all right?' he asks, opening a cupboard and taking out a packet of milk chocolate Digestives.

'Yup.'

I follow him through the open door into the sitting room, carrying the mugs. He has sprayed himself with aftershave or deodorant and I almost cough as I breathe it in. He giggles again. He's clearly still lit. Gesturing for me to sit on the sofa, he sinks into an armchair opposite me. I watch him gulp down the paracetamol and then open his packet of biscuits.

'This should help get rid of the headache,' he says, brandishing a Digestive in my direction.

I may as well get straight to the point. 'I wanted to ask you some questions about your mum.' His face darkens, but I carry on. 'My colleague and I are covering her story for *The Redcliffe*

Gazette, trying to get the miscarriage of justice out there as much as possible before her appeal.'

'What makes you think it's a miscarriage of justice?' he asks.

'Isn't that what you think?' When he doesn't answer, I change tack. 'How about telling me what she was like when you were little?'

'She was great. We were a happy family. Until she left my father and rode off into the sunset with a wanker.' His voice is flat, unemotional, but I think it's an act, hiding his hurt. And I don't mean the pain in his head.

'Not a big fan of Michael Slade?'

'You could say that,' he says, his mouth full of Digestive.

'Between you and me, I don't think much of him either.' That elicits a smile, which in turn causes him to scowl and groan. He bends forwards, leaning his elbows on the coffee table and cradling his head in his hands. 'Good night, was it?'

'You could say that,' he repeats. 'Some mean shit, though.' He rubs his head as if to illustrate his point. I wonder if he's on a cycle of good nights to obliterate the bad days.

I glance around the room. Grey carpet. The sofa I'm sitting on has dark grey upholstery and red cushions. Two framed prints on the wall. In one of the pictures, a street scene, a red umbrella contrasts with a grey day. In the other one, a black and white print, a monkey is wearing a sandwich board with the words *Laugh now, but one day we'll be in charge.* I recognise it immediately as one of Banksy's artworks. You can find this very print in every gift or tourist shop in Bristol. The overall effect of the room is rather nondescript and very masculine.

One thing stands out. A large framed photo on the sideboard of Melissa Slade in her thirties, standing between Callum, who must be about eleven years old, and Simon Goodman, who looks less worn in the photo than he does now, an effect heightened by the lack of facial hair on his chin, perhaps.

'Happy days,' Callum says, following my gaze.

174

There's a smaller photo next to it – a school photo. He's not smiling in this one. He sees me looking at it.

'I was thirteen in that one. It was just before my mother's trial.'

He looks older in the school photo than in the family photo, but he still looks a lot younger than thirteen.

'Did you attend your mum's trial, Callum?'

'Not as a witness, if that's what you mean. They read out my statement to the court. My grandparents took me one day and we watched from the gallery, but then they decided it wasn't a good idea – too traumatic for me or something – and I didn't get to go again.'

'And do you still visit your mum in prison?'

'No. I used to go when Dad made me. Haven't been for a while.'

'Why's that?'

He shrugs. 'I don't want to see her. She has ruined my life.'

That sounds a bit melodramatic, but I can relate to what he's saying. I know what it's like to grow up resenting one of your parents. If my father were still around, I probably wouldn't want to see him, either. As if on cue, an image of his face appears, as sharp as if he were standing before me. He might not be around anymore, but I still see him: in colour, in detail, in my head. The less I think about him, the better I feel. I haven't forgiven him.

'In what way has she ruined your life?' I ask, focusing on Callum's face instead.

He shakes his head. But then he says, 'People judge me because of who she is. When everyone found out who I was at uni, my life became a living hell.'

'People can be very unkind,' I say.

'I lost my sisters when they died, then my mother when she went to jail for it. But I also lost my stepsister.'

At these words, my heart clenches in a sudden stab of pain. 'I know what it's like to lose a parent and a—'

175

'My friends abandoned me. And my girlfriend has dumped me. All because of her.'

I wonder if Callum always feels this sorry for himself or if the weed in his system is making him open up more than he normally would. He has been talkative, but he hasn't actually given me anything I can use, either in an article or as a clue towards finding out the truth.

'So, you're not in touch with Bella anymore?'

'No. No one knows where she is.'

I can't get my head round that. 'Isn't anyone looking for her?'

'I think everyone assumed that if she took off, she didn't want to be found.'

This is one dysfunctional family. Even more fractured than my own.

'I understand how the police might not have the resources to continue to search for her, although I think that sucks, but I don't get how Bella's own family could just give up.'

It's only when Callum looks up at me through wide red-blue eyes that I realise I've spoken that thought aloud – and rather vehemently at that.

'Sorry,' I say. 'Subject close to my heart.' I reach over to the coffee table to put down my empty mug and stay sitting forwards on the sofa, studying Callum. 'What makes you think Bella took off?'

'She was fucked up, man.'

'Because of the twins' deaths?'

He puts his half-eaten biscuit down on the coffee table and furrows his brow. 'I think that tipped her over the edge. But she'd been teetering on the brink for a while.'

'Did you get on with Bella?'

'Yes. She was nice. Easy-going, you know. Bright. She had dark moods and she was quite introverted, but she could be fun.'

She sounds like a normal teen. 'What about your mum? Did she get on with her?'

'Yeah. Bella helped out with the babies and that. I think everyone liked her. Mike was always raving about how proud he was of her.'

'Mike? Michael Slade, you mean?'

'Yeah. Bella wasn't there a lot. And sometimes when she was there, I wasn't – I had to stay at Dad's every other weekend. Bella lived with her mother, mainly. I think she preferred it at her mum's.'

'Why was that?'

'Dunno. I liked it better at my mum's at the time. More people around. Better than just Dad and me. You know? Perhaps she liked that it was quieter at her mum's place.'

Sensing I'm heading into a dead end, I try to steer the conversation back to Melissa. 'You said earlier it wasn't just your mum you lost when she was sentenced. Do you think maybe your mum feels that she lost her daughters and then her son, too?' I ask.

His face changes, his eyes becoming blank, his lips pursed. 'She fucking asked for it. She deserves everything she gets. I hope her appeal fails and they leave her banged up for good.'

I can't think how to respond to his outburst, so I wait for him to continue, but instead he lifts the mug to his lips with both hands to take a sip of his tea. He's wearing a Black Sabbath T-shirt and my attention is immediately drawn to his left forearm. Pale white scars zigzag across it. Self-harm scars. He's evidently messed up. Did that start after his mother was arrested? Or was he already like that?

'Why's that, Callum?' He gives an almost imperceptible shake of his head. He's holding my gaze, but he's not going to answer me. I try again. 'What makes you think she deserves to stay in prison?'

He lowers his head and I think I've lost him. But then he whispers, 'She did it.'

'You mean you think your mum's guilty?'

A quick nod.

177

'What makes you think she's guilty?' I make an effort to keep my voice even and calm. 'Did she tell you that? Did someone else tell you?'

'I don't think she did it …'

'But you just said—'

'… I *know* she did. She killed Ellie.'

'How do you know?' He doesn't answer. 'How do you know that, Callum?'

I jump as I hear someone behind me. 'Hello again. Kelly, isn't it?' I whip my head round so quickly I crick my neck. Simon Goodman is standing in the doorway. He looks from me to Callum. 'I see you're up and about, young man. Feeling better?'

'A bit.' Callum looks sheepish.

'I should go,' I say, standing up.

'Yes, you should.'

Simon Goodman doesn't move and I accidentally brush his arm as I squeeze past him. My heart starts to thunder as for a second, I wonder how much of the conversation he overheard. I half expect him to lunge at me and prevent me from leaving the house. He turns around and I can sense him behind me. He reaches across me and I give a little whimper.

Then he opens the front door and holds it for me. Stepping outside into the daylight, I curse myself for letting my overactive imagination run amok. It was all too much, too tense. Callum's bitterness towards his mother. His belief that his mother killed his sister. Goodman bursting in on us like that.

The front door slams shut behind me. Taking a deep breath, I walk briskly down the drive and then slow my pace as I begin the walk back to my mother's. Hopefully she'll drop me home from there. Earlier I didn't want to walk, but now I think it will do me good. I need to clear my head, untangle my thoughts.

Did Callum mean what he said about his mother being guilty? How could he possibly know if she was? Maybe he doesn't know for certain and he was simply expressing his gut instinct. And why is nobody worried about Bella? Surely even if she did leave home of her own accord, someone must want to know where she is. She's a missing person that no one is missing. Unless someone does know her whereabouts.

I'm still deep in thought half an hour later, sitting at my mum's kitchen table, a steaming mug of hot chocolate in front of me.

'A penny for them,' my mum says, lowering herself into the seat opposite.

'Hips playing up?' I ask, noting her slow movements. My mum's in her late forties – she was in her early twenties when she had my sister and me – but she has stiffness in her joints. Arthritis, maybe. She won't see a doctor. She's a little plump and forever on some fad diet, convinced if she were slim her aches and pains would disappear.

'Never mind me. Tell me all about your interview with Melissa Slade's boy.'

I fetch the biscuit tin and take out a packet of Hobnobs. We had devilled eggs with avocado and iceberg lettuce for lunch, in keeping with Mum's latest food craze regime, and I'm starving now. Callum munched his way through at least five biccies while I was there, but he didn't offer me one, the sod.

I relate my discussion with Callum to my mum, who is all ears. She always listens to what I say, but I'm surprised at the keen interest she has been taking in my job since I started investigating the Melissa Slade case. It's bordering on morbid fascination. She grills me about it all every time I pop round.

I prepare myself for her volley of questions, but when I've finished, she is quiet and unsmiling. It must be all my talk about looking for Bella. I've made Mum think of Lily. Every time Bella's disappearance comes up, I'm reminded of Lily, too.

'I'm sorry, Mum,' I say. 'I've upset you.'

'No, you haven't. I'm fine,' she says, but I can tell she isn't. 'I do hope Melissa Slade gets justice. That woman's been through enough.'

'Do you remember the case, then? What do you remember about it?'

She heaves herself up, using her arms to push on the table. 'More than most,' she says, picking up the washing basket from where it was sitting on the worktop.

'You think she's innocent, don't you? What makes you think she's innocent?'

'She didn't seem guilty, put it that way.'

'What do you mean, she didn't seem guilty?'

'I meant … you know.' My mum lowers her head, avoiding eye contact. She's the one who brought this up and yet now she doesn't want to talk about it for some reason. 'Her picture on the TV and in the papers. She looked innocent … beautiful.'

'Hang on! You can't leave it there!' I call after her as she walks past me towards the door from the kitchen to the hallway. 'Talk to me.'

She turns around. 'I can't,' she says. 'I'm not allowed.'

'Why not? What do you mean, you're not allowed?'

'I'm sworn to secrecy.'

And with that, she disappears, armed with her basket of clean clothes. I hear her footsteps as she trundles upstairs. I won't get any more out of her on the matter. Not today, anyway.

CHAPTER 23

~

Jonathan

August 2018

'So, I went to pay Callum Goodman a visit while you were off galli-vanting in France,' Kelly says, flopping onto her swivel chair and dropping her bag at her feet. Her eyes are bright with excitement.

Kelly often starts her sentences with "So", which annoys the shit out of me, but I bite my tongue. At least she doesn't do it in her copy. It amuses me that she has dispensed with any form of greeting, even though I haven't seen her for over a week. 'Uh-huh. How did you find him?' I ask.

'Google Maps,' she says.

'No, that's not what I meant. I meant, what—'

'I was joking. I thought he was self-pitying, screwed up and immature.'

'He sounds adorable.'

She wheels her chair so close to mine that her knees brush my thigh. 'He says Melissa killed Ellie,' she says, lowering her voice.

'Really? How does he know that?'

'He didn't say.'

'Didn't you ask him?'

'Of course I did! But his dad walked in on us at that point.'

Her expression is so serious I can't help but laugh. 'Great timing,' I say. Kelly manages a smile, although I can see by the look in her eyes that this is no laughing matter for her. 'Did you believe him?'

'I think Callum believes his mother is guilty. Whether or not he knows for sure, I have no idea.' She manoeuvres her chair back to her workstation. 'And you were right and wrong, by the way.'

'How so?'

'You were wrong about August being a quiet month for news and right about Melissa Slade's appeal becoming national news. While you were across the Channel, it's all anyone has talked about here.'

'Hmm. I saw. I picked up a paper at the airport when I got back.'

'Not just in the papers. On TV, too. Everyone seems to be on her side this time.' Without taking a breath, she adds, 'So, how was France?'

'Good. The boys and I had a great time. I took a detour. Paid a visit to—'

'How come your wife didn't go?' Kelly asks before I can tell her about Clémentine. 'Was she working?' I frown. 'I'm so sorry. It's none of my business. That just came out. I shouldn't have asked,' Kelly gushes. She looks mortified. 'I've overstepped the mark. You're kind of my boss, after all.'

'It's OK, Kelly.' I rake my hair with my fingers. I think Kelly nearly asked me about Mel a couple of times before. Once when she looked after Noah and Alfie so I could go out with Holly and the second time when I said I was going on holiday with my sons. 'My wife is dead.' My voice cracks as it always does when I talk about this.

Kelly's mouth has fallen open. 'I'm so sorry,' she says again. 'I didn't mean to be nosy.'

'That's all right. You weren't to know.'

'How did she die? Was she ill?'

'No.'

There's a pause. Kelly holds my gaze. I don't ever talk about this. The last person I told was Holly and it took me several months before I was able to tell her all of it. But Kelly has a way of getting me to confide in her. And she has a right to know. She has looked after my boys.

I take a deep breath. 'It was a hit and run on a zebra crossing.'

'She was run over by a car, you mean?'

'A van, actually.'

I expect that to be the end of the conversation, but Kelly asks, 'Not deliberately?'

'No. The driver was texting. He didn't see her crossing the road. Mowed her down. She died in the ambulance.' I clear my throat.

'I'm so sorry.' She places her hand on my arm.

'Mel – my wife – was seven and a half months pregnant with our daughter Rosie.' My words come out as a whisper. 'Rosie died, too.'

'Bloody hell.' For a moment she says nothing else. I've shocked her into silence. Then she asks, 'Did they catch the driver?'

'Yep. His name's Adrian Pike. He's in prison. For now. Manslaughter.'

'I'm so sorry,' Kelly says again.

For a few seconds we don't speak. Then, just as I'm about to change the subject back to my trip to France, Kelly gets up and heads over to the vending machine, giving me a chance to compose myself. I watch her walk away, then look round the office. The renovation hasn't come along much since I've been away, although there's an overpowering smell of paint. At least it's quiet this morning. No drilling or banging.

183

'What's happened to the builders?' I ask, as Kelly comes back, handing me a plastic beaker of coffee.

'I think Saunders said they were working on several jobs at once.'

'Not that different to being a journo then,' I comment.

Kelly chuckles politely. 'You were going to tell me about something you visited in France.'

'Not something. Someone.'

Kelly's eyes widen and she gives a little squeal of excitement. 'You went to the wine place. Did you see the *au pair*? What did she say?'

I fill her in on my conversation with Clémentine. I don't tell Kelly that I was convinced Clémentine said something important that I didn't pick up on. I've mulled over her words several times, replaying them in my head. I'm no longer sure that she said anything helpful at all. The more I think about it, the more convinced I am that it was just wishful thinking on my part. I didn't want my trip to the *Château des Amoureux* to be for nothing.

'In the city centre, huh?' Kelly says when I've finished. 'Does Clémentine know Bella has left home? Do you think it's her mum who lives in the centre of Bristol?'

'I don't know.'

'That's my next step,' Kelly says, a determined expression on her face. 'Finding Bella.'

'Sounds like a Pixar animation.'

'Ha-ha.' Kelly isn't amused. 'Apart from the twins, there were eight people in the house the night Amber died. Between us, we've spoken to five of them – Melissa and Michael Slade, Callum, Clémentine and Jennifer Porter.' She counts each of them off on her fingers. 'I doubt there's any point speaking to Rob or Sophia Porter, so that only leaves Bella on the list. She's our last chance. If we find her, maybe we'll find out what really happened to those babies—'

'Maybe.'

'—and that's a good place to start. With her mum. So, what about you? What are you going to do?'

I scowl. I have no intention of continuing this so-called investigation now I'm home. I thought I'd made that clear to Kelly. I've been used. I played ball, setting the example by crying 'miscarriage of justice'. It seems to have worked – Melissa's case is receiving intense media coverage nationally and Melissa herself seems to be widely supported by the general public. Now it's time for me to get back to what I do best. Local news. School fêtes, job creations or lay-offs and roadblocks are more my bag. I'm a hack at heart.

'I've already told you, Kelly. I'm not interested in this,' I say. 'I've got work to do. Tons of it, in fact, now I've been away for a week.'

'But we have to follow this up.'

'Kelly, I don't—'

'Why did you go to see Clémentine Rouquier if you're so anxious not to have anything to do with this?'

'That was a mistake. It was a waste of time.'

'Why doesn't it mean anything to you?'

'Why should it mean something to me?' I'm shouting now, and an awkward hush descends on the office. I can feel the eyes of the other journos in the room on us.

Kelly doesn't answer straight away, but I can tell she has more to say; she's working out how to say it. I wait.

'You've just told me your story, Jon. Your baby girl was killed. Melissa Slade's baby girls died. Maybe they were killed, too.'

'Thanks, Kelly, but I don't need that pointed out to me.'

This is exactly what has been bugging me from the start. Do I have something in common with Melissa Slade? If she killed one or both of her babies, then we are poles apart, she and I. But if someone else killed them, then, yes, I should feel for her, for what she has gone through, what she's still going through. I should fight for her.

I can't come up with a counterargument, but I'm not about

185

to give in to Kelly's demands. 'Why do you care?' I ask her. I've turned down the volume a notch and everyone else looks away. The excitement is over. 'What's it to you?' Kelly sighs and looks down. I hope she isn't going to cry. 'Kelly?'

'Do you remember Lily Fox?' she says, still refusing to meet my eyes. Her voice is no longer raised, either.

'Lily Fox,' I repeat the name. The same surname as Kelly. 'No. Can't say I do. Is she a relative of yours?'

Kelly swivels her chair to face her laptop screen. I wonder if this is the end of our conversation. She types something, then angles her computer towards me. She has brought up an article, illustrated with a photo of a beautiful young blond-haired girl, maybe fourteen or fifteen years old. I recognise her. Her picture was in all the papers.

'You wrote this,' Kelly says, accusingly, tapping her computer screen with her index finger.

'Lily Fox,' I say. It's coming back to me now. It was all over the news, local and national. 'Was she your sister?' Then I think I get it. 'Was she your twin sister?'

'Not my twin, no. She *is* my big sister. She's two years older than me.'

I look at Kelly blankly. 'I'm sorry about your sister, Kelly. Did they ever find out—?'

'No. My sister's disappearance is the reason why I wanted to become a reporter. I can't help thinking if her story had been followed up by a dedicated journalist at the time, well, maybe we'd know …'

'But I don't see what this has to do with the Slade case.' No sooner have I spoken the words than it dawns on me. There are parallels in this case for Kelly, too. 'Lily is the reason you want to find Bella.'

Kelly nods.

Now it's my turn to sigh. I'm caving in. 'OK. There is something I can do.'

I send an email to Simon Goodman asking him if he can get me an address for Bella's mother. She won't be using the name Slade, and I have no idea if she has remarried or if she's using her maiden name or even what her maiden name is. I know nothing about the woman. But I bet Goodman does. And if not, he'll be able to find out. And that will give Kelly something to go on.

Just as I hear the swoosh of my email as it begins winging its way to Goodman, my phone beeps with a text. It's from Holly. My heart stops for a few beats when I see her name. I've been asking myself every day for the last three months if I should get in touch with her. Ever since she broke up with me. But I was too much of a coward to call or send a text.

Dare I hope that she has been thinking of me, too? Or is she contacting me because she has something else for me on the Slade case? Holding my breath, I open her text.

'Kelly, are you free this evening by any chance?' I ask when I've read it.

~

The boys protest that they're old enough to spend an evening alone without a childminder, but I beg to differ. Noah might come out with some precocious comments sometimes, but he's nowhere near mature enough to be trusted alone with his younger brother. Their objections stop instantly when I tell them Kelly is coming to look after them.

Leaving the boys in Kelly's capable hands, and leaving Kelly with strict instructions, I drive away to meet up with Holly. I'm trying not to get my hopes up, but I'm taking it as a good sign that she accepted the invitation to see me and I don't want to blow this opportunity of putting things right. In the car, I rehearse my speech. I want to tell her I've missed her and that if she'll give me another chance, I'd like to tell my boys about her and take it from there.

I have a little difficulty finding somewhere to park, but I arrive early at the café/bar where Holly suggested we meet on Cotham Hill. I've never been here before, but it's not far from Holly's, so it might be one of her haunts. According to the blackboard easel outside, it serves pizzas and platters until closing at eleven p.m. and has vegetarian options, which will suit Holly. I peer through the window. It looks relaxed and convivial. Perfect.

I see her sitting at a wooden table for two. Taking a deep breath, I enter the café. She smiles when she sees me, making my heart leap. She stands up to greet me and we kiss each other awkwardly on the cheek.

We exchange niceties and order food, although I'm so nervous I've lost my appetite. More than once we start to speak at the same time, then stop, then start up again. We've forgotten how to be natural in each other's presence, our attempts at small talk a jarring dissonance of false starts and uncomfortable pauses.

'What's the latest on Melissa Slade?' Holly asks at one point.

'My colleague – our junior reporter, Kelly – is working on that more than I am at the moment. She's trying to track down the stepdaughter, Bella, who seems to have disappeared without a trace.'

'How mysterious,' Holly says. She changes the subject. 'You're looking tanned, by the way. Did you go on holiday?' I can feel the tension between us lift slightly. Holidays and work. Safe subjects.

I tell her about our holiday in the Camargue. I even reel off what Clémentine told me.

'How about you? Did you go away?'

She shakes her head. 'I couldn't take the time off work.'

'How are things going at work?' I ask. It seems like the next logical question and I can think of nothing else to say, but Holly's face falls. 'What is it, Holly?' I reach over the table for her hand, although this feels inappropriate. She pulls her hand away. 'You can tell me.'

'Things have got bad again,' she says.

'I didn't know things were bad before.'

'Since Melissa Slade's trial, I've been pushed around and I'm essentially being pushed out. I lost credibility with that court case. As a woman working in a man's domain, it has been detrimental to my career.' She says this without a hint of self-pity.

'I'm sorry, Holly. I had no idea. You never told me about that.'

She makes a dismissive gesture with her hand. 'With Melissa Slade's forthcoming appeal, it's all got unpleasant again.' Then she smiles, a little maliciously. 'But with that hidden toxicology report, well … let's just say I hope Sparks gets his comeuppance. I'm glad he's retired.'

'Perhaps I should look into Sparks,' I say. 'See what skeletons he has in his closet.'

'Perhaps you should,' Holly agrees, her smile widening.

This whole conversation seems a little unreal to me and we lapse into an uneasy silence while we eat. I take in the room, the large round clock on the wall, which seems to have stopped, the wooden floor, the wooden tables and chairs, the dim lighting. Then I turn back to Holly. She locks her eyes onto mine. This is my cue. It's time for me to say the lines I rehearsed in the car.

It comes out in a rush. 'It's lovely to see you again, Holly. I almost called, on several occasions, but I bottled out. I was an idiot. I wasn't sure how my boys would react to the idea that their daddy had a girlfriend. I'm still not really. But …'

Holly's eyebrows pinch into a frown. I can't quite read her expression, but it halts me mid-sentence. Her frown deepens. Have I got this wrong? Why did she want to see me if she didn't want to give us another chance? Have I been too presumptuous?

'I'm pregnant,' Holly suddenly blurts out.

I open my mouth, then close it again. I have to replay those two words in my head a few times until they sink in.

'Wow. OK,' I manage eventually.

'It's yours. In case you were wondering.'

'No, no, I wasn't.'

I reach across the table and take both of her hands in both of mine. This time she doesn't resist. She looks down, at our hands linked together, and avoids my gaze. She's scared, I realise.

I have a sudden flash, a memory of Melissa Slade when I visited her in Haresfield Park, telling me her pregnancy with the twins had come as an unexpected surprise. I remember thinking if I found out at my age that I was about to be a dad again, it would be a complete shock. How ironic. Here I am.

But this is definitely more of a surprise than a shock. I'm thrilled. I can feel a smile stretch across my face as a warm sensation of happiness overwhelms me.

'Why didn't you tell me before?'

Holly sighs. 'Lots of reasons. I only found out after that evening in May when I suggested we should … take a break. I needed to get things straight in my head. And then, I wanted to see you, but I couldn't see you and not tell you. I kept thinking about Rosie. I didn't want to tell you too soon in case … not until I was past the twelve weeks' stage, anyway.'

'How far along are you?'

'Just over three months.' She looks up and sees my grin. She smiles tentatively then, too.

'And everything's going all right?'

'Yes. I'm well and the baby is absolutely fine.'

'That's good to know. Just over three months. January? February?'

'The very beginning of February. The due date's the second. It must have been the last time we … you know … just before …'

I let go of Holly's hands and bring my chair round so I'm sitting next to her instead of across the table. I put my arm around her and she leans in to me. I can smell the familiar fruity scent of her shampoo. I close my eyes for a moment and breathe her in.

'I have an ultrasound scan next week,' she says into my chest. 'It will be probably be too early to tell, but if you'd like to know the sex, I could ask then. Do you?'

'Yes. No! I don't know. I'd like to come with you, though. Can I? Can we do this together?'

'I was hoping you'd say that.'

'And I think it's time you met my boys.'

'I was hoping you'd say that, too.'

CHAPTER 24

~

Kelly

August 2018

Jon didn't get back home too late last night after his meeting with Holly, but he obviously had something on his mind, so I couldn't run my idea by him. I think it's a good one, but I'm not sure he'll approve, and I can't suggest it to Saunders until I've told him about it.

I've been thinking a lot about what Jon told me about his wife and the hit and run. Images of his wife keep streaming through my head. I know what she looked like from the photos of her with Jon and the boys in his house. I picture her walking across the zebra crossing, glancing up a split second before the van smashed into her. I hope it wasn't like that. I hope she didn't see the driver coming. I hate to imagine her feeling fear or pain. I wonder, too, if the driver glanced up just before he mowed her down. Did he slam on his brakes? Or did he only realise she was there at all when he felt the collision?

I see people on an almost daily basis holding their phones to their ears or smoking at the wheel. This morning, looking out of the window of the bus on my way to work, I saw a woman doing her make-up while she was driving. The traffic was slow, but it's not on. I felt a surge of anger rise in me. My mum often fiddles with the satnav while doing 75mph down the motorway.

Distracted driving. I'd like to write a feature on it, comparing it with alcohol and speeding as a cause of fatal accidents, checking out statistics for the Bristol area and maybe even doing a survey to determine habits according to age groups or sex. But I can't possibly do it unless Jon agrees.

'I think that's a terrific idea, Kelly,' he says when I've pitched it to him.

'You do? Are you sure you're OK with it?'

'Yes, of course. It will help raise awareness about the problem. I like the subjects you're tackling. Homelessness, distracted driving. I think it's great that you feel so strongly about issues like that.' He pauses, then says, 'But I've got something else you're going to want to look into even more.'

'Oh? What's that?'

He hands me a piece of paper with an address on it. I don't recognise the name. But I know instinctively whose address this is.

'Is this what I think it is? How did you get this?'

'Simon Goodman. Luckily, he didn't know it was for you. You're not flavour of the month, from what he wrote in his email.'

'Ah. He must have overheard more of my conversation with Callum than I thought.'

'I think it has more to do with you doorstepping his son against his wishes. He would prefer it if you didn't call back.'

I look down, embarrassed, and my eyes fall on the address again. Mrs Margaret Brock, 5 Greenditch Avenue, Hartcliffe. 'Where is that exactly?' I ask Jon.

'Hartcliffe? It's south-east of here. Not the most coveted area of Bristol to live in. A lot of unemployment and rundown council housing.'

'It's not in the city centre, is it? I thought Clémentine said Bella lived in the centre.'

'Not exactly, no. It's not far, though. It's an outer suburb, but maybe Clémentine did know Bella had moved out after all. Perhaps Clémentine meant Bella lived in the city centre after she'd left home rather than when she was living with her mum.'

I bring up Mappy on my laptop and type in Greenditch Avenue. It's about four miles away from here, so I text my mum, asking her to pick me up and take me there after work. I should take my driving test again one of these days, although after failing the test twice it might be time to give up. I'm lucky my mum never complains about taxiing me around.

~

Mrs Brock's home is a tiny terraced house that looks like it might once have been yellow. Now, though, the paint left still clinging to the façade is a dirty grey. The houses either side of it are in much better condition. On the outside, anyway.

There's no vehicle in the paved driveway.

'It doesn't look like she's in,' I say to my mum. 'I'll just check.'

'I'll wait in the car,' she says.

I walk up to the front door and ring the bell. To my surprise, the door opens almost immediately. A short woman stands before me, holding a cigarette in one hand and a ginger cat under the other arm. She's wearing a long dark skirt and a shapeless charcoal jumper. She has yellow teeth and long hair that was last dyed black several months ago, judging from the length of her grey roots. Her cat's the wrong colour, but other than that, she just needs a pointy black hat to accessorise and she'll be all set to trick or treat next Hallowe'en.

'Good evening, Mrs Brock. My name's Kelly Fox.' I rummage through my handbag, trying to find my press card.

'A friend of Bella's, are you?' She looks at me suspiciously.

'Er … yes.' Let's go with that. I zip my bag closed and paste a smile on my face. 'Yes, I am.'

'She's not here. I dunno where she is.' Mrs Brock starts to close the door in my face, but I put my foot out to stop her and push it open.

'I won't take up much of your time, Mrs Brock.' I try to sound firm. I step towards her, forcing her to take a step back. 'I'm just concerned about Bella.'

I'm shocked at my own audacity. I've more or less barged into the house. Once in the hallway, I close the door behind me. It reeks of cigarettes in here. Mrs Brock reluctantly leads me into the living room, where the stench is even stronger. The room is thick with smoke. On the coffee table, I spot an overflowing ashtray next to a bottle of gin and an empty glass. Mrs Brock turns and follows my gaze. 'It was a hard day,' she says by way of an explanation, looking slightly embarrassed. 'I needed a tipple.'

Through the choking fug, the whiff of gin on her breath wafts towards me. A familiar odour. My childhood memories are tainted with the miasma of gin or rum. I don't need to look at my watch to know that it can only be about five thirty.

'Would you like a cup of tea, Mrs Brock? I feel like one. I could make it if you like.'

'Thought you weren't staying long,' she mutters, stubbing her cigarette out in the ashtray. Then in a less hostile tone she adds, 'I'll do it. You sit down.'

I perch on the edge of one of the armchairs, which has certainly seen better days. Mrs Brock returns a few minutes later carrying a mug in each hand. She plonks them down on the coffee table. Some of the tea slops over onto the table, but either she doesn't notice or she's not bothered. The table has burn marks and the mugs are chipped. My tea doesn't look as if a teabag has been anywhere near it. Perhaps she won't notice if I don't drink it.

I try to get into character. I'm supposed to be Bella's friend. 'Mrs Brock, I haven't seen Bella for a while. Do you know where I can find her?'

'I haven't seen her for a while myself. The last time I bumped into her must have been a couple of years ago now.'

'Where was that, Mrs Brock?'

'Ooh, let me think. In the Old City, I think it was. Corn Street or Wine Street, maybe.'

The Old City isn't that far from *The Rag*'s offices in Redcliffe. I get the strange feeling Bella has been under my nose all along. 'What was she doing?'

'Just walking around, I suppose. I didn't get to ask her. As soon as she saw me, she scarpered.'

'Why?'

Margaret Brock narrows her eyes at me. 'Close friend of Bella's, are you?'

'I'm worried about her. I'd like to find her.'

'She blames me.'

'What for?'

'Everything.' Mrs Brock pours herself a generous gin and takes a slug. 'You know what happened to her, do you?' I freeze. I have no idea what to say to that. Fortunately, Mrs Brock doesn't look up and see my startled reaction. She lights up another cigarette and inhales deeply. I notice her nails are dirty. 'She blames me,' she continues, saving me from having to respond, 'for what that bastard did to her.' She exhales smoke as she talks. 'She accused me of turning a blind eye the whole time. She has never forgiven me for that.'

'Did you have any inkling at all it was going on?' I ask, improvising. Not what I want to know. What's actually racing through my head is: *What bastard? What did he do to Bella?* I just don't know how to word that without slipping out of character.

196

But as though reading my mind, she ignores the question I asked and sort of gives me the answers I want.

'I was going to leave him,' she says. 'When Bella told me, I promised to leave him. But he left me for that tart before I could.'

My brain is whirring, trying to keep up. She must be referring to Michael Slade. He's the bastard. That seems plausible. So the tart must be Melissa Slade. 'You mean Melissa Sl … Goodman?'

'That's right. Her. The copper. The one that killed Bella's step-sisters. Finished Bella off, that did. Sent her right over the edge.'

Her words hit me like a well-aimed blow to my stomach, winding me, wounding me. I shudder as my father's face swims into focus in front of me. Lily's disappearance was what sent him over the edge. Literally.

As I push away the image of my father, Callum Goodman's words come back to me. *That tipped her over the edge. But she'd been teetering on the brink for a while.* According to both Callum and Bella's mother, for Bella, the last straw was the twins' deaths. I picture Callum, stoned, in his pyjamas. He's not doing too well right now. The final straw for him seems to have been losing his girlfriend at uni after she found out who his mother was.

What was the pivotal moment for Margaret Brock? How long has she been an alcoholic? Since Michael Slade left her? Since Bella left home? Or before then? What exactly did she turn a blind eye to? She hasn't said what Michael Slade did to their daughter. An idea has formed in my head, but I hope I'm wrong. I wish she'd be more specific.

'I'd like to be alone now,' Mrs Brock says. Her voice is sad, but firm. 'Can you see yourself out?' I desperately want to know what Bella's father did, but it's clear I'm not going to get any more out of her mother. Her hand has closed around the gin bottle again.

I stand up and head for the door. Then something occurs to me. 'Mrs Brock?' She looks up. 'Could I trouble you for a photo of Bella? The most recent photo you have? It would help me find her.'

I'm sure she has sussed out I'm no friend of Bella's and she hesitates before pointing at a bookcase. I walk over to it. There are no photos on the shelves and I'm confused. Then I spot two rows of photo albums, one for each year from 1995 to 2012. I pull out the last one. 'Can I borrow this one, Mrs Brock?' When she doesn't object, I do as she asked and see myself out, the photo album tucked under my arm.

'Will you tell her I still love her?' she calls after me, her voice quavering.

Mum starts the car up as I buckle up, and presses the controls to open all four windows.

'Oi! It's freezing.'

'Sorry, Kelly. But you stink.'

'Thanks a lot!'

She closes the windows and I realise she's right. The smell of cigarette smoke has permeated my clothes and my hair. I'm minging. I'll shower as soon as I get home.

'Thanks, Mum, for taking me and waiting all that time,' I say.

'No problem. You weren't gone long. Any good?'

'Not sure yet.'

'Come on! Tell me all about it!'

Smiling at my mother's inquisitiveness, I fill her in on my conversation with Mrs Brock. Then I start to turn the pages of the photo album. There are several photos of a dark-haired girl. Bella. In a few of them she's next to her mother, who is almost unrecognisable, dressed nicely and wearing make-up, her black hair shiny and wavy, just like her daughter's.

My attention is drawn to one particular picture, a close-up. I trace my finger around her face, committing her features to memory.

'She's pretty. She must be about seventeen in these pictures,' I say aloud.

'Let's see,' my mum says, glancing down at the album in my lap.

'Keep your eyes on the road!' I pull the photo album around me, so she can't see. She laughs good-naturedly. I'll save the safe driving talk for another time.

'You've gone quiet,' she comments after a few minutes.

I can't seem to tear my eyes away from the photo of Bella. I tell Mum what's on my mind. 'She looks familiar.'

'All teenage girls look the same,' she says. 'They're like clones. Long hair, long faces, hoodies, Ugg boots.'

I raise my eyebrows at her. 'You're probably right,' I say, snapping the album shut.

But I can't shake the feeling that I've seen her somewhere before.

CHAPTER 25

~

Jonathan

August 2018

I've spent every spare second at my workstation this morning trying to find out as much as possible about Dr Roger Sparks. Well, if I'm honest, I suppose my aim is to dig up some dirt on the man. I'm furious on Holly's behalf that he can treat her with disdain simply because her findings in Amber Slade's post-mortem contradicted his conclusions for Ellie's. If anything, it's the other way round. After all, Amber died before Ellie. On top of this, I clearly remember Holly saying that Sparks is the best pathologist she has ever known. She described him as meticulous. She doesn't seem to have questioned his professionalism or the conclusions of his post-mortem, but he has had no qualms about casting doubt on Holly and her work.

I've gleaned some background information, mainly from online sources. He was educated at – and rowed for – Oxford. He comes from a wealthy Wiltshire family. He's married with four children: two boys and two girls. He hasn't bothered with privacy settings on his Facebook page and I scroll through his posts. But other than a one-liner about being in a "dead-end job", I can't find anything remotely distasteful on his wall.

There is something decidedly dodgy about his report appearing only now. Or perhaps it's more suspicious that it disappeared in the first place. Did Sparks deliberately conceal it? Was he paid not to include the toxicology analysis in the medical report? By whom? Who would want Melissa to be convicted if she were innocent?

At first, I can only think of one person with a motive: the real killer, if there is one. That isn't a lead I can follow up for now. Obviously. Then I wonder if the barrister for the prosecution could feasibly have had a hand in this. By securing a conviction in the Slade case, she would have furthered her career. And Dr Sparks's career certainly wasn't harmed by the outcome of the case. Until now. That's a bit of a stretch, and I don't fully buy my own idea, but I try to find a connection between Dr Roger Sparks and Eleanor Wood QC.

Then I have a Eureka moment. I stare at the screen. Wood read law at the University of Oxford. It comes up in the results when I google her name. But the feeling is short-lived. Wood is seven years younger than Sparks, so the chances that their paths ever crossed there are slim. The link is too tenuous.

To my frustration, I can't find a whiff of anything dishonest or damaging. Other than the toxicology report itself materialising after all this time, of course. I could write an article on that, and subtly hint that Wood and Sparks were at university together, but it's beneath me, even in an attempt to avenge Holly.

But Dan, a journo I know, has asked me a couple of times recently if I've got anything for him on the Melissa Slade case. He did a bit of freelance work for *The Rag* a while back when he lived in Bristol. He's working for a national tabloid in London now and thrives on building a story out of nothing. He's shrewd enough to point readers into drawing the conclusions he wants them to make without exposing himself – or the paper – to a libel suit.

I toy with the idea of calling him. Then I banish the thought. Holly is a capable, independent woman and she hasn't asked me to fight her battles. She doesn't need me to smear the reputation of one of her colleagues in order to succeed in her professional life. Even if he does deserve it.

I glance at the empty workstation next to mine. Kelly has been away from her desk all morning, covering a protest against a proposed car park on her patch. I've finished with Sparks for now, so I start looking through online articles about Kelly's sister. Lily Fox. I'm no good with names or faces and my memory is terrible.

But I do remember this story now. More details come back to me as I stare at Lily Fox's face on my computer screen. It was ten years ago. I remember interviewing the mother – Kelly's mother, Ruby Fox – a day or two after full panic mode had set in and a month before Ruby's husband committed suicide.

I click onto some of the headlines and read through several articles, getting a clearer idea of the timeline. When Lily Fox first disappeared in May 2008, no one was particularly worried. She'd run away from home a few times before. But when she hadn't resurfaced two days later, Ruby Fox phoned the police and reported her missing. The investigation quickly focused on any involvement her father might have had in the mystery. He "fell to his death" from the Clifton Suspension Bridge. There is very little information about the Fox family after that.

I start to write an email to Simon Goodman – he's proving to be a valuable contact at the moment. My fingers hover over the keyboard of my laptop. Then I change my mind, delete the draft and call him on his mobile instead. I expect him to be too busy to answer and prepare a message in my head, but then I hear his voice.

I ask about Melissa. Simon tells me a date in November has been set for the appeal hearing – 13th November. I note it down on my pad.

'It's much sooner than we expected,' he says. 'Lissa would like a few friendly faces in the courtroom. I'm hoping to persuade Callum to come to London with me. Can I count on you?'

'Absolutely. I was planning on going,' I lie. 'I'll be in the press benches. Is that OK?'

'Yes. Fine. She's just anxious. She'd like to see people on her side … you know?'

'Will her parents be there? And her friend Jennifer Porter?'

'I hope George and Ivy will come. I'm not sure about Jenny. Not if Rob has anything to do with it.' Without taking a breath, he says, 'I don't imagine you were calling to ask after Lissa?'

'That wasn't the only reason I called, no. I … my colleague … the one you met at the Watershed Café …'

'I remember. The girl who pestered Callum,' he says humourlessly.

'That's the one. Kelly Fox. She's a lovely person, Simon. She's been helping me with the research and interviews for the articles I've written about Melissa.'

'What about her?'

'Her sister was …' I recall Kelly's use of the present tense. She clearly isn't considering the possibility her sister is dead. '… *is* Lily Fox. Does that ring a bell? Do you know anything about her?'

'The girl who went missing? When was that? About eight or nine years ago?' Goodman's memory is a lot sharper than mine.

'Ten. She was fifteen.'

'From what I remember, it seemed likely she'd run away. An alcoholic father. A difficult relationship with her mother, although probably no more difficult than for most teenagers. The investigation had to be downscaled after a while due to lack of resources and evidence.'

'Was there anything to suggest Lily's father abducted her or was behind her disappearance in any way?'

'Not that I remember, although it was one of the avenues my colleagues explored initially. Lily Fox's father took her disappearance very badly, as you'd expect. He blamed himself; his wife blamed him. By all accounts, he was well on his way to drinking himself to death, but he topped himself by jumping off the Clifton Suspension Bridge in the end.'

'And Lily Fox has never been seen or heard of again?'

'Not as far as I know. No body was ever found. She's still considered a misper. I'll see what else I can find. Lissa would know more about her disappearance than I do. She worked on some aspect of the case for a while, and she certainly followed it more closely than I did. I'll ask her about it.'

'Thanks. I owe you one.'

'Yes, you do.'

I think he's probably joking, but his tone is deadly serious, so when he has ended the call, I ring Dan in London and give him what I've got on Roger Sparks and Eleanor Wood. I don't feel good about myself, but it may help both Holly and Melissa. And I doubt that one article will do much damage to the reputations of two eminent people if they've done nothing wrong, especially if it's written by a reporter with a bit of a bad rep himself.

I haven't got much to do today except rewrites and updates, but I'm stuck in the office. Turning back to my laptop, I stare again at the photo of Lily Fox on my screen. She looks just like Kelly. Same wide smile, same button nose, albeit without the stud. She looks innocent and happy in this picture.

I catch sight of Kelly entering the offices, so I quickly close the window on my computer.

Dropping her bag by her workstation, she turns to me and says, 'So, I went to see Mrs Brock, Bella's mum, after work yesterday.'

'How did that go? What's she like?'

Kelly's face screws up in thought. Or maybe disgust. 'She's an alcoholic chain-smoking witch,' Kelly says eventually. For good measure she adds, 'And she's not big on personal hygiene.'

I remember Kelly describing Callum as self-pitying, screwed up and immature. It occurs to me she's an even harsher judge of character than I am. I'm about to make some quip about this, but then I think the better of it. Kelly's father was an alcoholic. That might be why she's so critical of this woman.

'Brock said she hadn't seen her daughter for two years and last time she just sort of bumped into her in town, but apparently Bella bolted and wouldn't talk to her.'

'Odd. That would seem to confirm she's a runaway, though.'

'It's what she ran away from that's interesting,' Kelly continues, the serious expression on her face matching her tone of voice.

'Go on.'

Kelly swallows hard and takes a deep breath. 'She said Bella blamed her for what Michael Slade did to her.'

'What did he do to her?'

'She didn't elaborate. But Bella told her, apparently. Brock claims when she found out about it, whatever it was, she decided to leave Slade, but it seems he got there before her and walked out on her to move in with Melissa Goodman.'

'It was something pretty bad then, if she said she was going to leave him.'

'Yes. I've only come up with one explanation.'

Kelly doesn't need to spell it out for me. 'I know what you're thinking,' I say, 'but let's not jump to conclusions. For the moment, all we have is an incomplete account by a drunk and probably embittered ex-wife.'

'You'd think the mother would have realised if something serious was going on, though. Perhaps she did. Perhaps that's why Bella accused her of turning a blind eye.'

'Hmm,' I say, noncommittally.

'Deffo something very abnormal about the guy, anyway.'

On that score, I agree with Kelly. I wouldn't put anything past Michael Slade. I don't trust the guy at all.

'The mother's not all there, either,' Kelly continues. 'I'm surprised she recognised her daughter when she saw her in town. She was probably pissed. Oh! I've just remembered! I've got a photo of her.' Kelly's voice is high-pitched with excitement.

'Who? Bella's mother?'

'No! Well, yes. But I meant Bella herself!' She picks up her handbag, rummages around in it and pulls out her phone. Then she brings up a photo, which she shows me. 'Look! I took a photo of one of the pictures in the album Mrs Brock lent me. I'm convinced I've seen this girl somewhere. Does she look familiar to you?'

I study the picture. Nice-looking teenager. Raven-black hair. Troubled eyes. Fake smile. 'Nope.' Kelly's face falls. I've burst her bubble. 'Sorry. Maybe Michael Slade had a photo of her on the mantelpiece or on one of his beige walls and that's why you think you recognise her.'

'Maybe.' Kelly sounds unconvinced. 'But you went to his house with me. You would have recognised her, too.'

'Not necessarily. I'm hopeless with faces. Bad memory, as I'm sure you've noticed. Anyway, most teenage girls look the same to me.'

'That's more or less what my mum said. She's obsessed with Melissa Slade, you know. She keeps questioning me about the progress we're making.'

'Well, I expect she remembers the media frenzy surrounding Melissa's arrest and trial. Melissa Slade was headline news for months, and around here, well … you can imagine … everyone was obsessed with her.'

'Because she was local.'

'Yes. She was also intelligent and beautiful. Not most people's idea of the profile of a murderer. She'd been accused of a heinous crime, but she looked like an angel. The fact that she had an excellent track record as a police officer added to the whole furore.'

Kelly seems to ponder this, but then she says, 'So, I've told you all about my evening. You didn't say how your date went the other night. How's Holly?' Her abrupt change of subject throws me for a second, but we're onto a topic I'm only too happy to talk about.

'She's fine. She's …'

I've arranged for her to meet Noah and Alfie. We're taking them to the caves at Wookey Hole this weekend and then Holly will come back and the two of us will cook a meal. Together. While the boys watch a film. That's the plan. Afterwards I'll talk to them. I haven't told them they're going to have a baby brother or sister yet. I'm dreading that discussion, actually. But I have a sudden urge to confide in Kelly.

'Holly had some news for me the other night. It came out of the blue, but I'm over the moon—'

'She's pregnant!'

'How on earth did you guess that?'

'You were using too many idiomatic expressions,' she says, which makes me laugh. 'Congratulations! Are you excited?'

'Yes. Happy and excited.'

I'm also terrified. Lightning doesn't strike twice. That's what Melissa Slade's friend Jenny told her. But it did for Melissa. Amber died, then Ellie died too. Melissa lost both her daughters. I lost Mel and Rosie, the woman I loved and our baby. I can't go through that again.

'Boy or girl?'

I feel my face cloud over. 'I'm not sure.'

'Do you want to know?'

'I'm not sure,' I repeat. I need to make up my mind before the scan at the end of the week, but I don't tell Kelly this.

She nods sagely. 'Everything will be fine, Jon,' she says. 'Don't worry.' She's too wise for her years, sometimes, is Kelly. 'And you'll be an excellent father. Either way,' she says.

'How do you know that?'

'You already are,' she says earnestly. She lowers her head, seemingly embarrassed by the compliment she has just paid me. Her signature smile has transferred to my face.

But I feel it slip as my thoughts turn again to those two missing girls. What happened to Bella Slade? And what became of Lily Fox?

CHAPTER 26

~

Kelly

September 2018

People find different ways to alleviate their pain. Some join a support group or an online forum. Others find temporary oblivion in drugs. This, I suspect, is what Callum is doing. Jon's grief is palpable sometimes. He finds it hard to let go, channelling his energy into bringing up his sons, but at the same time he has done his best to move on and he's besotted with Holly.

And then there's my parents. My father, who, to use my mother's understatement of the year, was already "a bit partial to the bottle", hit it even harder when Lily disappeared. My mum, well, she's in denial. Still, after all these years. For her, Lily is alive somewhere, and it's just a question of time before she comes home. With her arthritis, my mum struggles with the stairs and the house is too big for her, but she won't consider moving. The fact that my sister would be a twenty-five-year-old woman now and probably wouldn't think of Mum's house as home doesn't enter the equation.

She lost a lot, my mum. She lost her daughter and her husband. She swore not to lose me. And she has never lost hope. I've always thought that's what gets you. The not knowing, the maybe, the what if. But my mother is fuelled by hope. So I'm not allowed to say *would*. It's *will*. And it's not *if*; it's *when*. *Is* instead of *was*. Because that's how my mum copes with Lily's disappearance.

Mum and I are close. We were before, but I think the fact we've stayed so close has a lot to do with Lily going missing. Afterwards, there was just Mum and me. She pinned her hopes and dreams on me but she also doted on me, cared for me, gave all her love to me. We were frank and truthful with each other. We confided in each other.

And right now, I'm using that against her. I'm stinging her with the very words she used to say to me throughout my teens.

'We always tell each other everything.' I can hear the whine in my voice.

'Yes, but I can't tell you this.' She's sitting on the sofa, doing her cross-stitch, and she doesn't look up.

'Why not? I only want to know why you think you're more clued up than most people on the Melissa Slade case.' I've picked up from where we left off the last weekend I was here. 'Just tell me why you remember it so well.'

'I told you, I'm sworn to secrecy.'

I open my mouth to argue, then close it again as a thought strikes me. That's what she said last time. Why didn't she say *I promised not to tell anyone*? What's with the *sworn to secrecy* crap? Who did she swear to?

I don't remember much about Melissa Slade's trial. I was eighteen. I'd just started university in Cardiff and even though I wanted to be a journalist, I didn't follow the news that regularly. I was studying for an English degree and I had too many books to wade through. Too little time. It's easy to shut out the real world when you're a student.

I do remember my mum watching a news programme one evening after the trial had ended, though. I was home for a weekend, or maybe for Christmas – the decorations and the tree were up. I was sitting on the floor, hunched over the coffee table, working on an assignment, while my mum was sitting on the sofa. I remember her crying in front of the TV. She changed channels and then she poured herself a glass of sherry. She never drinks, my mother, not even a drop, because of my dad. But she always had sherry in the house at Christmas time for neighbours and guests. And she drank that evening.

My forehead pinches into a frown and my lips pucker. I'm trying to grasp a memory that's hovering stubbornly just out of reach. It was a few weeks before the glass of sherry. A phone call when I was at uni. And then it comes back to me and floors me. My mother telling me that she'd received a summons. I can hear her voice as clearly as if she were sitting on the sofa telling me that now instead of over the phone ... how long ago? The trial was in 2013. Five years ago.

'You were on the jury,' I hiss at my mother. 'That's why you said the other day that she didn't seem guilty. It wasn't because she looked innocent in her photo in the press. You saw her in the dock *with your own eyes.*'

'Ouch,' she says, pricking her finger on her needle. Or pretending to.

'You told me you'd been summoned to do jury service, but you wouldn't talk about it. You didn't even mention for which trial. That's it, isn't it? You were a juror for the Melissa Slade murder trial?'

She carries on sewing as if I'm not even there. This isn't like my mother. She doesn't usually ignore me. My mind races through the relevant pages of Melissa's journal. My mum must have been the juror Melissa Slade described as "matronly". She thought my

211

mum was about the same age as her and hoped she'd be on her side. Was she? She also wondered if my mum had lots of children. Little did she know. They had more in common than she could have imagined.

In a different diary entry, Melissa had described the shock end to the trial no one could have anticipated. The verdicts. The jury failed to reach a unanimous decision and returned two majority verdicts. Ten out of the twelve jurors said she was not guilty of murdering Amber, and ten out of twelve jurors found her guilty when it came to Ellie. Melissa wondered if the two women her age, the thin one and the plump one – my mother – had voted in her favour.

What happened there? Was this some sort of arbitrary compromise? *We're not sure, your Honour, so we'll say guilty for one count, but not for the other?* My mum could shed some light on this mystery, but she won't.

I try again anyway. 'Mum?' I turn to her on the sofa, dipping my head to try and get her to look up. But she's still avoiding eye contact. 'What happened, Mum? Why were the verdicts different?'

She puts her embroidery down on her lap. 'I can't reveal what went on in the deliberation room.' She sounds less resigned than before and I think she's going to cave in.

'Mum, this is me. I won't print it, if that's what you're worried about. But I'd like to understand.'

She sighs, then shakes her head. She has never been one to blab, my mum, but we don't keep secrets from each other. I sigh, too. I throw her a look, but she doesn't catch it. Picking up the remote, I start flicking through the channels. I don't want to hound her. If she won't talk, frustrating as it is, I have to leave it at that.

Her voice, when she speaks, is barely audible. 'For what it's worth, I think she's innocent.'

I snap the TV off. 'Is that the way you voted?'

'Yes. On both counts.'

Both of us are silent for a few seconds and I realise I'm holding my breath. 'How did you—?'

'It was all very confusing. The pathologist for the first twin, Amber, was adamant she died of natural causes. She was very convincing. But for Ellie, all the medical evidence pointed the other way. I suppose some of the jurors felt happier sitting on the fence that way.'

'But even being found guilty on one count of murder meant a life sentence for Melissa Slade.'

'I know that. There was a lot of pressure on us to reach a majority verdict,' she says. 'A lot of pressure for some of us to change our minds and our votes. Otherwise the court would've had to declare a mistrial.' She pauses. When she speaks again, it's in a whisper. 'We'd already spent two nights in a hotel. I think a lot of people wanted to get home to be with their families. It was coming up to Christmas.'

'So some jurors allowed themselves to be swayed. Is that what you're saying?'

'I wouldn't put it—'

'Who else believed Melissa?'

'I can't remember all of it. And even if I did, I don't feel comfortable talking about it. I'm sworn—'

'To secrecy. I know.'

'I've got nothing new to bring to the table.'

I have one last question, though. 'Was there no doubt in your mind about her innocence?'

'Of course there was! But it's supposed to work the other way round, isn't it? I didn't think she was *guilty* beyond all reasonable doubt.'

I think that's the end of it, but then my mum adds, 'The woman lost her babies. She didn't come over well on the stand. She was detached. Unemotional. But she didn't strike me as evil. And I think that losing her daughters, even if she was in some way responsible, well, maybe that was punishment enough.'

213

I let that sink in.

'It's a remarkable coincidence,' I say. 'Me investigating the case you did jury duty for.'

My mum shrugs, picking up her embroidery hoop and resuming her sewing. 'Not really,' she says. 'You're a journalist. It was a huge news story. It happened locally. It was bound to crop up again one day.'

I wonder if my sister's case will "crop up" again one day.

It's raining and I wait for the shower to dissipate before I leave Mum's. I'm going to walk home. It's not far. Mum offers to drop me off, but I need some headspace.

I've walked a couple of blocks before I start to feel uneasy. It's just a prickling of the hairs at the back of my neck at first, but my senses are immediately on high alert. Then I hear the tyres on the wet road and the purr of the engine. I'm being followed. I whirl my head round. I'm right. There's a red car behind me, hugging the pavement and going so slowly that I know I'm not mistaken. I check again. The only cars around me are parked – no one is driving down this side road. There's no one else out walking in this weather, either.

My heart tightens. Why is that car following me? It's making me feel nervous, vulnerable. I steal another glance over my shoulder.

I know who it is. His car is unmistakeable. It's a Mercedes Benz SLK. My father was a car dealer. He knew his cars and he went on about them so much that I learnt a fair bit, too.

Trying not to quicken my pace, I get my mobile out of my handbag and call my mum, but she doesn't answer. I keep the phone pressed to my ear to give the impression I'm talking to someone. I'm hoping this will buy me time to think. What does he want? I reason if he wanted to run me over, he could have mounted the pavement. Is he going to somehow force me to get into his car? Why would he do that? Is he just trying to scare me?

Curiosity is going to get the better of me. I'm nearing a junction, where this lane joins the main road. I feel safer. There are cars, lots of cars, just a few feet away from me now. I open the Voice Memo app on my smartphone, and pressing the red button to record, I lower my arm to my side. Then, stopping dead in my tracks, I turn to face the car. He brakes and stops, too. I step out into the road and walk round to the driver's window. He hesitates before lowering it.

'Mr Slade, what are you doing?'

'I thought it was you,' he says, all fake surprise and chirpy.

'Don't play games with me, Mr Slade. This isn't a chance meeting. You were following me. Why?'

'You're the one playing games, Miss Fox,' he says. 'Role-playing, in fact. Pretending to be a friend of Bella's.' I've been caught out. The alcoholic witch has squealed on me. 'Stay away from my ex-wife,' he hisses.

I know full well he means Margaret Brock, but I can't resist it. 'Which one?' That makes him angry. His face reddens.

'What is it you want to know?' he asks. 'Can't you leave me and my family alone? What are you hoping to prove?'

I look at him. He makes my skin crawl. But not because he frightens me. He doesn't. No, he makes my skin crawl because I find him repulsive. I look down at him as he sits in his car, his knuckles white as they grip the steering wheel. And I see a coward.

If he won't tell me why he's following me, he probably won't answer the only other question I have for him. But I ask it anyway. 'Did you sexually abuse your daughter, Mr Slade?' He might not scare me, but I sound bolder than I feel even so. I study him for a reaction. His face turns from red to white. 'That's what I'm trying to prove,' I say.

I expect him to deny it. Or not say anything at all. And indeed for several seconds he says nothing. He just gapes at me.

'You'll never prove that,' he says eventually. 'Bella will never talk to you. Even if you do find her.'

Then he drives off, turning into the main road without giving way and causing another driver to hoot his horn. I'm left standing in the middle of the road, staring after him, feeling chilled by his words, which play on repeat in my head.

CHAPTER 27

~

Jonathan

September 2018

Holly and I are making dinner in my kitchen when the shrill ringtone of my mobile makes us jump.

'I hope that's not my parents to say they can't take the boys out tomorrow,' I mutter, easing my phone out of my back pocket. Holly and I have planned to spend the day together. Just the two and a half of us.

Peering at the caller ID, I frown. It's not like her to call me at the weekend. She has never done it before. 'I'll have to take this,' I say to Holly, swiping the screen. 'Kelly? Is everything OK?'

I can tell immediately that it's not. She's babbling breathlessly down the phone and I can't make out what she's saying.

'Calm down. Start from the beginning. What's wrong?'

I keep quiet, listening while she tells me the whole story. Hearing a sudden drumming at the kitchen window, I whirl round and find myself face to face with my own ghostly reflection, slashed by the rivulets of rain racing down the black pane. When Kelly has finished, I ask, 'Where are you now?' She shouldn't be out alone in this dark night. She needs to get somewhere safe. And dry.

She gives me the name of a road that means nothing to me.

'Do you want me to come and pick you up? Take you to your place or to your mum's?' I shoot a quick glance at Holly, who is chopping tomatoes. She nods at me.

'No, that's fine. I'll be home in a few minutes. I'm all right.'

'Maybe he just happened to be in the same area as you, Kelly,' I say. I don't really believe my own words. I've got a feeling Slade was stalking Kelly. 'But if he does anything like this again, it might constitute harassment and we could go to the police. I will mention it to Simon Goodman, though.'

I think about how brave – and reckless – Kelly was, stepping up to Slade's car and challenging him for following her, then daring to ask him if he'd sexually abused his daughter. 'Tell me again what he said?'

'He said, *You'll never prove it. Bella won't ever talk to you even if you find her.*'

'Those were his exact words?'

'I think so. I recorded it on my phone. I'll play you the conversation on Monday.'

'It does sound rather like he's admitting it.'

'He didn't deny it.' Her voice is breaking up now. It has started to rain her end, too. 'Sorry, Jon, to bother you on a Saturday,' she says. 'I'll leave you in peace now. I just had to talk to someone, you know? I think my mum has had enough for one day – she's not answering her phone. And you're the only other person I could think of.'

'Kelly, you did the right thing calling me. I'm going to stay on the phone with you until you get safely home. OK?'

She doesn't object. For all her bravado, I can tell her confrontation with Slade has left her shaken. Understandably. There's a pause, then Kelly says, 'Tell me about your day?'

The change in subject takes me by surprise. 'Ah, well, Holly and I took the kids to Wookey Hole.' I can hear the lift in my voice, and I turn to smile at Holly.

'Oh, that's right. How did it go?'

'Well, it was wet, but a lot of it's underground, so it didn't matter too much. The boys enjoyed it.'

'I remember going when I was little.'

'They've developed it quite a lot since I last went. They've recently blasted open a new cavern.'

'Ah. So, did you have free tickets to write a review?'

That makes me chuckle. 'No, I didn't, actually. I got money off for booking online, but it still cost a small fortune! Well worth it, though.'

There's a pause. I try to think of something to ask Kelly, to keep the conversation going. 'Have you got enough battery in your phone to keep talking to me until you get home?'

'Yes. I'm nearly there now.'

'Good. How was your day, by the way? Until Slade ruined it, I mean.' Walking over to the fridge, I pull out a bottle of beer. As I've only got one hand free, I go to crack it open with my teeth, but Holly snatches the bottle from me, finds a bottle opener in the cutlery drawer and does the honours. She hands me back the beer and I give her a silent kiss on the lips.

'A bit weird, actually,' Kelly says. 'Can you keep a secret?'

I'm intrigued. I'm hopeless at keeping secrets. I can't even surprise the boys – I have to tell them what I've got in store for them before it comes around. 'Yes, of course,' I lie, taking a swig of my beer.

'I found out today that my mum was on the jury for the Melissa Slade trial.'

I almost spurt lager out of my nose, and instead I swallow it and choke. 'What?'

'My mum, she was a juror for the—'

'Yes, I heard you. Are you sure? Ruby Fox? Kelly, I interviewed your mother after … you know, when your sister … Her photo was in the news. I would have recognised her in the courtroom.'

Kelly snorts. 'Jon, no offence, but you have a crap memory and you're not good with faces. It wouldn't surprise me if you didn't recognise your own mother.'

I laugh at that. 'Fair point.'

'Anyway, my mum put on a lot of weight after Lily went missing. She looked very different by the time of the trial.'

'Oh.'

Then Kelly tells me what her mum told her about what went on behind the closed doors of the deliberation room and as she does, I know this is one secret I will keep. It helps explain the contradictory verdicts, but even if Kelly's mum were to go into more detail, it probably wouldn't help us to determine if Melissa truly is the victim of a miscarriage of justice. As I listen to Kelly, I get that familiar gut feeling that we'll never find out for sure what happened to those baby girls.

'Kelly, I don't think you should mention this to anyone else,' I say when she has finished. I lower my voice and add, 'I think a juror who reveals anything that happened in a deliberation room is in contempt of court and liable to a hefty fine or …' I break off. I don't want to scare her too much.

But Kelly finishes my sentence for me. 'Prison.'

'Yeah. Let's keep this to ourselves, OK?'

'Definitely.'

I don't catch what she says after that and I have to ask her to say it again.

'You couldn't make it up,' she repeats, more loudly to make herself heard over the noise of the rain. 'I mean, it's one hell of a coincidence, right?'

'Yes, it certainly is.'

'Jon, I'm home. Thank you so much for this.'

'Not at all, Kelly. Any time.'

'Have a nice evening, Jon. See you on Monday.'

Kelly ends the call and Holly bombards me with questions. I fill her in on Slade, but I don't mention the jury service. If Holly heard any snippets of my side of that conversation, she doesn't probe. I push Kelly's phone call to a recess of my mind for now. I've got to concentrate on something else.

I pull Holly in for a hug.

'Now I know I've chosen the right man,' she says.

'Because I give good hugs?'

'No! Because you have wonderful paternal instinct.' I think she's referring to Noah and Alfie, but she adds, 'You're very good to Kelly, you know.'

I straighten my arms, holding Holly away from me so I can look at her – my bright, beautiful girlfriend, who is carrying my baby. She's wearing a thin waistcoat over a warm shirt. I keep staring at her tummy, but you can't see she's pregnant yet. For the moment, the boys only know that Daddy has a girlfriend. We're going to break the news to them about the baby this evening over dinner.

Holly and I have decided to put her flat and my house on the market and start looking for a place together, with the boys. We'll be looking in the Kingswood area so that they don't have the extra upheaval of changing schools. How soon we can start house-hunting depends on the boys' reactions. It's big enough for all of us, including the baby, here, and I'd like Holly to move in with us in the meantime, if the boys are all right with that, but both Holly and I would like to choose a place together and start over. I'm worried Noah and Alfie won't jump on board with all our plans, but I'll do my best to sell it to them.

'One thing at a time,' Holly reminds me as I call the boys to the table. This has become her motto when we're discussing Noah, Alfie and the baby.

As the boys are tucking in to their meatballs and pasta, I feel a tightening in my stomach. I play over in my head exactly what I want to say. This is an announcement I need to rehearse a bit. I can't just wing it.

'Now, before dessert—' I begin, adopting a serious tone of voice and a serious expression on my face.

'What's pudding?' This from Alfie.

'You can have ice cream, if you like—'

'Yay!' says Alfie.

'But Holly and I have something to tell you first.'

'You're getting married,' Noah says. It doesn't sound like a question.

'No. Not quite. Not yet. We're having a baby. You're going to have a little …' We went for the scan yesterday. I was overjoyed when I found out we were having a boy, although I think I'd have been delighted either way. But a boy, well, it really does feel like a new beginning. '… baby brother. Next February.'

Holly squeezes my hand under the table. It gives me support and warmth at the same time. I squeeze back.

Alfie looks crestfallen. 'Does that mean we'll have to turn the games room back into a baby's room?'

'Er … no. The baby can sleep with … me … us … Holly and me, to begin with.' This could get awkward. 'And when we're all ready, we'll move into somewhere a bit bigger. It will be somewhere near here so that you can keep your friends and stay at the same schools.'

The boys are silent as this sinks in.

'You can help us choose the new house,' Holly says gently. 'The baby will have his own room in the new house. And we'll make sure we find somewhere where you can have a games room.'

'Maybe we should share it with the baby. He can have a play area,' Alfie suggests, making me choke up. That's my boy.

'Can we help choose the baby's name, too?' Noah asks Holly.

'Yes! That would be very helpful!'

'The baby can sleep in my room with me until we move house,' Noah offers. Now I'm struggling not to cry.

'Can we have our ice cream now?' asks Alfie.

~

Holly doesn't stay over. She thinks it's better to let Noah and Alfie digest what we've told them. The boys are surprised she's not there when they get up. But Holly's right. One thing at a time. And it's one thing telling the boys they're going to have a baby brother. It's quite another announcing to my parents when they pick up Noah and Alfie the next morning that I'm going to be a father again. I can't be sure of their reactions and I'm glad Holly's not there for that part. I'll go round to her place when the boys have left with my parents.

It goes better than expected, my mum reminding me that I promised her a third grandchild once before, and my father congratulating me by thumping me on the back so hard that I nearly fall over. Then they're ushering their grandsons out of the door. They'll have a great day out. Mum and Dad are far better grandparents than they ever were parents.

I grin like a loon on the way to Holly's, feeling relieved. I'm looking forward to building my future with Holly and the three boys. We'll be a family. I'm trying to enjoy this as much as possible and not let what happened in the past – with Mel and Rosie – make me paranoid.

'That went well last night,' are her first words as she lets me into her flat.

'Couldn't have gone better,' I say, taking Holly into my arms and kicking the front door shut behind me.

'Tea?'

'Yes, please. Shall I make it?'

'No, you take a seat.' She nods towards the sofa. 'I'll do it.'

Leaving my shoes by the door, I flop down on the sofa, while Holly makes her way to the kitchen. I've always liked Holly's place. She has good taste in interior design and I hope with her eye for deco, we'll make our new house into a beautiful home.

Holly's slippers are under the coffee table and her laptop is on it. I smile, reminiscing about evenings when I would watch the news and she would work, her feet up on the table and her computer on her thighs.

My eyes rest on the wallpaper picture on Holly's computer screen. It's a photo she took on a safari holiday with some friends in South Africa. Two zebras standing next to each other, facing in opposite directions, the one behind bigger than the one in front. What's great about this photo is that the stripes of the two animals are perfectly aligned, as if they have been painted across both mare and foal with long, sweeping movements.

Then I spot it. A Word document, nestling among the numerous folders on the desktop. It only catches my eye because no other Word documents are visible, presumably all tidied into the folders. Its name consists of two capital letters whereas the folders all seem to be clearly labelled in lower-case letters.

At first, I think nothing much of it. Sitting back comfortably on the sofa, I cross my arms and put my feet up on the table, the way Holly always does. Then it hits me. I sit bolt upright as if I've been stung by a wasp. I think I know what those letters stand for.

I glance to my right. The door from the living room to the kitchen is ajar and I can hear Holly bustling around, but I can't see her. More importantly, she can't see me. Leaning over, I double-click to open the file. But a dialogue box appears, asking me to enter a password. The document is encrypted.

Now I'm convinced I've guessed correctly. I even have a hunch I know what this document is about. *Oh, God! Oh, no!* From the corner of my eye, I notice the door from the kitchen open. Quickly, I close the dialogue box and sink back into the sofa again, just as Holly comes in, carrying our mugs of tea.

'Everything OK? What do you fancy doing? We have the whole day to ourselves. Wa-hey!'

I paint a smile on my face as Holly sits down beside me and I try to answer naturally. Everything I say echoes strangely in my ears and my voice no longer sounds like my own. Our conversation is out of step with the question going through my head. *What should I do now?*

We decide to go for a walk, so we head to the Clifton Suspension Bridge and cross it to stroll around Leigh Woods. It's sunny and the view over the Avon Gorge is spectacular. I do my best to relax and enjoy the moment.

But my mind keeps wandering back to the document I've just seen on Holly's laptop. Could this be a coincidence? I hear Kelly's words in my head. *One hell of a coincidence.* That's what she said on the phone. This whole Melissa Slade case is riddled with coincidences and it's making me feel uneasy. Did both Amber and Ellie die of cot death? Or would that be too much of a coincidence? Melissa Slade asked herself the same question. On top of that, Ruby Fox was one of the jurors and Dr Holly Lovell, my Holly, was the pathologist who carried out the post-mortem on Amber.

But this document. This can't be a coincidence. Not if my hunch is right. A chill runs down my spine, as if someone is trailing their cold fingers down my back.

CHAPTER 28

~

Kelly

September 2018

On arriving at *The Rag*'s offices, it's obvious that something is different, but I can't quite figure out what it is. I'm still half-asleep. As I flop down at my workstation, I notice everything has gone from Jon's desk – the lamp, the notepads, the pen pot, the pile of books, his wastepaper bin, the computer cables, everything. Then I get it. Jon won't be working next to me anymore. The thought unsettles me a little, although I'm not sure why. I guess I've just got used to him sitting there, keeping an eye on my copy and keeping me company.

I make myself wait for a few minutes before knocking on the door of his new office. Unlike the Aquarium, it's not glass-walled – the walls are made out of plywood or plasterboard or something flimsy – and I can't see if he's there or not.

'Come in,' he calls.

Pushing open the door, I peer cautiously round it. He's

unpacking books and things out of a cardboard box. 'Hi,' I say. 'I wanted to play you the recording, you know, of Slade. Is now a bad time?'

'Good morning, Kelly. No, it's fine. Have a seat.' He gestures at the chair on the opposite side of the desk to his and sits down on his own swivel chair.

'Nice office.' Jon raises his eyebrows at that. I look around the room. Small. Dark despite the white walls. One desk, two chairs, three shelves. 'Well, it's a bit minimalist, but it could be all right.'

'It's dark and stinks of paint. And there's not even enough room to hold meetings with more than one colleague at a time. Now, let's hear what Slade had to say for himself.'

I sit down and play Jon the recording. It's patchy in places, but you can just about make out the whole conversation. 'What do you think?' I ask, when it's finished.

'Well, as you said yourself, he doesn't deny it when you accuse him of abusing Bella. On the contrary, it sounds more like he's admitting it, but knows he'll get away with it.'

'That bit about me not being able to prove it, right? Can I tell you what I think?' I'm aware I'm speaking too fast. I couldn't sleep last night and now I'm wired after drinking too much caffeine this morning. It's an effort to sit still and not jump up and start pacing across the limited floor space.

Jon looks amused. 'Go on,' he says.

'I think Slade's words could have a darker, hidden meaning. He said Bella wouldn't talk to me even if I found her. What if she's dead? If he knew that, he'd know there was no way I'd find out anything from Bella even if I could find Bella herself.'

Jon makes a disgusting snorting sound. I realise I'm not pitching this idea very well. I'm not making much sense. 'What makes you think she's dead?' he asks.

'Think about it. It would explain why no one knows where she is and why no one is even looking for her.'

'But her mum spotted her. Mrs ... what's her name?'

227

'Brock.'

'Brock, that's it. Mrs Brock told you she saw her daughter in the Old City.'

'Yes, but she didn't get to talk to her. According to Brock, when she called out, Bella ran off. And perhaps she didn't see Bella at all.'

'You mean she was mistaken? She called out to someone who looked like her daughter, who bolted?'

'Well, yes, maybe. She might have been bladdered and thought it was Bella when it wasn't. Or she might have been lying, covering up for her ex-husband. She made up the story so that everyone would think Bella was still alive.' Jon doesn't say anything. 'So, what do you think?' I prompt.

'Honestly?' I nod. 'I think it's pure conjecture.' He says this gently, which softens the blow. 'Slade may well have sexually abused Bella, which would make him a paedophile and a pervert. But it doesn't make him a killer. What possible motive could Slade have for bumping Bella off? And why would Mrs Brock cover up for it with a fake sighting of their daughter? I'm sorry, Kelly. I don't buy it.'

Jon's scepticism is rubbing off on me. My theory seemed watertight when I came up with it at three a.m., but now I can see it's full of holes. It's one of those flawed ideas that seem like a brainwave in the middle of the night, but in the cold light of day you realise it's total crap.

'I just wondered if there might be a connection between one daughter being missing and the other two being murdered,' I say.

'*If* they were murdered.'

'I can't help thinking Slade's involved somehow.'

'Listen, I want to ring Simon Goodman about Michael Slade following you on Saturday evening. I'd like his take on it. I'll ask him if he's got anything on Slade. I expect Goodman will tell me Slade is a prick, but a harmless one, but in the meantime, Kelly, stay clear of him. And don't go looking for Bella without me. It might provoke Slade. We haven't got any proof he's a murderer, but he does seem to have a predilection for young women and we don't know if he's dangerous.'

~

Around half eleven, we have the usual Monday morning editorial meeting, only today it's being held upstairs. For once, we all arrive on time, keen to check out the new "conference room".

It smells like Jon's office, of paint and turps. But the windows the length of the far wall make it much lighter in here. Most of the space is taken up by a long Formica table with more than enough room – but not enough chairs – for every member of the reporting and advertising staff to sit around it. I remain standing, leaning against the wall, while the more senior employees of *The Rag* claim their seats. Jon, however, stands next to me.

'I've arranged to see Goodman in a day or two, hopefully,' he whispers, his eyes on Claire as she struts across the room to open a window.

That sounds like a vague sort of arrangement. Does Jon need to see Goodman? I thought a phone call would do the trick. 'Should I be worried?' I ask. 'That you're actually discussing this with him in person, I mean.'

'Oh, no, not at all, Kelly. I need to see him about another matter. Fairly urgently.'

'So, in a day or two, hopefully.'

'Yeah. Just … um … busy schedules, that's all.'

'OK.' Jon's not telling me everything, but it probably has nothing to do with me.

'Careful!' Jon gently pushes my shoulder away from the wall. 'I think the paint might still be a bit wet.' He points with his other hand at the floor and I follow his gaze. We're standing on sheets of newspaper, speckled with paint and littered around the perimeter of the conference room.

Claire starts to talk and the excited buzz of chatter peters out. She likes everyone to attend these meetings, encouraging us all to participate and moderating our lively debates. Most of the input, though, comes from Jon, who drafts a list of stories beforehand and pitches them to Claire. All the decision-making ultimately comes from Claire after we've discussed which stories to run in that Thursday's print issue. She's the one who determines what stance the paper should adopt for any controversial articles.

Today's meeting will be a long one as we're starting to work on the October edition of *The Mag*. I can sense my concentration waning when we get to that point. I make a conscious effort to stay attentive. But after a while, I tune out. I need more coffee. Even my legs feel tired. Some of the others are sitting on the floor, so I allow myself to sink down to the ground, too. Careful to keep my back away from the wall in case the paint isn't dry, I hug my knees to my chest and rest my chin on them. I let my mind wander back to Bella and Michael Slade.

Was my theory that far-fetched? No one knows for sure what happened to any of Slade's daughters. Two died in suspicious circumstances and one is missing. He can't be squeaky clean. But Jon's probably right. How did he put it? There's a huge difference between being a molester and a moron and being a murderer. Not those exact words, but that was the gist of it.

I can feel my eyelids getting heavy, so when I see it on the floor beside me, I'm not sure if I'm dreaming. It's a double-page spread. Written by me. Picking it up, I study the photos illustrating the article. I'm awake now. This has had the effect of ten cups of coffee on me. My article is punctuated with white spots and stripes, but one of the pictures is unblemished. It's like it was protected from the paint spattering so it would grab my attention. I can't tear my eyes away from it. I can't move, although I'm vaguely aware that everyone else is filing out.

'Are you all right, Kelly?' Jon asks. He reaches out his hand, as if to pull me to my feet, but then retracts it. Too familiar a gesture, maybe, especially with Saunders still in the room.

'A quick word, Jon?' she calls.

'I'm fine,' I say, leaping up. 'Look!' I hold the newspaper page out to him.

He frowns, then says, 'Oh, don't worry. There are loads more copies in Archives.'

He's not on the same wavelength and it takes me a second to work out what he's thinking. I wrote that feature and it's covered in paint. He must think I'm devastated the decorators used that edition to protect the floor. It's sort of funny, but I'm not in a laughing mood. This is it! This is the clue that's been right under my nose. I can't believe I didn't join the dots before.

'It's not that.' Sensing Saunders approaching, I lower my voice. 'She's alive, Jon.' I wave the article at him and he takes it from my hands.

'Excellent piece on distracted driving, Kelly,' she says. 'I can't wait to see what you come up with next. Well done.' Saunders doesn't often give praise. I get the impression it's really a dismissal in disguise.

'Thank you.'

Jon throws me a bewildered look as Saunders takes him by the elbow and leads him back to the table. I hear him enquire politely after the health of Saunders's son.

Our conversation is over for now. I'll have to wait to talk to him. But I'm not waiting to go to her. I run out the door and downstairs to fetch my handbag.

CHAPTER 29

~

Jonathan

September 2018

I hardly take in a word Claire is saying. It's nothing important, nothing urgent. It could have waited. I can't. I'm desperate to get out of here.

Claire's in full-monologue mode, but it's Kelly's voice I hear in my head. *She's alive, Jon.* At first I think she means her sister, Lily. But I reject that thought as soon as it enters my head. She means Bella. Of course she does. I'm not sure what Kelly is up to, but I don't think she should be doing it alone. Something is niggling me, but I can't put my finger on what it is. I need Claire to stop droning on so I can think straight.

'We're done here.' Claire's voice breaks into my thoughts. It's my cue to leave.

I leg it down the stairs to the newsroom, but Kelly's not there. Neither is her bag. Damn!

'Does anyone know where Kelly is?' I get a few blank looks in response, but most of the reporters don't even glance up from their screens. They obviously haven't even noticed she has left the building.

I realise I'm still holding the double page of newspaper I took from Kelly. I sit down at her workstation and examine it. The article is stippled with so much paint that it's unreadable and two of the photos are defaced, too. But not a single drop has fallen onto one of the pictures, which stands out, framed by white drops and splashes. It's the photo Kelly took of one of the homeless women. As I stare at it, it seems to morph into the photo Kelly showed me, the one from the album she'd taken from Margaret Brock's house. A close-up of Bella, a beautiful girl with shiny black hair and sad dark eyes. And a forced smile.

The homeless woman in the newspaper illustration looks very different. She has shabby clothes and knotty lank hair. She wasn't smiling at all when Kelly snapped that shot with her phone. But there's no doubt about it. This homeless twenty-something is Bella Slade.

Kelly was right. She did recognise Bella when she saw her photo in Mrs Brock's album. But it wasn't because Michael Slade had a photo of his daughter on the mantelpiece, as I'd suggested; it was because Kelly had interviewed Bella for her article on Bristol's female beggars and buskers.

Kelly must have gone to find Bella. Pulling my mobile out of my back pocket, I call her, but it goes straight to voicemail. I leave her a message. Drumming my fingers on her desk, I wait for her to call back. *Kelly's a capable, bright woman. What is it that's bothering you, Jon?*

It suddenly occurs to me that this article came out before we went to Slade's house. He'd behaved in a lecherous manner, ogling Kelly. Didn't he realise Kelly had written that feature? What was Slade playing at? Why did he let us in?

Then I remember he didn't ask Kelly her name when we paid him a visit. This only struck me because he'd interrupted me

233

when I was introducing her and I'd found it ironic that he then insisted on Kelly calling him by his first name when he hadn't bothered to find out hers. *Call me Michael.*

He can't have known Kelly had written that article when we called round. He probably hadn't even seen his daughter's photo in the paper. Otherwise, he wouldn't have talked to us. When we showed up on his doorstep, he knew we wanted to ask him about Melissa. He didn't ask if it was about Bella. He can't have realised we were on to him at the time. We didn't realise ourselves.

But Slade has certainly put two and two together now. He may have googled Kelly after she interviewed him. I seem to recall she left her business card when I gave him mine. Or maybe he only stumbled across Kelly's article recently. Perhaps he did his home-work after talking to Margaret Brock.

One thing's for sure – he has worked out that Kelly has all the pieces of the jigsaw puzzle and just needs to put them together to see the whole picture. That would explain why he followed her. He was stalking her, but not in a sexually predatory way. He was trying to scare her off. Threaten her. Because he's wary of her.

I need to find Kelly. We were originally investigating the Slade babies' deaths and tracking down Bella feels like going off on a tangent. Maybe a risky one. I know Kelly is determined to find her, but she can't go looking for her alone. Slade might be one step ahead. *Where are you, Kelly?* Where's Bella? Because that's where Kelly will be.

Squinting, I try to find the answer in the article. But it's no use. The print is obliterated by white paint, as if someone has deliberately put copious amounts of Tipp-Ex all over it so that I can't make out the words. And although the photo of the home-less Bella is clear, I can't tell where it was taken.

Then, remembering we ran Kelly's article on our website too, I leap up from Kelly's chair and head for my office. I bring up the online article on my laptop and scroll down to the bit about

Bella. She didn't give her name, unlike Rose, the homeless violinist Kelly interviewed. I read Bella's story to refresh my memory. Abused by her father, failed her exams, started taking drugs, kicked out by her mother, sexually assaulted on the streets. *The poor girl.* Here, in Bella's own words, we have the confirmation we were looking for. Spelt out in black and white. Michael Slade abused his daughter. *The sadistic bastard.*

Pero's Bridge. The words seem to leap off the page at me. Kelly interviewed Bella at Pero's Bridge on Harbourside. Snatching my jacket from the back of my chair, I sprint out of my office, across the newsroom, through the door and down the steps to the exit. It's probably about a mile from here. There's no point in taking the car. I'll be quicker on foot if I run. Besides, Kelly will have headed there on foot.

I regret taking my jacket almost immediately. I haven't put it on and it's impractical trying to jog with it slung over my shoulder. I regret not taking the car when I reach Redcliff Hill – only three or four minutes from *The Rag*'s offices. God, I'm so unfit. Walking now, I decide I really need to do some regular sport, find a moment to slot some jogging or cycling into my working week. Then I remember I'm about to be a father for the third time and shelve that plan. Sleepless nights aren't conducive to mustering the energy and willpower required to get fit.

Passing a pedestrian sign for the city centre, an image of the wooden wine tasting sign at the Rouquier family's vineyard flashes before my eyes. Clémentine's words come back to me. *I don't 'ave an address for her, if that's what you mean.* I can hear her chuckle in my head. She was making a joke, albeit one in poor taste! Bella doesn't have a fixed address. *The last I 'eard she was always in Bristol, in the centre.* I'd assumed Clémentine had meant "still" instead of "always" and got the wrong adverb. But now I realise she knew all along where Bella was.

A thought hits me and I feel a wave of fury flood through me, winding me for a few seconds. I stop running. Clémentine got that information from Michael Slade. He knew his daughter was in the centre of Bristol, living on the streets! He didn't want us to find her, so he was careful not to let that slip. Mrs Brock must have known, too. She caught sight of her daughter one day in the Old City. Why didn't she tell Kelly? Was Mrs Brock ashamed of Bella? Did she assume Kelly knew Bella was homeless? Maybe she simply didn't trust Kelly. Whatever her reasons, she has failed her daughter.

Poor Bella. What hope was there for the kid with parents like that? I realise I've clenched my fists at my sides and I force myself to take a deep breath and calm down. I'm of no use to Bella or Kelly if I let anger override me.

I half-jog, half-walk the rest of the way and when I get there, I have to bend over, my hands on my knees, to catch my breath. I hear someone curse behind me, and turn to see a cyclist who has braked to avoid hitting me. He gives me a tight smile, dismounts and starts to push his bike over the pedestrian bridge.

I expect Kelly found Bella somewhere back from the waterfront on the opposite bank when she interviewed her, so I start to cross the bridge. How ironic that Bella was only a mile away from our offices the whole time Kelly was trying to track her down. Even more ironic that Kelly has met her. What was it Clémentine said when we discussed the possibility that both Slade babies died of cot death? *I don't believe in coincidences.* I think *I* am starting to.

Then I spot Kelly leaning on the railing, peering out over the murky waters of the Floating Harbour with its boats moored along the quay. She's partly hidden by one of the bridge's peculiar horn-shaped counterweights, which Alfie always says look like Shrek's ears. But I can see it's her.

A bubble rises inside me and transforms into a giggle, surprising me as much as an elderly lady walking the other way. I think it might be more relief at seeing Kelly than the Shrek memory. Or perhaps it's just the adrenaline from worrying about Kelly and the endorphins from the fresh air and exercise.

'She's gone,' Kelly says, seeing me approach. 'I couldn't find her.'

'It's been cold and wet recently,' I say. 'It's probably a good sign she's not outdoors. Maybe she's got accommodation in a hostel.'

Kelly straightens up and turns towards me, brightening at this idea. 'You're right,' she says.

'While we're here, why don't we walk around and see if we can find her? Where was it Mrs Brock claimed to have seen her? Somewhere in the Old City?'

'Yes, Corn Street or Wine Street, she said.'

'That's not far. Shall we?'

For the next hour, we walk around the Old City. We even go through The Arcade, although I can't see why Bella would have come here. Kelly asks some of the shoppers along Wine Street and Corn Street if they come here regularly and brings up both photos of Bella on her phone – the one she took of Bella on the streets and the one from the photo album – to show to anyone who does. No one recognises Bella.

As we walk past the Exchange for the second time, Kelly points up at the clock. 'Did you know Bristolians refused to adopt Greenwich Mean Time at first and insisted on keeping local time? That's why there are two minute hands on that clock. Bristol time was ten minutes behind.'

'That's fascinating, Kelly,' I say, although it comes out sounding sarcastic as I'm fed up tramping around the Old City now. 'GMT or local, I think it's time to call it a day.'

We trek back to Redcliffe and get back to work, Kelly at her desk and me in my smelly, sterile office. I think of The Exchange clock. There's no clock in here. I need to get one and maybe a framed print of something, decorate the walls a bit.

I have things to do – Claire is planning a special supplement of *The Rag* for the Armistice Centenary – but my mind keeps wandering. I check the time on my mobile again. I seem to be doing that every five minutes. Two hours until I can bunk off work. Then I've got a job to do.

I'm going round to Holly's this evening to give her a hand. She's clearing out some things from her flat so she can make it look good for viewings. It's going on the market in a few days. I'm picking up some of her stuff to take back to my place.

But there's one thing of hers in particular I need to get hold of. And I doubt she'll put it in the bags of clothes and boxes of books for me to take home. I'll have to try and slip it into a suitcase when she's not looking. Holly's laptop. I have to know for sure what's in that document. It might just hold the key to everything – I can't pretend I never saw it or give Holly the benefit of the doubt. I feel dishonest about this, but I think Holly has been dishonest with me.

CHAPTER 30

~

Kelly

October 2018

All anyone can talk about at work at the moment is the special supplement for the centenary. Saunders wants true stories from local people, about war heroes and heroines in their families, soldiers who fought and fell in The Great War and nurses who braved the bombs to save lives.

She also wants us to remember those who died in more recent wars. I've already written one article, after interviewing some local veterans, mostly over the phone, who fought in Iraq and Afghanistan. The focus of my piece is on their hidden war wounds: depression, Post Traumatic Stress Disorder, insomnia ... I find their accounts of struggling to readapt to normal life heartbreaking. Writing up their stories, I want readers to remember and honour not only those who fought and died on foreign battlefields, but also those who survived and came home, for whom the fight is far from over.

It's only when I've handed my copy to Jon one afternoon later that week that I can finally get back to my quest to find Bella. Sitting at my workstation, with the help of the Internet and a local charity, I find ten places that accommodate homeless people in and around Bristol. I ring a hostel for the homeless in the city centre, but the person I speak to refuses to give me any information. I try another one. This time I'm told there's no one there by the name of Bella. This makes me wonder if Bella would give her real name. So, instead of ringing round the hostels, I make a list.

I leave work an hour or so early and walk into town to check out a night shelter near Pero's Bridge. Jon has made it clear he doesn't want me looking for Bella without him, but this might take a while and he gave me the impression that he has something important to do this evening. I send him a text message before I go.

The double white doors of the night shelter are closed. I ring the bell and wait, then knock, but there's no answer. Maybe it opens later in the evening. I've noted the name and address of a hostel about fifteen minutes away on foot. I decide to go there.

Just then my mobile goes. It's Jon.

'Where are you?' he asks.

'I'm on my way to check out a hostel along Cheltenham Road.' There's a pause and I wonder if we've been disconnected. But then Jon says, 'Kelly, can you text me the exact address and send me a message as soon as you're done? I'd feel happier knowing where you are and I don't want you taking any risks.'

Not for the first time, I'm touched by how much Jon looks out for me. He's almost paternal, in a way my father once was, before alcohol consumed him. With a wistful smile, I end the call, text Jon the address, then bring up Google Maps on my phone.

The hostel is inside a large grey stone townhouse. It's both the oldest and most beautiful building in the street. I'm surprised by this, although I don't know what I was expecting. Something resembling a school sports hall, maybe. This time the door opens when I push it, so I go inside. I'm immediately accosted by a young woman with a ponytail wearing an orange fleece. She's also wearing a badge identifying her as MATHILDA VOLUNTEER but she introduces herself anyway and asks how she can help.

'I'm looking for someone who was on the streets a few months ago,' I say. 'Bella Slade?'

'Bella. That name's familiar,' Mathilda says. 'I'd need to check the books. Can you tell me why you're looking for her?'

'I'm a journalist.' I find my press pass and flash it at her for good measure. 'I've written a feature about the plight of homeless women in Bristol. I interviewed Bella for it, and I'd like to do a follow-up.' I'm shocked that the lie slips so easily off my tongue. But it's close to the truth, I guess.

'I'd need to check with someone if it's all right for me to give out information. It might be better if you leave your mobile number or business card and I can try and track down Bella, then ask her to get in touch with you.'

'You can't tell me if she's here now?'

'There's no one called Bella here at the moment. This is an emergency hostel. People tend to stay here temporarily before moving on somewhere else.'

I'm about to ask where when someone calls my name.

I whirl round. 'It *is* you!' A girl in khaki trousers, a beanie and fingerless gloves is marching down the disinfectant-smelling corridor towards me. 'Remember me?'

'Of course I do.' It's Rose, the busker I also interviewed for my article. 'How are you?'

'I'm good. I've got a flat in a housing project now. I work here a bit. Try to help the homeless like the volunteers here helped me. Pay it forward, you know? What are you doing here? Are you writing another article?'

'Sort of. I'm looking for someone, a woman about your age

who was also living on the streets.' I'm still holding my mobile, which I used for directions to get here, so I flick through the photos until I find the one I took of Bella.

'I know her!' My heart skips a beat and soars, but then plummets when Rose adds, 'That's one of the other girls you wrote about. I bought the newspaper, you know. I'd never been in the paper before.'

'That's right,' I say, trying to keep the disappointment out of my voice. 'Her name's—'

'Bella.' Rose is grinning. It takes a second for my brain to kick in. I didn't put Bella's name in my feature. She didn't want to tell me her name. Before I can ask Rose how she knows, she says, 'She lives in the same block of flats as me, you know, in the project.'

'Can you tell me where that is?' I ask.

'Great Ann Street. St Paul's. It's a ten-minute walk from here,' Rose says. 'I'll take you if you like.'

'Would you, Rose? That's very sweet of you.'

As we leave the shelter, I text Jon with an update. Rose chats away as we walk along. She now plays the violin once a month in a local Irish bar, where she works in the kitchen.

'The owner says I can do a bit of waitressing in the summer,' she says, her voice and face attesting to her excitement.

'I'm thrilled for you, Rose,' I say, realising I'm going to do that follow-up after all. 'I'll come along the next time you play.'

The block of flats isn't somewhere I'd like to call home. Rabbit cages, piled five storeys high, loom over me and some kids in their late teens loiter in front of it, smoking. I can smell the marijuana before I get anywhere near them or their ugly albino dog.

'They're harmless,' Rose says, leading the way down the path and through the entrance hall, which smells strongly of piss.

It strikes me that Bella may not be in. 'Does Bella work now?' I ask, following Rose up the steps to the third floor.

'She has an evening job,' Rose replies. 'Pretty sure she said she's off tonight though.'

I'm about to ask what Bella does when Rose says, 'This is her flat, here.' She hammers on a door with blue paint peeling off it. She calls, 'It's Rose. Bella? Open up.'

And she does. There she is, standing in front of me. I can hardly believe it. I've found Bella Slade. Finally.

'Hi, Bella. Remember me? I'm Kelly. You talked to me for my article about homeless women in Bristol. Would you mind if I came in for a chat?'

Bella's eyes flick from left to right, like a trapped animal that doesn't know which way to run.

'I'm writing a follow-up on my story.'

'Sure,' she says, uncertainly. I can't read her expression. Surprise? Anger? Unease, perhaps.

'I have to get back to the shelter,' Rose says, turning to go. 'Laters, Bella.'

Bella holds the door open for me to come in. Her flat is clean, if a little sterile, and sparsely decorated. There's a faint smell of cat litter by the front door. She leads me to the living room, which has a kitchenette in the corner. Moments later, I'm sitting next to a more relaxed Bella on her sofa – the only piece of furniture in the room apart from a small plastic coffee table. Bella's tabby is sandwiched between us, purring loudly. She tells me about her job, washing up dishes in a restaurant.

'The restaurant owner is nice to me. I get to eat my evening meal when everything's been cleaned up at the end of the evening.'

I take notes and sip the tea she has made.

'I'm doing a course, too,' she says, stroking the cat. 'The hostel put me onto it. It's to help people in recovery from alcohol and drug abuse. People like me.'

I decide this gives me my lead-in. 'I came to see how you were getting on and I'm super pleased you're doing so well. I'd like to talk to you about a different matter now, if that's OK.' I make a show of snapping my notebook shut and putting it in my handbag to indicate to Bella that this is between her and me. 'I want to ask you about a different form of abuse.'

I sense her stiffen next to me and notice her hand stop on the cat's back. 'On the streets?' she asks.

'No, not on the streets. Before you left home.' Turning to look at her, I notice her eyes fill with tears. 'Why didn't you report it?' I ask gently.

'Is this … what's the expression? Off the record?'

'Yes. I promise.'

But she shakes her head. 'I don't want to talk about it. Why do you want to know anyway?'

Good question. How do I answer that? It's not really clear in my own head. To begin with, I was investigating the Slade babies' deaths and I thought Bella might be able to throw some light on it seeing as she was there the night Amber died. I thought it odd no one knew where Bella was and this made me all the more determined to find her. Then I discovered Michael Slade had been abusing his daughter and I have such a low opinion of him that I've convinced myself he had a hand in his babies' deaths. But, as Jon says, the fact Slade abused one daughter doesn't mean he killed the other two.

'Well, you see, I'm trying to help someone, too. Someone who's in prison right now and who may have been wrongfully imprisoned.'

'Melissa.'

'That's right. I think your father's hiding something – I'm not sure exactly what – that might help prove Melissa's innocence.' Or guilt, I think, but I don't say that. 'I believe he knows more than he's telling us, or the police, or anyone else. And I'd like to find out what it is. I'm trying to work out who your father is, get a full portrait. And what he did to you, well, that's something else he's been keen to keep quiet about, isn't it?'

Perhaps it doesn't sound any more logical to Bella than it does to me, for she remains silent and tense beside me.

Then she says, 'I'd like to help Melissa, I really would. She's nice. But I don't want to … I left that behind me when I left home.'

'OK. I'm sorry. I understand. Let's talk about Melissa. And your sisters. Would that be all right?'

She gives a faint nod.

'Do you remember the night Amber died, Bella? Can you tell me what happened?'

At first she doesn't answer. Then she starts stroking the cat again, in slow sweeping movements. The cat's not purring anymore, but perhaps caressing it soothes Bella. 'It was a dinner party. Dad and Melissa's friends were there with their daughter. Callum, my stepbrother, he was there. Clémentine …' she spits the name out '… the twins' *au pair.*'

The unspoken words hang in the air between us, but I'm sure we're both thinking the same thing. Clémentine was also her father's lover. Michael admitted in court that they'd been having an affair. Bella didn't attend the trial, but I'm sure she followed it. I remember Jon telling me that Bella had written an angry email to Clémentine after it came out about the affair.

'Clémentine brought Ellie downstairs and gave her a bottle,' Bella continues. 'Melissa was sitting there with the baby monitor, waiting for Amber to wake up. And, of course, Amber didn't wake up. My stepmother went to check on her eventually. It was just awful … the screaming. We heard Melissa screaming and I just knew … something terrible had happened. Clémentine put Ellie down on the rug and we all raced upstairs. Clémentine tried to … you know, do mouth-to-mouth. Someone rang for the ambulance.' Bella's voice breaks here. 'But it was … too … late.'

The cat leaps off the sofa with a yowl. Bella must have pulled its fur or pummelled it.

'What do you think happened to Amber?'

'She died of cot death, like they said.' She sounds very sure of herself.

'And Ellie? Do you think that was cot death, too?'

Bella doesn't answer immediately. Just when I think she's not going to answer at all, she says, 'No. Ellie's death was deliberate.'

'You mean she was killed?'

'Yes.' Her voice is almost inaudible, or perhaps it's drowned out by the roar of blood in my ears.

'Do you know who killed her?'

She nods.

I'm aware I'm holding my breath, but she doesn't offer the information. 'Was it Melissa?' I ask.

'No.'

'You're sure?'

'Yes.'

'Then who was it?'

She shakes her head. I try to think of a way of teasing this out of her. 'Does anyone else know who killed Ellie?'

'Yes,' she says.

'Who?'

'My father. He was there that night.'

'Where?'

'On the landing. Outside the babies' bedroom. He knows everything.'

CHAPTER 31

~

Jonathan

October 2018

It's two days before Simon Goodman gets back to me. Of course Holly noticed her laptop was missing immediately. I'd barely arrived back at my place with her stuff when she phoned to ask me to check the bags for it. Then she wanted to know if she could come and get it. I had to lie and say Alfie had a temperature and I didn't want her near him, with her being pregnant and all. Nor did I want to leave Alfie to bring her the computer. She didn't insist. Luckily. But her silence down the phone spoke volumes that I couldn't quite comprehend.

I'm consumed with guilt for taking Holly's computer and for not trusting her, and I regret handing over the laptop to Simon, but I simply had to know if I could trust Holly. Beyond that, I haven't thought anything out. I don't know what I'll do if my suspicions turn out to be founded. I'm convinced I'm right. But I've never hoped so hard that I'm wrong.

As Holly is spending the weekend with the boys and me, I heave a sigh of relief when I get Goodman's phone call on the Thursday morning. He won't give me any details over the phone. He won't even say if his "guy" managed to unlock Holly's password-protected file. We arrange to meet in a pub near his home in Totterdown that evening. And I imagine all will be revealed then.

'Banco Lounge. It's on the corner of Wells Road and some other road – I don't know its name, or even if it has one.'

'OK. And it's near your place, you say?' I ask, wondering how he doesn't know the name of the road.

'Yeah. About fifty feet from my front door. You can't miss it. It used to be a bank. Hence the name. Six-ish?'

'No problem. I'm free,' I say, thinking I'll have to ask my parents to look after the boys this evening. 'You'll bring the laptop, right?'

'Of course.'

Despite thinking Goodman's directions were a bit vague, I find it easily, even in the dark. You can barely make out the words Banco Lounge on the glass windows, but the building has got Lloyds Bank splashed across the wall in huge stone letters. Arriving bang on time, I slot my trusty Ford into a space in the unnamed road. Goodman passes on foot as I'm getting out of the car. With the laptop tucked under his right arm, he shakes my hand a little awkwardly. Then together, we make our way to the pub.

It turns out to be more of a café slash bar and it's very noisy. There's an excited crowd, wearing fancy dress and obviously celebrating something. Even the bartender is dressed up as a policeman, while, somewhat ironically, Simon is in jeans and a bomber jacket.

Goodman spots a couple, also in normal clothes, putting on their coats. We grab their wooden table for two, right in front of the bar and underneath three rows of paintings, hanging on the maroon wall. My eyes travel over the paintings: brown landscapes, portraits, flowers – varied subjects, but they're all hideous and faded, and look like they've been picked up in a car boot sale.

When the pair have left, Goodman shrugs off his jacket and sits down on one of the chairs.

'Erm ... I'll get these,' I say, picking up the empties from our table.

'Mine's a bitter,' Goodman says as I turn to the bar.

'What have you come as?' the bartender asks, looking me up and down before blowing a streamer across the bar in my face.

I feign a chuckle, then order a pint of bitter and a pint of lager. As an afterthought, I ask for two chicken and chorizo paninis, too.

When I take my seat opposite Goodman, the laptop on the table between us, he gets straight to the point.

'I passed the laptop to a colleague and friend of mine – he's a forensic computer analyst. Fortunately, your girlfriend has an old version of Microsoft Office on her laptop. Recent versions of encrypted Word documents are much harder, sometimes impossible, to break into.' He hands me a printout.

'Is this ... it is ... isn't it?' The first time I laid eyes on this document was in a Thai restaurant in Clifton with Holly. The very words that caught my eye then grab my attention now. *Antimony, liver.*

'It's Ellie's post-mortem toxicology report, yes.'

'Is there any way Holly could have saved the document to her desktop after it resurfaced?'

'No. She's definitely the author of the document. And the date of the last revision precedes the date Ellie's toxicology report was discovered. By two days.'

'So she forged it.' It's not a question. It's what I've suspected since I saw the file on Holly's desktop. A Word document with the title ES. Ellie Slade.

'It certainly looks like it.'

'Holly said the toxicology analysis was found in her colleague's papers as well as on his computer. Wouldn't it be easy to prove that he didn't write it?'

'It's easy enough to change the author name. You need to be a bit tech-savvy to change the time stamp and so on, but it can be done. She must have changed all the document properties after transferring it to her colleague's computer.'

I'm appalled at what Holly has done, but I can't help but feel a grudging admiration for her at the same time. She has damaged Sparks's reputation to get him back for damaging hers.

Our paninis arrive and Simon bites into his ravenously. I've lost my appetite.

'Will she …? What do we …?' I've also lost the ability to speak, apparently.

'No. Nothing.' Goodman puts down his panini, and steeples his hands. He gives me a look, a strange amalgam of a warning and a plea. 'All trace of the encrypted document has been deleted from this computer.'

My first thought is that Holly will notice. She'll know I know. Then something else dawns on me. Simon Goodman is a police officer in the CID. And he has just destroyed evidence. Evidence that my fiancée faked a report to exact revenge on her colleague. Holly's forgery is Melissa's lifeline, her get out of jail card.

'Neither you nor I have ever touched Holly's computer,' he says, as if to drive his point home. 'OK?'

An entry in Melissa's diary comes back to me, when she related how Simon persuaded her to ask for leave to appeal. She described a man used to getting his own way. Simon says. He's turning his intense blue eyes on me now, waiting for me to consent to this. He knows I'll agree. He's got me by the short and curlies.

I maintain eye contact with Goodman, as he continues to stare at me, stroking his stylish stubble. It crosses my mind that he upholds the law in his own way, but at the same time, he holds himself above the law, making decisions on his own initiative, according to his own sense of right and wrong. I think of Claire's son, whose misdemeanour – whatever it was – Goodman essentially buried. Goodman saw a boy who needed a second chance and made sure he got it.

And Melissa. Simon is convinced she's innocent. He'll do anything to prove that. Even if he has to rely on fabricated evidence. He wants Melissa to be freed at all costs – for her sake and for their son's sake, but also for himself.

'Sure,' I say, ripping up the printout. It's about more than the secret that now binds us. We both have the same ulterior motive behind our actions. Because like Simon, I would do anything to protect the woman I love. And just as Goodman has his son Callum's interests at heart, I'm desperate to do what's best for my sons – all three of them.

'Great,' he says, sliding Holly's laptop across the table towards me. 'Now, there was another matter you wanted to run by me?'

I'm amazed he can jump to a different subject so easily. Deep down I knew it was the fake report Holly had on her computer, but the confirmation of that has knocked the wind out of me. I'm still trying to catch my breath, get my bearings.

'Er … yeah.'

'I'll get another round in, shall I?'

While Simon places his order at the bar, I pull myself together and when he gets back, I tell him what's on my mind.

'My colleague—'

'Kelly Fox.'

'Yep. Michael Slade followed her the other night. She was walking home from her mother's; he was at the wheel of his poncey red Merc. Do you have anything on him? I mean, is he dangerous?'

Simon narrows his eyes. 'Could it have been a coincidence he was in the same neighbourhood as Kelly?'

'I don't think so.'

'Why would he follow her?'

'I think he got wind that she was on to him and he was trying to intimidate her. You see, Kelly believes Slade sexually abused his daughter.'

Goodman holds his hand up, like he's directing traffic. 'Hang on. Rewind a bit. Abuse? I don't know anything about abuse.'

I bring him up to speed, telling him about Kelly's article on the homeless for which she happened to interview Bella Slade. 'Kelly may know more,' I say. 'She went to visit Bella today in some hostel or housing project, but I haven't seen her yet to get a full report.'

There's a manic glow in Goodman's eyes as he drinks all this in. I know he can't stand Slade – I'm sure he hates him with a passion – and I dread to think what's going through his mind right now. I get the uncomfortable impression that the information I'm giving Simon is feeding his shady side.

He asks for Bella's address. Against my better judgement, I get out my mobile and bring up Kelly's text message, then pass him the phone. Typing the details into his own phone, he finally answers my questions.

'He doesn't have a police record. He was arrested three times, in the eighteen months or so after Melissa's imprisonment.'

'Oh?'

'Twice for dangerous driving – he was speeding near a school on one occasion and he jumped a red light on another. And once on suspicion of trying to pick up underage prostitutes.' I raise my eyebrows at that. 'But there was nothing in it.'

The corner of Simon's mouth twitches suddenly, but he recovers his poker face so quickly that I think I may have imagined it. *In the eighteen months or so following Melissa's imprisonment.* What a strange thing to say. What does Slade being arrested have to do with his ex-wife – no, she would have still been his wife at the time – going to jail?

I'd be willing to bet Goodman tried to pin something on Slade but couldn't make anything stick. Or perhaps he merely wanted to get at him. I already know he can show clemency to those he considers worthy; does he mete out punishments to those he deems unworthy? The thought sends a shiver down my spine. *Better stay on the right side of him, Jon.*

'You're sure Slade's harmless?'

'Well, I can't be one hundred per cent certain, but we've got nothing on him. He was charged, a couple of times, but the charges were flimsy.' When I don't comment, Simon continues, 'The speeding near the school, it was at midnight. And as for the underage prostitute thing, the women were in their twenties and they weren't soliciting. In fact, they weren't even prostitutes. They were out on a hen night, smoking outside a pub. He got lost, pulled over and asked them for directions. That was his story. The fact his poncey red Merc, as you call it, has a satnav is irrelevant. He wasn't breaking the law.'

He's telling me all this to reassure me about Kelly's safety, but he has also just reinforced my suspicions. Despite the positive connotations in his name, Goodman can be rather devious. There's no doubt in my mind that Simon had Michael Slade arrested deliberately. Simon had to drop his trumped-up charges as quickly as he'd dreamt them up, but now I've supplied him with ammunition. There's nothing flimsy about an allegation of abuse. No wonder he has a malicious glint in his eye.

The din around us seems to increase a notch and jolts me out of my thoughts. I notice Simon's glass is empty, so I drain mine, and we get up and leave. When we reach my car, Goodman shakes my hand.

'Leave this with me,' he says. 'I'll look into what that bastard Slade did to his daughter.'

That wasn't why I'd told him about it and I pull my coat around me, my blood running cold all of a sudden.

'I very much doubt he's dangerous,' Simon adds, 'but keep Kelly away from him. Just to be on the safe side.'

Watching Simon in the wing mirror as he walks down the road towards his flat, my thoughts turn to Holly. I should never have taken her laptop. I wish I could un-see what I saw on it and un-know what I've just found out. I wish I could go back in time. I wanted to know if I could trust Holly. Now I know I can't. How can I when she is capable of such deceit? I feel angry, hurt and betrayed, although what Holly did has nothing to do with me personally. Looking down at her laptop on the passenger seat, I decide to confront her.

I call home to say goodnight to the boys and tell my mother I'll be later than I thought. Then I turn the key in the ignition and head for Holly's place in Cotham. As I drive, I become ablaze with indignation. Holly has done something very wrong.

It occurs to me that her colleague was wrong, too. Not necessarily in his post-mortem findings, although possibly there too, but in his treatment of Holly. He bullied her. Her reaction, her fabrication of evidence against him, may free an innocent woman in a couple of weeks. *Be careful, Jon. You're starting to reason like Simon Goodman. Two wrongs don't make a right and all that.* Although, in this case, they just might.

When I get to Saint Michael's Hill and Holly opens the door, the sight of her takes my breath away. She has showered and is in pyjamas, her wet hair combed back from her make-up free face. She has a small bump showing now, but she looks petite and frail. I'm overwhelmed with the desire to wrap her in my arms, breathe in the clean smell of her and protect her. Any trace of a fight I had left in me hightails it out of my system. I wanted answers, but suddenly I can't think of the questions.

'My parents are with the boys, so I thought I'd return your laptop,' I say. Holly gives me her killer smile and I know that was the right move. 'In case you need it.'

'Thank you.'

She offers me a beer, which I decline, but I accept her invitation to come in for a while. I make us a cup of tea and when I come out of her kitchen into the living room with the mugs, she's sitting on the sofa, hunched over her computer, which she has booted up.

'Just needed to send a quick email,' she says by way of an explanation, but it sounds hollow. Snapping down the lid, she smiles again, but this time it doesn't reach her eyes. She has seen the document has been deleted. She knows I know.

Putting the mugs on the coffee table, I sit next to her and put my arm around her. She's shaking and I rub her shoulder.

'Do you still want me to come this weekend?' she says in a voice that tugs at my heartstrings.

I kiss her and hope that answers her question.

CHAPTER 32

~

Kelly

October 2018

'Say that again,' Jon says. He sounds as shocked as I was when I heard it. 'Slowly.'

He gestures for me to sit down in the chair opposite him at his desk, but I can't stand still. I certainly wouldn't be able to sit still. So I stay standing, hopping from one foot to the other.

'Bella said Amber died of cot death but Ellie was killed,' I repeat. 'Deliberately.'

'That was the jury's verdict,' Jon points out. 'Are you sure Bella's not just repeating the outcome of the court case?'

'Yes, I'm sure. She said she knows who killed Ellie. And so does her father. I've already told you all this. I left a message on your phone last night.'

'Sorry. I didn't listen to it. I got in late. Carry on.'

'She didn't actually say that her father didn't murder Ellie. She just said Melissa didn't do it. And that her father knew who did.'

'What else?'

'Nothing. She wouldn't say any more. She, like, totally clammed up.'

'Kelly, sit down!' Jon orders. His voice is stern, but I can tell from his expression he's amused.

'What's so funny?'

'Alfie used to do that when he needed the toilet.'

'Do what?'

'Jump around like you're doing.' His face falls. 'Mel called it his "wee" dance.' He does the air quotes to make sure I get the pun.

I would laugh if he didn't look so sad at the memory of his wife. I do as I'm told and take a seat. I wonder if everything is all right between him and Holly, but I don't want to pry. 'Will you come with me to see Michael Slade?' I ask.

'No! Simon said to stay away from him.'

'What else did Superintendent Goodman say?'

'Nothing. Just that.'

I don't believe him. He knows more than he's letting on. 'Does he think Slade's dangerous?'

'He doesn't know,' Jon says. 'Why don't I come with you to Bella's?'

'She won't tell me any more.'

'She might, if I'm there. It's worth a shot.'

Jon's right. He has a way of making me feel secure and I bet he's protective of Holly, too. If Bella feels comfortable in his presence, she might open up.

'OK. Let's go.'

'We'll take my car.'

I think we'd be quicker walking, but I keep quiet and follow Jon out of the building to his car.

When we get to St Paul's, Jon parks on the street in front of the block of flats. I lead the way to the staircase, turning around once to catch him wrinkling his nose at the smell.

Bella's in, and she doesn't look surprised to see me.

'Hello, Bella, this is Jon.'

'Hi,' Jon says. 'I'm Kelly's colleague. Do you mind if we come in for a few minutes?'

It shows on Bella's face that she does mind, but she steps back and lets us in. In the living area, she pushes the cat off the sofa and motions for us to sit down.

'Bella, Kelly and I have been doing some investigative journalism,' Jon begins. 'We've been trying to find out if Melissa has been a victim of a miscarriage of justice. There's fresh evidence ... to suggest that she was wrongfully imprisoned ...' Jon breaks off. I look from him to Bella. She's staring at him, waiting for him to continue, but he seems to have lost his own thread midsentence. Either that or his mind has wandered off somewhere.

'The new evidence – a toxicology report – suggests Ellie died of cot death,' I say, coming to Jon's aid. 'Just like her sister Amber. And so we're intrigued as to why you seemed so sure the other day that Ellie's death was deliberate.'

Bella shakes her head, but I think she's refusing to talk rather than changing her story.

'You say someone killed Ellie,' I say. Bella nods. 'And you know who that person is.' She hesitates for a few seconds, then nods again.

'Are you scared of what might happen to you if you tell us, Bella?' Jon asks.

'Yes.' It's the first word she has spoken since we entered the flat.

Jon leans forwards, closer to Bella. 'Are you worried that the person who killed Ellie might harm you if they find out you've told us?'

She doesn't answer. We've lost her again. She sucks her bottom lip. Then she asks in a small voice, 'Will this new evidence be enough to get Melissa out of prison?'

'We don't know,' I say.

'Her appeal is in a few weeks' time,' Jon adds. 'She may have to go through a retrial or she may get to walk out of the main entrance.'

'What are her chances?' Bella asks.

'Hard to say,' Jon says.

Bella bursts into tears, leaning forward and hiding her face in her hands. Jon and I exchange a perplexed glance over her head. Jon shifts awkwardly on the sofa. I remember crying in front of him one day after Saunders had just ripped into me. He was uncomfortable then, too.

Putting an arm around Bella's shoulder, I gesture at Jon with my other hand to make a cup of tea. He looks relieved at the opportunity to get away for a moment, even if it's only as far as the kitchenette. Bella has calmed down by the time Jon comes back, juggling three steaming mugs, a teaspoon and some sachets of sugar I think Bella might have taken from the restaurant where she works. Jon puts the mugs on the plastic coffee table and perches on the edge of the sofa.

'Don't you want Melissa to be released, Bella?' I ask.

'Of course,' she says, sniffing loudly. 'She's innocent.'

I don't think we're getting anywhere. In fact, we've gone round in circles without getting any more information out of Bella than she gave me yesterday. I look at Jon, hoping he'll take over, but his attention is on his tea as he pours sugar from the sachet into his mug.

It's Bella who breaks the silence. 'He called them his little darlings.'

'Who?'

'My father.' Her voice is so quiet that I have to strain to hear. 'He used to call me his little darling. I knew they'd be in danger when they got older. He calls it love, but it's not the right kind. It's twisted and deformed. No father should love his daughters that way.'

For a second or two she says nothing, sitting as still as a statue

259

apart from picking unconsciously at the skin around her thumb with her forefinger. As she wipes her nose with the back of her sleeve, I sip my tea and try to come up with something to say. Jon gets there before me.

'How old were you when it started, Bella? How old were you when your father started to abuse you?'

'It was my seventh birthday.' She looks at Jon, eyes filled with a mixture of sadness and hatred as she is forced to remember her past.

'And you never told anyone what your father was doing to you?'

'My father made me promise not to tell anyone. I was too young to know any better. I told my mother when I was a bit older – twelve or thirteen, maybe. But nothing changed. At the time, she said she'd leave my father, but she didn't. Then she said she didn't believe me. I think she did. She just didn't want to. In the end, he was the one who left her. For Melissa.'

Bella breaks into sobs and Jon hands her a cotton hanky. I remember him giving me a handkerchief the day I got upset. Bella attempts a grateful smile and blows her nose loudly into it.

'It stopped for a while when my father met Melissa. I think he lost interest in me. But then after the babies were born ... I tried to make sure I was never alone with him ... but ... he wouldn't let me leave. He kept me there ... in that house, so he could ... abuse me. He said he wouldn't pay for my studies if I left. He said if I tried to get a job without qualifications I would always be dependent on him. He threatened me with all sorts of things. I felt trapped.'

'Why didn't you tell Melissa what was going on?' I ask.

'I don't know ... I wanted to tell her. But I thought if my mother hadn't wanted to believe me, there was no way Melissa would. I wanted to do what was best for the twins. But I was confused. I thought they'd be all right, Amber and Ellie. As long as there were two of them. I thought Melissa might believe them if it happened to them. I thought maybe he would leave them alone because there were two of them.'

'Two against one,' I say.

'Yes. But then Amber died.' Bella starts to cry again.

'Go on,' I say, setting down my mug and putting my arm around her again.

'I wanted to save Ellie.'

'Oh, God.' I hear Jon's murmur above Bella's sobs.

'I didn't want her to have to go through the same thing as me. I thought she would be better off with her twin. She was sleeping. She looked so p ... peaceful.'

Her whole body is racked with sobs now. It's getting hard to make out what she's saying. 'So I let her go. I thought it was the right thing to do. I thought she wouldn't suffer that way. I held her in my arms first so that she'd know she was loved. Then I lay her in the cot and I held ... I held the cushion from the rocking chair over her face.'

For a long time, no one speaks. I can't seem to move. I can't even move my hand on Bella's shoulder. The only sound is Bella's weeping. It's like I'm in a film and someone has pressed pause but it hasn't muted the sound.

I run through the whole conversation again in my head. I had a gut feeling there was a link between Slade abusing Bella and the twins dying. But I got it completely wrong. Slade didn't kill his daughter. Bella killed her sister. I can't get my head round that. She was messed up, although that doesn't excuse what she did. But at the same time, I can't quite condemn her for it. She's not blameless, far from it. She wanted to protect her little sister. She did that by smothering her. It's majorly fucked up, all this. And terribly sad.

When I start to recover from the shock, I say to Jon, 'We need to go to the police.'

Jon nods. I feel Bella stiffen beside me. She has stopped crying now. Turning to her, I say, 'Bella, an innocent woman is in jail. You have to tell the police what you told us. Can you do that?'

'Yes.' It's almost a whisper.

'We'll take you to the police station and help you explain. Won't we, Jon?'

'Of course.'

'I'm sure everyone will understand that there were mitigating circumstances,' I continue.

'That doesn't matter,' Bella says. 'I want to do the right thing. For Melissa.'

I get up, my hand under Bella's arm to pull her to her feet, too.

'Sit down,' Jon says. 'Sit down, both of you.'

We do as we're told. I throw him a puzzled look.

'I'll ring Simon,' he says.

'Are you sure that's a good idea? He's too involved in all this. Ellie was Melissa's daughter.'

'Yes, but she wasn't *his* daughter. He'll know what to do.'

I don't think this is a good idea, but I say nothing as Jon extracts his mobile from the back pocket of his jeans, taps the screen a few times and then holds his phone to his ear. 'Simon? I'm with Kelly at Bella Slade's flat. I think you need to come round. It's urgent … Yes, that's right, the address I gave you last night … Thanks.' He turns to me, sliding forwards on the sofa to push his mobile back into his jeans pocket. 'He'll be here in fifteen minutes.'

It's a long fifteen minutes. Bella starts to cry again. Jon gets up and paces the room. He has picked up a pen from somewhere and he's holding it between his fingers. He keeps bringing it up to his lips absent-mindedly and then looking at it like he has just realised it's a pen, not a cigarette. I know he's a non-smoker, but he looks like he needs a fag.

We're expecting Superintendent Goodman to arrive any minute, but the gentle knock at the door makes us all jump.

Jon lets Goodman into the flat. Goodman sits down the other side of Bella on the sofa and Jon remains standing. Putting the pencil down, he rakes his fingers through his hair.

The superintendent stays composed as we go over Bella's story, and even though it's mainly Jon and I who retell it, he never takes his cool blue eyes off her.

When we've finished, the silence stretches out, enveloping us all.

'Have you told anyone else any of this, Bella?'

'No,' she whispers. 'No one. Nothing.'

'Who else knows?'

'Only my father.'

'Could he have told anyone?'

'No.'

'How can you be so sure?'

'Because of what he did to me. He doesn't want that to get out.'

'How did your father find out about what you did to your sister?' Goodman asks. I notice he's choosing his words carefully.

'He saw me come out of the nursery.'

There's another long silence. Bella is no longer crying and it's so quiet that a weird stillness starts to descend on the room. After several minutes, I hear a dog bark faintly from outside. This seems to give Jon his cue.

'What do we do now?'

I think we're all asking ourselves the same thing. Superintendent Goodman looks a question right back at Jon, but I'm not sure how to interpret it.

Jon shrugs. 'It's your call, Simon,' he says.

Goodman stands up. 'None of this is to leave the room,' he says. 'Understood?'

From the corner of my eye, I see Bella look up sharply at him.

'Yes,' I say with more conviction than I feel. Bella nods.

Jon doesn't seem so sure. 'But Melissa—'

263

'If Lissa ever finds out about this, she'll start grieving all over again. She thinks Ellie died of cot death, peacefully, in her sleep. Let's leave her with that version of events, shall we?' His voice is no-nonsense, non-negotiable. 'Melissa's appeal is coming up in just a few weeks' time. The whole process will take a lot longer if this comes out now.' He lowers his voice as he adds, 'Lissa's innocent. The main thing is that she is released from prison as soon as possible. With a bit of luck, we won't need the full truth to do that.' He looks at Jon, who shifts uncomfortably. I get the impression the two of them know something I don't.

'I want you all to promise you won't mention any of this to anyone.' Goodman waits while the three of us solemnly vow, each in turn, never to speak about this again. 'I'll sort this out.' His voice is cold as he says this and it makes the hairs at the back of my neck tingle.

Superintendent Goodman tilts his head towards the door, an order for Jon and me to leave. I pat Bella's shoulder one last time and get up. My limbs feel heavy and my movements are in slow motion. I can't find my tongue until I'm doing up my seatbelt in Jon's car.

'What do we do now?' I ask, aware that I'm echoing the question he put to Goodman just a few minutes earlier.

'We go back to the office and put our heads together. We've got one hell of an article to write.'

'But we've just given our word we won't ever mention—'

'Not about Bella. About Melissa. We need to paint such a pretty portrait of her that the public will not only be shouting for her to be freed, they'll also be demanding that she be canonised.'

Judging from the coverage in the news recently, public opinion is very much in Melissa's favour anyway, but I get why Jon wants to do this. Well, partly. He seems to think he owes Goodman for something – I'm not sure what – but it's also about protecting Bella. If Melissa's appeal is unsuccessful, it doesn't bode well for Bella. I doubt her story could stay a secret. In other words, if the recovered post-mortem report isn't enough to free Melissa, Bella will have to confess to killing Ellie.

'Is she safe? With Superintendent Goodman, I mean?'

'Yes,' Jon says. '*Bella* is safe.' He emphasises her name and I wonder if he's implying that someone else is in danger.

But maybe he's thinking of Melissa, innocent and languishing in prison while she waits for her appeal.

Not long to wait now. Just a couple of weeks.

CHAPTER 33

~

Jonathan

November 2018

Kelly and I get an early train from Bristol Temple Meads to London Paddington, then we take the Circle line to Temple. There's already a crowd along the pavement on the Strand when we arrive. Journalists and photographers, armed with takeaway coffees and cameras, are noisily preparing to broadcast live updates to their networks. Behind them and to either side are groups of people, some looking curious; others anxious. Scanning the whole throng, I recognise a few faces. Simon, Callum, Melissa's parents. George Moore gives me a taut smile when he sees me. There's a slim, attractive woman standing next to Simon who I think must be Melissa's friend, Jennifer Porter.

But I don't see Michael Slade. That surprises me. This is about his baby after all, even if he has known the truth about her death all along.

Someone hits me hard on the back, knocking me forwards. Whirling round, I find myself face to face with Dan, the journalist who used to work with me at *The Rag*. He managed to concoct a salacious article from the coincidence I mentioned to him about Eleanor Wood QC and Roger Sparks having attended the same university.

'All right, mate?' he greets me with another clap on the back.

'Great piece you wrote, Dan,' I say.

'Yeah, proper job, that. The boss liked it. Cheers for the tip.' His Bristol accent has broadened somehow since he's been living in London. I introduce him to Kelly.

Together, we make our way inside the Royal Courts of Justice.

'Impressive,' Kelly comments, staring at the carvings of judges' heads over the porch arches, 'and a bit creepy.'

Kelly's mouth is wide open as she takes in the vast Main Hall with its high ceilings, Gothic arches and ornate floors. I bump into Simon as we go through security. He is smartly dressed, but haggard.

'She'll be out of here tomorrow, or the day after that at the latest,' he says. 'She'll be walking out the main door.' He gestures behind him. 'And then she'll be coming home to Callum and me.' He rubs his stubble furiously, belying his confident tone.

I watch Goodman step into the courtroom ahead of me. He's closely followed by Callum, his shoulders slumped and his eyes to the ground. There's a sign on the wall by the heavy wooden door. Court Number Three.

Kelly points to it. 'Melissa's lucky number,' she says.

Kelly and I make our way inside. The door behind us closes on a courtroom that is bursting at the seams. There are so many journalists that there's not enough seating room on the press benches for us all and some reporters are standing; others have squeezed into the public gallery instead.

Melissa is led in by a security guard. She's wearing a straight black skirt and flimsy white blouse, like a waitress's outfit. I'm sure she's aiming for smart, but she must be cold. She looks terrified. The three judges – one woman and two men, all in their forties or fifties – look kind, though. Let's hope they are. Melissa's freedom and future depend on their decision. Her eyes flit from one to another as they take their seats in comfy-looking red leather chairs, their faces half hidden by green lamps. I shift enviously, only half of my arse fitting onto the end of the hard wooden pew next to Kelly.

I spot Simon, whose face has gone grey. Despite his prediction that Melissa will be leaving through the main entrance when this is over, in his mind the outcome of this appeal is obviously not the foregone conclusion he has made it out to be.

Even Martin May QC, Melissa's barrister, seems nervous, adjusting his wig repeatedly and stuttering once or twice.

Kelly has had the same thought. 'He doesn't seem very sure of himself,' she whispers. 'That's not a good sign. Melissa described him as confident in her diary, didn't she?'

'It's probably the most important case in his career,' I whisper back, although I'm inclined to agree with her. He's acting like Melissa has already lost. Or maybe he thinks she's guilty.

It's obvious that the thought going through everyone's minds is that this is Melissa's last chance. If she loses, she'll stay in jail and serve out the rest of her life sentence.

Melissa's barrister clears his throat and makes his opening statement. His voice is tremulous at first, but he soon gets into his stride.

'This is a clear case of non-disclosure, which has caused a grave miscarriage of justice,' he says. 'There is irrefutable evidence of a natural cause of death for Ellie Slade, as for her sister Amber. It is evident that had the toxicology results been made available earlier, as they should have been, Melissa Slade would never have been charged with the murder of either of her twin daughters, much less convicted of murdering Baby Ellie.'

The judges agree that the main issue here is the toxicology

analysis. They instruct the prosecution and the defence to call only one expert witness each.

Listening to the experts, an imminent toxicologist and a paediatric pathologist, and knowing the truth about the missing report, I feel more and more restless as the day goes on. I catch Simon's eye once, but he looks away.

Before the court adjourns that evening, Lord Justice Hartley says, 'Since the failure to disclose the toxicology analysis calls into question the reliability of Dr Sparks's expert testimony and by extension the cause of Baby Ellie Slade's death, Dr Sparks will be given the opportunity tomorrow to explain the circumstances surrounding the omission of this vital document from the original post-mortem report.'

As we stand up and the judges leave the courtroom, I mop my brow with my sleeve.

Kelly and I spend the night in a Premier Inn near Victoria station. Tired after our early start, we eat dinner in the hotel before turning in. My room is quiet and the bed's fine, but I hardly sleep. Anxious to avoid having to give Holly a full account of the day's proceedings, I send her a quick text to say goodnight. There will be extensive coverage on tonight's news anyway. She doesn't need me to bring her up to speed.

The knot in my stomach tightens as we head back to the Court of Appeal the next day. Kelly tries once or twice to talk about the case but soon gives up, perhaps assuming I'm not a morning person. I can't discuss what's on my mind, so I keep my thoughts to myself. I'm worried about what Holly's colleague will say when they call him to the witness box. Will he claim the document was planted? Will he destroy Melissa's chances of freedom? These questions have been going round in my head for most of the night. And today I'll find out the answers.

All eyes are on Dr Sparks as he takes his place in the witness box. The courtroom is swamped by a surge of disapproving groans, but they quickly die down. He's of average height, of slight build with an ordinary face. His jacket does little to pad out his slim shoulders. He's clean-shaven and wears frameless glasses. He appears frail despite an effort to stand up tall.

Martin May QC asks Sparks if he can explain how part of the original post-mortem for Ellie Slade came to be missing. The judges take notes while Sparks speaks. So does Kelly. I keep my eyes fixed on the Royal Coat of Arms, carved in the wood behind the judges, but I don't miss a word of what he says.

'I can only imagine that it was an oversight,' he says. 'A terrible mistake.'

He dodges the question, though, when May asks if Sparks was the one who made the mistake. He looks as if he's about to cry at this point. He's buckled over, broken, no longer able to hold himself up straight. It is hard to imagine this man harassing Holly, but I suppose bullies come in all shapes and sizes.

Sparks looks contrite when he is asked if he can confirm that he is the author of the toxicology report.

'I have no recollection of writing it, but I recognise this as my work,' he says. 'It was on my computer and the technical phrases would be the same for any pathologist, but there are expressions in this report that do indeed appear to be mine.'

I feel sorry for Sparks. He is used to working with evidence, and now the evidence is working against him.

'What will happen to him?' Holly whispers.

'No idea. Maybe he'll have to face trial himself. He has just retired, so he won't be suspended or struck off, at least.'

In her cross-examination, Eleanor Wood QC implies that there was no failure to disclose the toxicology report, but rather a failure on the part of the defence at the original trial to request it.

'It was never concealed deliberately or kept separate from the rest of the post-mortem report.' Eleanor Wood QC concludes.

But it's irrelevant. Sparks isn't the one on trial here. Melissa is. And I think it's very likely she'll be given the benefit of the doubt now even if Sparks isn't.

Glancing at my watch, I groan inwardly. I don't want to come back here again for a third day, but it's getting late in the afternoon, and it looks like the court will shortly adjourn. I shift uncomfortably on the bench.

But then Eleanor Wood QC is on her feet again. 'My lord,' she booms, her powerful voice contradicting her petite stature, 'the prosecution no longer seeks to uphold this conviction.'

I sense Kelly stiffen beside me. The only sound in the courtroom is a collective, sharp intake of breath. After that, it's deathly silent as everyone awaits Lord Justice Hartley's response.

'Understood, Ms Wood,' he says. 'Which leaves the matter of a retrial.'

I observe Melissa as she looks from one barrister to the other, then to the judges, before seeking out Simon's blue gaze in the gallery. I see him nod at her, in an attempt to reassure her, and probably himself.

'My lord, given that Ellie Slade was cremated and another post-mortem cannot therefore be carried out, the Crown does not seek a retrial.'

It's over. I turn to Kelly, sitting on the press bench next to me. Tears are streaming down her cheeks. I pull my handkerchief out of my jacket pocket and pass it to her, receiving a watery smile in return.

'Is Melissa free?' Kelly asks.

Not trusting myself to speak past the lump in my throat, I nod towards the Lord Justice of Appeal to indicate that Kelly should listen to him. I try to listen, too, but the words are muffled, as if I'm underwater and someone is talking to me from above the surface. I catch only phrases: *unsafe conviction … no retrial … sentence quashed*.

I glance again at Melissa, who appears to be rooted to the spot, her eyes wide in disbelief, and then at Simon, who has jumped to his feet and is punching the air. When Lord Justice Hartley has finished talking, the judges retire. And now it really is over.

Kelly and I stand outside the Royal Courts of Justice to get our shot of Melissa stepping into freedom.

'What's taking so long?' Kelly asks after about half an hour. 'I'm freezing my … sorry. I'm—'

'It will take a while for Melissa to be processed out,' I explain. 'Forms to fill in, formalities to complete.'

We freeze our unmentionables off for another hour before Melissa appears. She comes out of the main door, just as Simon predicted. As I take photos, Kelly frantically tweets snippets of the short statement Melissa makes on the steps to the courts, under the arch of the porch. There are camera crews with cumbersome equipment and microphones, jostling each other and us to get closer.

'I'd like to thank everyone for the overwhelming support I've received. First and foremost, my family …'

Melissa is flanked by Callum and Simon; her parents, George and Ivy, are standing nearby, at the bottom of the steps, both smiling. Again it occurs to me that Michael Slade is conspicuous in his absence. I wonder what message that sends. Is he trying to make a statement? Does he want people to think that he believes Melissa is guilty of murdering their daughter? He knows better than anyone that she's innocent.

I tune back in as Melissa says, 'I will not be celebrating my release. I'm overjoyed to be free, but my babies died. My imprisonment was a miscarriage of justice that has been righted, but nothing can bring back my babies, and because of my loss, I do not consider this to be a win.'

In the train on the way home, I type up an account of Melissa's successful appeal, resisting the urge to sleep for a bit, while Kelly fiddles on her phone next to me.

'Oh my God! Jon!' she suddenly shouts, causing several travellers to look up in alarm.

She hands me her smartphone. Looking at the screen, I see she has been reading an article published online by *The Post* a few hours ago.

272

I read the headline: MAN'S BODY FOUND ON ROCKS AT PORTISHEAD BEACH

'It doesn't say how he ended up there,' Kelly says.

'Shhh.'

'It doesn't say if he washed up onto the rocks or fell over the cliffs and landed there.'

Shutting out Kelly's voice so I can concentrate, I scroll down the text on her phone and skim-read. Then my eyes are drawn to one particular sentence.

The body has not yet been formally identified, but is thought to be that of local Bristol builder Michael Slade, missing since yesterday.

'What do you think?' Kelly asks excitedly before I can get through any more of the article.

'I think Slade would be furious if he knew they'd written "builder" instead of "chartered surveyor".'

'That's not what I meant. I—'

'I know what you meant.' My tone is serious now. 'Don't say it.'

She doesn't. But I'm sure she's thinking it, as I am, for the rest of the train journey. Did Goodman have a hand in this? He didn't use his own hands, that's for sure. If Slade went missing yesterday, Goodman has the perfect alibi. He was in court. I guess we know now why Slade wasn't.

CHAPTER 34

~

Kelly

November 2018

I can hear the music from outside Superintendent Goodman's flat. The place is practically vibrating with the bass of some metal or hardcore track, Callum's choice, I presume, rather than his father's. I have to hammer hard on the front door a couple of times before it opens.

It's Melissa. Wearing make-up and a navy blue woollen dress, a flute of bubbly in her hand, she looks far more relaxed than the last time I saw her, about ten days ago, standing on the steps of the Royal Courts of London, making her statement to the press. So much for not celebrating the outcome of her appeal, though.

'Come in, Kelly,' she says, leaning forwards to kiss my cheek. 'I'm so glad you could come.'

'Thank you for inviting me.'

I follow her into the living room. Jon and Holly are already there. Superintendent Goodman hands me a glass of Prosecco as soon as I enter the room.

'Darling, do you think you could lower the volume a bit?' Melissa says. I turn round to see Callum sitting on the sofa. I do a double take when I see who is sitting next to him. Bella. She gives me a little wave as Callum points the remote control towards the stereo next to the television set.

'It's a bit risky, inviting Bella, isn't it?' I whisper, joining Jon and nodding towards Bella and Callum in greeting. I watch Holly and Melissa as they pick up plates and bowls from the coffee table and offer crisps, olives and various other nibbles to Bella and Callum. 'Isn't Goodman worried Melissa will find out about what Bella told us?'

Jon doesn't reply as Holly chooses that moment to come up to us, armed with her bowl of crisps. Jon grabs a handful of Doritos and I do the same.

'How are you?' Holly asks me.

'Good, thanks,' I say, my mouth full of crisps. 'You?'

'Yes, fine.' Her voice is shaky and she doesn't sound fine. In fact, she seems edgy, like she doesn't really want to be here.

I look down at her bump. 'Everything going OK? When's the baby due?'

Her face breaks into a smile at that and she looks lovingly at Jon as she answers. 'Beginning of February. Only another three months to go.'

When Holly has moved on, I say in a low voice to Jon, 'Looks like Slade fell over that cliff.' I read the latest online article from *The Post* on the way here. I wanted to cover his death, but Saunders, who usually gets off on that sort of story, forbade it.

'Better to stay away from that. Leave it to *The Post*,' she'd said. When I pressed her, she said it was a "conflict of interests".

'Hmm,' Jon replies now.

I check both Goodman and Melissa are still out of earshot. 'You think he was pushed?'

'I'm not allowed to think anything about it at all,' Jon says. 'You heard Claire. I doubt he was short of enemies, though.'

'But—'

'Kelly, Michael Slade wasn't a nice man.' He looks over to the sofa and I follow his gaze. Bella is laughing at something Callum has said. 'And I doubt he'll be sorely missed.'

'Poetic justice, then?'

The corners of Jon's mouth turn up, but don't quite make it into a smile. 'Something like that, I suppose,' he says.

'Lady Justice has many faces,' I comment wryly.

'Wears many masks, more like.' He mutters this so quietly I'm not sure if he intends me to hear. I frown at him, not sure I've got his meaning, but his eyes are on Goodman who is striding back into the living room with a tray of sausage rolls in one hand and a bottle of Prosecco in the other.

I remember the day we left Goodman in the flat with Bella. Jon assured me Bella would be in safe hands. Goodman's hands. *Bella* is safe, Jon had said. As if she wasn't the one in danger. I know Jon has the same suspicions as me. He won't voice it, and he won't let me say it, either. And we couldn't prove it even if we wanted to, but it seems like too much of a coincidence that Slade was found dead on Portishead beach just after Goodman learnt he'd abused Bella. Then again, this whole Melissa Slade case has been full of coincidences. Perhaps this just makes one more.

Goodman tops up my glass, and I make my way over to the sofa, plonking down my handbag and sitting next to Bella.

'I'm surprised to see you here,' I say. Immediately I berate myself. I shouldn't have said that. It makes it sound like she has no place being here. 'I read about your father. I'm sorry for your …' The word "loss" is on the tip of my tongue, but it sounds way too formal in my head, and besides, it's not the right word.

I think of my own dad. He fucked up spectacularly and then he topped it all off by topping himself. When he took his life, it was a loss for mum and me. But "loss" doesn't cut it. We resented his death as much as we grieved it. We were as angry as we were bereft. My dad didn't help us cope with Lily's disappearance. He didn't help us look for her. Instead, he added to what we had to go through. It was only years later that I started to understand how desperate and depressed he must have been.

And Bella? She has lost her father. But didn't she lose him a long time ago? Just as I'd lost my dad long before he threw himself off the bridge? I lost mine to alcohol. Bella lost hers on the day of her seventh birthday, the day he started to abuse her. He was no longer a father to her after that. I still treasure my childhood memories of Dad, back when we were a family of four. What memories does Bella have? Certainly none that she treasures.

'I hope you're OK,' I finish lamely.

'Thank you, I'm all right, I think,' Bella says, picking at the skin around her thumb. 'In shock, obviously. Confused. I'm not sure how I feel, or how I should feel, to tell you the truth. But I am supported, and that feels nice. Melissa invited me today. She says I'm still her stepdaughter.' She smiles, and turns shyly to Callum. 'It's been good, catching up with Callum.' He mirrors her smile, his own just as bashful.

'That makes you still my stepsister,' he says. He's more with it than the last time I was here. A little tipsy, but a lot less stoned.

So Melissa invited her. I wonder what Goodman thinks of that. I bet he'd have liked to keep Bella away from Melissa and Callum.

As if reading my mind, Bella says, 'Simon said in time I should try to patch up things with my mum, but that he, Melissa and Callum will always be my family. They're here for me.'

I turn my head to look at Goodman and find him standing next to Jon and Holly, talking to them, but his eyes are on me. I whip my head back to Bella.

'Kelly,' Melissa has poked her head around the kitchen door. 'I wonder if you'd give me a hand.'

'Of course, Mrs …' Crap! I know she uses her maiden name,

but I can't think of it off the top of my head. Then it comes to me. 'Moore.'

'Melissa,' she says as I step into the kitchen. 'Or Lissa.'

She closes the door behind us and gestures for me to sit down at the small kitchen table as she sits down in the chair opposite me.

'I wanted to talk to you about something,' she begins. There's a thick blue folder on the table and she drums her fingers on it, as she appears to be working out what she wants to say. I notice the tattoo on the back of her hand. BKB. *Baby Killer Bitch.*

'It has faded a bit,' she says, noticing my gaze. 'Not as much as I'd hoped. I might see if I can get it removed. Or maybe not. It serves as a reminder.' I want to ask what of, but she continues before I can speak. 'I have a lot of things I want to sort out now I'm out of prison. The tattoo is not at the top of the to-do list.'

'What are your plans?' I ask politely, wondering why she has called me in here.

'Well, I need to look for a flat of my own and find a way of making some money to pay for it. Simon can't sleep on the sofa forever.'

She pauses, but I don't know what to say to that. I think Goodman is completely infatuated with Melissa and probably has other ideas, but it's not my place to say that. Melissa has a wistful look on her face and I wonder if she regrets walking out on her marriage, too. Perhaps they'll get another chance.

She clears her throat. 'No, that's not what I wanted to say. I have two projects I want to work on now I'm out. Firstly, I made a close friend in prison. Cathy. I'd like to campaign for her release. Theoretically all her avenues to freedom have been explored and blocked. Her appeal was unsuccessful. She did kill her husband, but he was a violent bastard. And I don't think enough has been made of that.'

I'm not sure why Melissa is telling me this. 'I remember reading about Cathy in your memoirs,' I say. 'I didn't know her appeal had failed.'

'No. I wrote about it, but it was after I'd given Simon my diary.'

Melissa stops drumming her fingers and clutches her hands together in her lap. I wonder if she's resisting the urge to start drumming with the other hand. As my mind wanders to Melissa's OCD and how she has been damaged, I realise there must be a long road to recovery in front of both her and Bella.

Lost in my thoughts, my eyes fall on the white label on the cover of the folder. I hear myself gasp as I read upside down what's written on it. I look up at Melissa and then down again at the folder, as if I've read it wrong.

'That's the second thing,' she says. 'If you agree, I'd like to take a look at what's in here. With you. Go through it all together with a fine toothcomb.'

My eyes fill with tears and when I look back at the label, I can no longer make out the writing on it. But I know it's there. A name. My sister's name. In capitals. LILY FOX.

'I'll understand if you don't want to.'

'No. No,' I hear myself say. 'I do.'

'Simon has smuggled me photocopies of the case notes and so on.' She taps the folder. 'Everything's in here. I've only flicked through it. We'll need to go through all this more thoroughly, of course, but I think … well, there might just be some leads that weren't followed, or not followed through completely. This will be unofficial. To begin with, anyway. I've decided not to work in the police force again. But Simon will help, and if we uncover anything …' She doesn't finish her sentence. 'You must try not to get your hopes up. We may not … Your sister might not still be …'

I nod. I know exactly what she's trying to say. We may find out what happened to Lily, but it's unlikely we'll find her. Not alive, not after all this time. But this might put an end to the torture, the not knowing. Unable to speak past the lump in my throat for the moment, I lean forward and put my arms around Melissa. She hugs me back.

'Why?' I manage. It comes out croaky.

'You helped me,' Melissa says. 'You and Jon. Without you both I'm not sure I'd be here today. Anyway, I worked on the original case. I like to see things through.'

'Everything all right, ladies?' It's Goodman. I didn't hear him come into the kitchen. Letting go of Melissa, I wipe away my tears and sit back. 'I think you may need some more of this,' he says, refilling my glass. 'Bella has had to go. She's working this evening. She says goodbye. She didn't want to disturb you.' And with that, he disappears back into the living room.

Some time later, Jon, Holly and I walk down the steps away from Goodman's flat. My legs are shaky. I've drunk way too much Prosecco.

'How are you getting home, Kelly?' Jon asks.

'I'm going to give my mum a ring. She'll come and pick me up.'

'Holly and I can give you a lift home, if you like. Save her coming out for you.'

'Oh, no, thank you, though.' I think the fresh air will do me good. I'll walk some of the way. That will sober me up as well as help me get my head round the discussion I had with Melissa in the kitchen. 'You two get back to the boys.'

'OK. If you're sure.'

'Yes. I'll see you on Monday.'

I realise that I've left my handbag inside the flat. I dumped it by the sofa when I went to sit with Bella and Callum. As Jon and Holly walk away from me towards Jon's car, I turn and make my way back up the path and steps.

The music is up loud again and when I knock on the door, no one hears. I try the door handle. The door is unlocked, so I go in.

Outside the living room, I hear raised voices. Callum's and

Melissa's. I stand there, rooted to the spot, not knowing what to do. Should I go outside and knock again, louder this time? Should I cough and hope that attracts their attention? Should I just walk in and grab my bag?

'You're such a hypocrite!' It's Callum.

'What do you mean?' Melissa says.

'Don't speak to your mother like that.' Goodman's voice.

'Don't tell me what to do. I heard you just now. Whispering in the kitchen.'

'What did you overhear?'

'I heard you telling Mum she wasted those years in prison, thinking she was doing the right thing when it was cot death all along. Start again. Start over. Blah bloody blah. You know what you said.'

'Callum—'

'Darling, it's not what you think,' Melissa says, her voice quavering.

'Yes, it is! It's not what *he* thought! He thought you covered for me!'

I gasp, and then smack my hand to my mouth. But no one has heard me.

'Dad, did you really believe I could have killed my own sister? Is that what Mum told you? And *you* …' I imagine him, his face red with anger, turning to Melissa. 'How can you celebrate your release after what you did? You and I, we're the only people who know the truth.'

'Callum, calm down!'

'Can't you see what she has done, Dad? She killed Ellie and blamed it on me.'

'Your mother didn't kill Ellie, Callum. She—'

'Yes, she did! I saw her!'

The track has just finished playing through the speakers and there is a brief, terrible silence before the next track starts up. No one speaks. Then the music stops suddenly and everything is

281

quiet again. Someone has turned off the stereo; no one is talking. I realise I'm holding my breath, terrified of being discovered, but unable to move.

'What did you see?' Melissa asks.

'I saw you lift the cushion out of the cot and put it back on the rocking chair. Then you saw me watching you. You took Ellie out of the cot and pretended to try and resuscitate her. I only understood afterwards why you sent me out before the ambulance arrived and why you told me never to tell anyone I was at home that evening. I lied for you. And you still went to prison.'

I hear sobbing now – Melissa.

'Callum, the cushion was in Ellie's cot, at her feet. I thought it had been used … I thought you … I don't know how I thought my own son … You just stood there while I tried to ring for the ambulance and bring your sister back to life. I misunderstood why you did that. You must have been in shock. I told you not to admit you were there so that no one would suspect you.'

'But you … what made *you* suspect me?' At first I don't realise it's Callum who has said this. His voice is a high-pitched wail. 'How could you think I would do that?'

'Well, you'd been an only child for so long and then I left your dad and—'

'So, you thought I killed Ellie because I was jealous? Or angry?'

'Not just that, no.'

'Then what?'

'You said something that evening, when you came into the nursery,' Goodman says. 'Do you remember what you said to your mother?'

'Yes. No. Sort of.'

'You said it was better that way. Ellie and Amber—'

'—would be together,' Callum finishes his father's sentence. His voice is choked, but calmer. 'Ellie wouldn't have to grow up without Amber, with half of herself missing.' Callum is crying now, too. 'I didn't know what to say. I was trying to comfort

Mum. I couldn't find the right words. And what I said made you think I'd killed Ellie so she would be with Amber?'

'Yes,' Melissa says softly between sobs. 'I'm so sorry. Can you ever … forgive me for thinking you … capable of that?'

I stay behind the living room door, my heart pounding so loudly I'm convinced it will give me away. For a few seconds no one speaks. Melissa and Callum are crying in harmony now. I have tears in my own eyes. I hope they're holding each other.

Then Callum says, 'I thought the same thing of you. Can you forgive me?'

'So, as I was saying to your mum,' Goodman begins, pragmatic as ever, 'we need to make a fresh start.' I don't hear any more because I slip back down the hallway and let myself out. Then I run down the steps and the path and out of the gate.

For several minutes, I sit on the wall, my back against the hedge, replaying in my mind what I've just overheard. Melissa thought her son had killed her daughter. Callum was convinced he'd seen his mother kill his sister. It's unbearably sad. No wonder Melissa accepted her fate. She even wanted to plead guilty to begin with. She'd lost her daughters and had to cover for her son, take the rap for him. And no wonder Goodman was so sure his ex-wife was innocent. Until Bella confessed, Goodman was convinced his son was guilty. Callum's parents tried to protect him.

Angry words from the argument I've just overheard still echo in my head. *Did you really believe I could have killed my own sister? Your mother didn't kill Ellie, Callum. It's not what you think.* I'm still reeling from the shock of it all and I can only imagine how Melissa, Callum and Simon are feeling right now.

The cushion in the cot. I can see the image in my head. Bella must have used the cushion to smother her little sister and then left it at her feet. Ellie died in her cot, but it wasn't cot death. That's the story Goodman is sticking to, though. Easier for Melissa, he said. I think I understand him now. He is driven by his loved ones – his family – and he does everything in his power to make the world a better place for them to live in.

I get up and walk back up the drive. I hammer on the front door hard this time, although there's no noise from inside. No more music, no more shouting. The calm after the storm.

Goodman opens the door. He's holding my handbag. 'You came back for this,' he says.

'Yes. I got all the way down the hill before I realised I'd left it behind.'

'Would you like me to call you a taxi? I'd drive you home, but I've had too much to drink.'

'No, that's fine. My mobile's in my bag. I'll ring my mum.'

'OK. Well, we hope to see you soon, Kelly. You'll come and see us again?'

'Of course. Thanks. I had a lovely time.'

He closes the door, leaving me on the doorstep. As I turn away and stroll back down the drive, feeling sober now, I tell myself that the argument I listened to was never meant for my ears. This is between Goodman and his family. It should stay within their four walls. It's none of my business. And it doesn't change anything. I resolve not to tell anyone about it. Not a soul. Not a word.

EPILOGUE

~

Melissa

Today I'm going to allow my most traumatic memory to surface. I've tried to bury it, but it continues to haunt me. I've tried to rewrite history in my own mind, but I can remember everything too clearly.

My hands are shaking over the keyboard and tears are already streaming down my cheeks. The prison psychiatrist said writing a journal would be therapeutic. It has certainly been cathartic.

This will be the last chapter in my journal and the hardest thing I've ever put into words. I don't really know why I'm so determined to write this part. I have no intention of sharing this diary entry with anyone and I don't see how reliving this experience can help me. But I suppose that although I can't confess my innermost thoughts to anyone, I owe it to my daughters to at least admit this to myself. So, this is for them. And for me.

April 2012

They would be here any minute. I was running out of time. At first I hadn't wanted them to come. It had been Michael's idea. I didn't feel like hosting a dinner party. But I'd made an effort, been to the hairdresser's, bought a new dress, that sort of thing. I wouldn't look anywhere near as elegant as my friend Jenny, but I could scrub up pretty good. If only I had a few minutes.

'Hush, little baby, don't you cry,' I sang, but Amber wasn't having it. She screamed louder, covering my tuneless singing, making me feel – not for the first time – utterly useless as a mother.

I walked up and down the floor of the nursery, Amber in my arms, rubbing her back. She threw up. I had a cloth over my shoulder, but most of it went over my new dress. I sighed. It didn't matter. It would wash off with a flannel.

Once I'd changed Amber into clean pyjamas, I sat down on the rocking chair and rocked her. She was still crying. I held her across my arm, her head in my hand. She was getting big and I had to shift in my seat as the arm of the rocking chair was getting in the way. Sometimes it soothed her when she lay with her tummy across my forearm and so I often held her in this way. That evening, though, I couldn't stop her crying.

I'd tried everything. My GP had shrugged and referred me to a paediatrician. She'd said, 'Babies cry. Some more than others. There's nothing wrong with her.' I tried Calpol and various homeopathic and herbal remedies to help her digestion. I'd even prayed for the first time in decades. Nothing worked. I suggested getting a dummy for her. 'No way,' Michael had said. 'Babies look so ugly with those bloody things in their gobs. And then they won't speak properly when they get older. None of that for my little darlings.'

Amber's screams grew more anguished and I moved her so that I was holding her upright, her head against my shoulder.

Standing up, I placed my hand on the back of her head, pushing her into my neck to encourage her to suckle on my bare skin. It seemed to quieten her and I held her tightly to me, rocking my upper body. I thought about calling Clémentine, but she was busy in the kitchen. And anyway, she was great with Ellie. With Amber, not so much. But as the thought entered my mind, I realised Amber had stopped crying.

I think I gathered that wasn't a good sign, but I was still for a moment longer, frozen in time and frozen to the spot. After a few seconds, I lay Amber gently in her cot next to her sister's cot. Ellie had slept through the whole racket. I tiptoed out of the nursery.

In the bathroom, I took off my dress and sponged off the baby sick with a flannel. Then I slapped on some make-up – too much foundation and blusher, and some mascara and lipstick. I was zipping up my dress again when the doorbell went.

At the dinner table, I tried to act normally. I felt like such an impostor. I felt like I didn't belong here, in my own home. I didn't feel like myself, but rather like someone who had stepped into my life and was pretending to be me. Even before I felt the effects of the alcohol in my bloodstream, I struggled to speak coherently.

I spent the whole evening willing the baby monitor to sputter into life. All the while I gripped it in my hand, I was convinced Amber would wake up screaming. Hours ago I'd wanted her to stop crying. Now I would have given anything – *anything* – for her to start up again.

When it crackled with Ellie's gentle cries, but Amber made no sound, I knew for sure. I turned up the volume, but there was no point. Not because when Amber screamed with hunger you could hear her from anywhere in the house without the baby monitor, but because she wouldn't scream with hunger ever again.

I delayed the moment. I didn't want to face it, or face up to it. So I went outside and smoked a cigarette with Jenny, much to Michael's disgust. Strangely, the nicotine relaxed me slightly, or perhaps it was the getting out of the house and the cold night air that did it.

Then it was time to go to Amber.

Standing outside the nursery door, I sobered up in an instant as the reality of what I'd done hit me. I dared to hope I was wrong and that Amber was still breathing in her cot. I strained my ears, but it was calm. Too calm. I couldn't make out Amber's snuffles, the sound of her breathing.

I still don't remember walking into the nursery or looking into the cot. I only recall hearing myself scream when I could no longer convince myself and no longer pretend to everyone else that nothing was wrong.

I was convicted of murdering Ellie. I accepted it. But I didn't kill Ellie. It was Amber I killed. Technically, I suppose, it wasn't murder. It was manslaughter. It was a tragic accident, a fatal mistake. I held her against me to stop her crying. It hadn't felt too tight, but I'd obstructed her airway by pushing on her little head. I should have tried to revive her immediately, but instead I laid her in her cot and went to put on my make-up.

I deserved to go to prison. I deserved to die. Not Amber. Not Ellie. Me.

I was given a life sentence for a crime I didn't commit. Recently I was freed. But I'm not free. I will spend the rest of my life paying for the crime I did commit.

ACKNOWLEDGEMENTS

A MASSIVE thank you to …

… Clio Cornish, my brilliant editor. This book is far better than I could have achieved alone thanks to your hard work and insightful feedback.

… the whole team at HQ Digital.

… my amazing agent, Sam Copeland, at Rogers, Coleridge & White. Thank you for always replying so quickly to my messages even when I ask stupid questions! Thanks also to Eliza and Honor at RCW.

… my writing buddy, Amanda Brittany, author of *Tell the Truth* and *Her Last Lie*. Your suggestions, encouragement and ideas during the writing process were invaluable.

… Andy Keeble. Thank you for taking the time to tell me about your career as a North Devon journalist and editor. You gave me loads of ideas for the character of Jon as well as some journalist jargon.

… my beta readers: my mum, Caroline Maud, my friends, Emmeline Blairon and Bella Henry, and my cousin, Anne Nietzel-Schneider. Thank you for your time, comments and support.

… my fellow authors: Caroline Mitchell, author of *Silent Victim* and *Witness*, and Imran Mahmood, author of *You Don't Know Me*, who answered my questions about women in the police force and criminal law courts respectively. A special thank you to the Savvies.

… all the wonderful, supportive bloggers who have helped me along the way. A special mention for Mark Fearn, Book Mark!

… and above all, my family: my husband, Florent, and our children, Benjamin, Amélie and Elise, for putting up with me writing and making me endless cups of tea while I'm typing away, as well as to my Labrador, Cookie, who keeps my feet warm while I write.

And finally, a huge thank you to all my readers, whoever you are and wherever you are, for taking the time to read my books. I hope you enjoy reading my novels as much as I enjoy writing them.

Diane
xxx

Dear Reader,

Thank you so much for reading *The Guilty Mother*.

It was quite a challenge writing this novel as I sometimes felt out of my comfort zone. Firstly, I had to get into the head of a male protagonist, but it was great fun creating Jon. I'm going to miss him as well as Melissa and Kelly with whom he shares the narration.

There was also a lot of research involved for this book and a few people kindly helped me by answering my questions. Any inaccuracies are mine and I have also made liberal use of artistic licence. Melissa's second appeal, for example, would almost certainly have been conducted via a video link, but that wouldn't have made for a very interesting prologue and I wanted Melissa present in the court scene at the end!

One of the best parts about writing is hearing from my readers. If you'd like to get in touch with me, I can be contacted on Twitter @dianefjeffrey or on Facebook.com/dianejeffreyauthor. If you enjoyed *The Guilty Mother*, please take the time to write a short review. Not only is your feedback useful for me, but it can also help other readers decide if they might enjoy my book.

All the best,
Diane
xxx

Dear Reader,

Thank you so much for taking the time to read this book – we hope you enjoyed it! If you did, we'd be so appreciative if you left a review.

Here at HQ Digital we are dedicated to publishing fiction that will keep you turning the pages into the early hours. We publish a variety of genres, from heartwarming romance, to thrilling crime and sweeping historical fiction.

To find out more about our books, enter competitions and discover exclusive content, please join our community of readers by following us at:

🐦 *@HQDigitalUK*

f *facebook.com/HQDigitalUK*

Are you a budding writer? We're also looking for authors to join the HQ Digital family! Please submit your manuscript to:

HQDigital@harpercollins.co.uk.

Hope to hear from you soon!

ONE PLACE. MANY STORIES

Turn the page for an extract from *He Will Find You*, another
gripping psychological suspense
from Diane Jeffrey – out now!

CHAPTER 1

2017

This can't be it, I think, my heart sinking as I see it for the very first time. I pull in to the side of the country lane. Resting my arms over the steering wheel, I lean forwards and study the house through the windscreen. Even from this distance it appears austere. Isolated. Built in cold, dark grey stone, the building dominates the valley from the top of a steep gravel driveway. It is prison-like with its barred sash windows. It must be at least five times the size of the two-bedroom semi my boyfriend – ex-boyfriend – and I bought as our first home ten years ago in Minehead.

I look to the right, observing the lush green grass speckled black and white with sheep, and beyond that the blue-brown water of Lake Grasmere. I'm struck by how incongruous this residence seems against the surrounding countryside. *This isn't the right place.* But a quick glance at the black and white chequered flag on the satnav screen confirms that I have arrived at my destination. Even so, I remain hopeful that the right house might be situated a few metres further along the road until I see the slate sign on the wooden gate. *The Old Vicarage.*

I can't quite believe it. It has taken me nearly eight hours to drive all this way, but I'm here at last. The Old Vicarage, my new home. I've left everything and everyone I know; I've left my whole life behind in Somerset. Here I am, moving to a region I've never visited, into a house I haven't laid eyes on before. This is the start of a new existence for me. It should be exciting, but I feel so scared. Butterflies are hurtling around in my stomach. It's only to be expected, I suppose. This is such a monumental change.

As I get out of the car to open the gate, I notice a mailbox. To my surprise, my name is on it. He has handwritten it on a scrap of white paper and stuck it next to his own name, engraved on the rectangular metal plate. It must have rained since it was added because the ink has run slightly where the Sellotape has come away. I can still make out my name, though. KAITLYN BEST. But even that is about to change.

There is a cattle grid and I'm careful walking over it as I push the gate open. I have to get out of the car again to close the gate once I've driven through it. It's only then that I realise how cold it is outside this evening. Even as I shiver, I can't help but admire the view of the fields and the lake. The daylight is fading fast now, but the scene is breathtaking. I could get used to this place.

But then I turn around and see the house again. It's late Georgian, although it makes me think of a Gothic castle. It's been in his family for years, this place, and I know he loves it. Telling myself it's probably more welcoming inside, I drive up to the house.

I use the heavy knocker to bang on the front door. I wait for several seconds, but there's no sign of anyone moving inside. I step down from the porch and pace up and down in front of the house, looking around me and pushing my hands into my coat pockets for warmth. Creeper covers part of the wall. I imagine in any other season it must look beautiful and detract from the drab colour of the stone, but at this time of the year the web of spindly branches looks dead and bare. There's a light on upstairs. He must be here. I'll try again and then I'll text him.

Am I making a terrible mistake? I wonder, not for the first time. My dad and my elder sister both tried to talk me out of coming here. After all, I've only seen this man once in the past twenty years. I step forwards again and go to grab the knocker, but then I spot a metal handle hanging down to my right and so I pull on it instead. I hear a loud chime sound inside the house. Seconds later, the door opens and he's standing there. Alexander Riley. My heart beats madly. He's smiling and it warms me through. Any doubts I had evaporate as I look up into his handsome face.

'Katie,' he says, sweeping me into his arms and squeezing me so tightly I can hardly breathe. He smells amazing. 'Come in. Welcome.' He releases me, takes my hand and leads me into the house. 'Would you like something to drink?' He doesn't pause for me to answer. 'I hope your drive wasn't too long,' he gushes as we walk side by side through the entrance hall, away from a huge pine staircase leading upstairs.

'Here's the sitting room. Go on through and I'll bring you some tea.' He pushes me gently into a spacious room to the left with high ceilings and a log fire burning at the end of it. 'I'll bring your stuff in from the car later. I'm so glad you're finally here.' And with that, he disappears.

I stand with my back to the fire for a couple of minutes, admiring the built-in bookshelves. Many of them have books on them, but there's more than enough space for some of my paperbacks when I bring up the boxes I've stored at my dad's house.

Feeling exhausted after the journey, I sink into an armchair. I look out of a sash window at the other end of the room. This one has thin wooden bars, too, in keeping with the Georgian period, no doubt. They're supposed to be decorative, I imagine, but I find them disturbing. The windowpanes are black now; night has fallen quickly.

Alex soon comes back carrying a tray with sandwiches, biscuits, a teapot and two mugs. He puts it down on the coffee table. Then he walks over to the sideboard and pours himself a Scotch. Holding the glass in one hand, he puts his arm around me from behind my armchair and, stroking my breasts and then my tummy, he plants a kiss on the top of my head. Then he bends over the coffee table, and from a little bowl on the tray he takes two ice cubes, which chink as he drops them into the amber liquid. He drags a heavy armchair nearer to mine and sits down.

I watch him as he does all this, his blue eyes bright with excitement. Tall with dark curly hair, he's very good-looking. I know he has an incredible, muscular body under those jeans and that sweater. When he smiles, dimples appear in his cheeks. He has an aquiline nose. His sideburns are way too long, but I find this endearing. His face has the healthy glow – even in winter – of someone who spends a lot of time outdoors. I have so many photos of him – I've kept all the photos he sent me in his emails –but none of them really do him justice.

'I'm finding it hard to believe we're finally together,' he says, picking up the teapot and swirling it around. Then he pours tea into a mug that already has a little milk in it. 'Do you take sugar?' he asks.

It seems strange, this question, when we know each other so well. At school, I hardly talked to him. I fancied him like mad, but I kept that a secret from everyone, especially him. Both my sisters had more to do with him than I did back then. But since we reconnected about seven months ago – initially thanks to Facebook – we've exchanged hundreds and hundreds of emails and phone calls. We've spent hours and hours chatting on FaceTime.

We've talked about our respective families in detail. I've never met Alex's children, but he has told me all about them so I feel as if I have. I know that Alex's favourite dish is shepherd's pie and that his favourite dessert is tiramisu. I could tell you his place of birth, his date of birth, his hobbies and interests and his tastes in music. I know so much about his education and career that I could probably write his CV.

He read *Wuthering Heights* when I told him it was the best book I'd ever read and he watched *The Piano* because I told him I loved that film. Once, he sent me a purple silk scarf and another time, I received a pink T-shirt because these are my favourite colours. He knows I adore roses and lilies and he has had bouquets delivered to both my place of work and home. He knows I hate take-offs and landings on planes. He's familiar with my deepest fears and darkest secrets. He could even describe my sexual fantasies.

But he has no idea how I drink my tea. I do take sugar, usually, but I can see that Alex hasn't put any on the tray, so I shake my head.

Alex talks non-stop when he gets excited – I know this from our numerous phone calls – and he babbles away as we eat. He says that tomorrow we'll visit Grasmere. He mentions a famous gingerbread shop, which he says is open almost every day of the year. And he promises to show me William Wordsworth's house and his grave.

I love the idea that this Romantic poet, whose works I studied at school, links my old home to my new home. I've come from Somerset to the Lake District; William Wordsworth did the opposite. He moved from Cumbria to the village of Nether Stowey, which is only about fifty miles from Porlock, where I grew up. And slightly closer to Minehead, where I lived until this morning. Eventually, Wordsworth returned to his roots. He was homesick. I hope I won't be.

I have that familiar nervous feeling in my tummy as I wonder again if I've made the right decision coming here. But it's a bit late to be asking myself that question now. The rain starts to beat down all of a sudden and Alex gets up to pull the thick curtains across the two sets of bay windows. Before sitting back down in his chair, he kisses my cheek, and once again I'm reassured and content.

We chat for ages, although Alex does most of the talking. Even though it can't be that late, I yawn. Alex immediately leaps up and clears away the tray. Then he insists that I stay by the fire while he brings in my things. I protest and get up to help, but he won't hear of it.

'You lost a lot of blood,' he says. 'You're not to take any more risks.'

It wasn't a lot, really, but I'm not going to argue.

The car is packed to the hilt with boxes, suitcases and bags, and it takes him about forty minutes. I feel a bit bad about letting him lug in all my stuff by himself, but I really don't want to go out in the rain. I've had a long drive and it's all too easy to persuade myself I'm only doing what I've been told. So, closing my eyes, I enjoy the heat emanating from the fire.

When he has finished, Alex comes back into the sitting room, combing his wet hair with the fingers of one hand and holding his other hand out to me. He pulls me out of my chair and leads the way upstairs. He has left the boxes and bags in the entrance hall, which he calls 'the vestibule', but he has brought my cases upstairs to the master bedroom, which is similar in size to the entire ground floor of the house I've just moved out of in Somerset.

It's cold up here and I'm almost reluctant to take off my clothes. After taking a shower to warm myself up a bit, I climb into bed naked, next to Alex, who is waiting for me. He makes love to me with just the right mixture of passion and tenderness. This is only the second time I've been to bed with him and I'm surprised at how natural it feels.

He falls asleep with his arms around me. At first, I relax and breathe in time with him, but after a while he starts to snore. I'm cold again and I begin to shiver. I slip out of his embrace and get out of bed. I manage to feel my way to the en suite bathroom and I turn on the light in there. Leaving the door open just enough to see what I'm doing, but hopefully not so much that the light will wake up Alex, I move silently across the carpeted floor of the bedroom to the suitcase that contains my nightwear. I look over my shoulder as I unzip the case, but he doesn't stir.

When I climb back into bed a minute or two later, I'm snug in my fleece pyjamas, but I'm wide awake. I can't get comfortable. The bed is lumpy and the quilt is tucked in tight around my feet, which I hate. For a while, I toss and turn.

After a few minutes, I realise I've disturbed Alex because he turns over and asks, 'Are you all right?'

'I'm fine. Sorry,' I whisper, feeling a pang of guilt for waking him. 'Go back to sleep.'

'Night, princess,' he says into my ear as he rolls towards me and puts his arms around me.

I lie still even though I can feel a spring digging into my lower back. Reminded of the story of *The Princess and The Pea*, I smile wanly in the darkness. Alex's body is like a hot water bottle against me and now I'm sweating slightly. Listening to the rain outside, I wait for sleep to come. It's a long wait.

~

The phone rings, waking me up with a start. It takes me a second or two to remember where I am. By the time I'm fully awake, the ringing has stopped.

I've been dreaming about Louisa, but I can't remember the details. I reach out for Alex, but he's not there. I get out of bed, stretch and walk over to my suitcase to find my slippers and dressing gown. I wonder if he could be in the bathroom, but I don't hear any water running. I open the door anyway and peep inside. Just as I thought, he's not in here. I freshen up a bit, and then I make my way downstairs to find him.

'Alex?' I call out.

I go into the sitting room, where the fire was crackling last night. It's chilly in here this morning, and I wrap my dressing gown around me and knot the belt.

'Alex?'

I walk down the hallway and peep into the kitchen. He's not in here, either. There's a strong smell of coffee, which makes me feel queasy even as my tummy rumbles.

As I'm hunting in the cupboards for teabags and a mug, I catch sight of the note. He has written a message on a Post-it and left it next to the kettle.

Gone training. Back in a bit.

Make yourself at home.

Mi casa es tu casa.

Alexxx.

I'm disappointed, of course I am. But it was nice of him not to wake me. He has left out some bread, butter and jam on the worktop.

As I wait for the kettle to boil, I look out of the window at a large tree in the back garden – I remember Alex telling me there was a damson tree, so this must be it. Its trunk is leaning at an angle that seems to defy gravity, but perhaps it's the visual effect created by the grassy slope. Not far from the tree, there's a swing set, and behind that, a thick wood.

The window bars give me the unnerving impression that I'm being kept prisoner. The rain is lashing down outside and the sky threatens to keep this up for a while. I don't expect we'll be wandering around Grasmere today after all.

The toast pops up and startles me, and this is followed by the telephone ringing again. I'm tempted not to bother answering, but then I think it might be Alex trying to get hold of me. I haven't turned my mobile on yet, I realise, so he would have to use the landline. I run out into the hall, where the sound is coming from, find the phone and pick up the handset.

'Hello?'

There's no answer.

'Hello?' I say again.

Still no answer.

'Alex, is that you?'

I wait for a second, but then there's a beep as if the caller has hung up. I dial 1471. I think I'd recognise Alex's mobile number if it was him. But the last caller's number is withheld. Shrugging, I go back into the kitchen to eat my breakfast.

Sitting at the long wooden table, I feel a bit lost and very alone. To shake off that sensation, I picture Alex and me feeding our children at this table one day. I see myself making cakes with my stepdaughters, whose mother has finally forgiven Alex – for whatever it is she thinks he's done – and let them come to stay with us. I close my eyes and inhale, imagining the mouth-watering smells wafting towards me from the oven and almost hearing the girls' laughter.

I've always wanted lots of children. At least four. Ideally, two boys then two girls. Having kids was a dream that didn't come true for me with Kevin. It wasn't for want of trying. It was the overriding desire to have a baby that killed the passion in our relationship and made it go stale. Looking back, I think it was over long before I left. Or perhaps I'm just telling myself that so I don't feel so bad about walking out on him.

Alex still isn't back when I've showered and got dressed, so I decide to explore the house. On the ground floor, there are several rooms I haven't seen yet. There's another lounge, which also has an open fire, and opposite it, a study. It has alcove built-in wooden cupboards and when I open them, I see they're empty.

As I discover my new home, I keep mentally comparing it with the house Kevin and I lived in, which we've just put on the market. The upstairs bathroom in Minehead would easily fit into either the laundry room or the cloakroom in the Old Vicarage.

Coming back through the hallway, just outside the kitchen, I notice a door near the staircase. I turn the handle, but it's locked. Briefly, I hunt around for a key – on the wall, in the cupboard under the stairs – but then I leave it. I realise the door probably leads to a cellar and I don't want to go down there anyway. I walk on towards the staircase.

Upstairs, there are five bedrooms altogether. Ours is the only one with an en suite bathroom, but there is another bathroom and a separate loo along the landing.

Although the views are better from the master bedroom – you can see Lake Grasmere – I prefer the bedroom at the back of the house, which, like the kitchen below, looks out onto the garden. It's smaller and cosier, with some sort of period fire grate and surround. The walls are painted a warm peach colour, but I notice there are no pictures on them, and it strikes me that I've seen no paintings or photos – not even of Alex's daughters – anywhere in the house.

While I ponder this, I push the last door open wider and step inside. Decorated in pink and lilac, it is a large room with two single beds. Fairies fly around on wall stickers and a giant stuffed cuddly dog lies on a multicoloured rug on the floor.

This must be Poppy and Violet's bedroom. Then a thought pushes its way into my head. Alex's daughters would be too old now for fairies and teddies. Alex's wife walked out on him five years ago and the girls are in their teens now. He said he hadn't seen them for a year. Surely if they'd come to visit a year ago, they wouldn't have wanted to sleep in such a childish environment. They would probably each want their own space at their age anyway.

Briefly, this puzzles me. But then I reason with myself. Alex didn't say the girls had ever come to stay with him before his ex-wife cut off all contact. Maybe they haven't slept at the Old Vicarage since his wife – ex-wife now – left him. That would explain it.

Sitting down on one of the beds, I run my hand over the hearts on the quilt cover. Quite unexpectedly, a chill runs down my spine. I scan the room. It's beautifully decorated. There are toys, games and children's books everywhere. And yet, there's something I don't like about it. I can't quite put my finger on what it is. The sense that someone was very unhappy in here? No, that's not it. Scared more than unhappy. In danger, even. As if something bad once happened in here.

I laugh at my silliness. I've always had an overactive imagination. Julie would have taken it seriously, though. My elder sister is into feng shui and mental wellness. She's reluctant to set foot in Dad's house now on the pretext that it has had negative energy and bad vibes since Mum died. I'll have to invite Julie to stay with us at the Old Vicarage. She'll have the chi flowing, or whatever it is you need to do, in no time.

I decide to start unpacking. Maybe when I've tidied away all my things, I'll feel at home in this house.

Mi casa es tu casa.

Hopefully Alex will be home soon. That will help, too.

Today is the first day of the rest of my life, I say to myself. A completely different life to the one I've had until now.

If you enjoyed *The Guilty Mother*, then why not try another gripping thriller from HQ Digital?

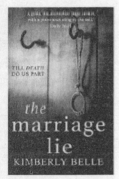

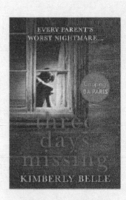

Diane Jeffrey grew up in North Devon, in the United Kingdom. She now lives in Lyon, France, with her husband and their three children, Labrador and cat.

Diane's debut psychological thriller, *Those Who Lie*, was a Kindle bestseller in the USA, Canada and Australia and spent several weeks in the top 100 Kindle books in the UK.

He Will Find You, set in the Lake District and Somerset and published in August 2018, is her second novel. *The Guilty Mother* is Diane's third book.

Diane is an English teacher. When she's not working or writing, she likes swimming, running and reading. She loves chocolate, beer and holidays. Above all, she enjoys spending time with her family and friends.

Readers can follow Diane on Twitter @dianefjeffrey or on Facebook.com/dianejeffreyauthor

Also by Diane Jeffrey

Those Who Lie
He Will Find You